An Unlikely Truth

by

John Rachel

Published by
Literary Vagabond Books
Los Angeles • London • Tokyo
literaryvagabond.com

Trade Book ISBN: 978-0-615-97410-1

Cover Art by Thelonius Fotochop

An Unlikely Truth

by John Rachel

Martin Truth wasn't just an underdog. He was an invisible dog. A practically non-existent dog.

This was his fourth run for U.S. Congress representing Ohio's 3rd District, which included Dayton, Ohio, home of Wright-Patterson Air Force Base, and a lot of Republican farmland. His main opponent, GOP pretty boy Matt Gardner, was a sixth-term incumbent, ex-military, slick, patriotic, arrogant, always smiling and full of hot air, which voters sucked in with steadfast loyalty. The only question this time around seemed to be how big his landslide victory would be.

Things looked really bad for Martin. His fiancé and girlfriend of eight years left him. His 9-to-5 job rendered him a zombie. His campaign was broke and as the Green Party candidate, he wasn't even on the radar screen of 99% of the voting public. His chances of winning the election appeared to be less than zero.

Then a way to turn everything around arrived in a most unexpected form.

Jamila Parks was an African-American grad student from Rutgers University. She joined Martin's campaign on a practical internship required to complete her masters program in political science. Jamila had the face and body of pop music star Rihanna, and the IQ of Albert Einstein. She brought with her a unique and untested campaign strategy which had been work-shopped in a graduate seminar at Rutgers. It had been precisely designed to take on the likes of smooth-talking, two-faced toadies like Martin's nemesis, Congressman Gardner.

How effectively it would play out in this election remained to be seen. But one thing was certain.

Politics in America would never be the same.

Acknowledgements

First off I'd wholeheartedly like to thank the personable and quite mentally stable residents of Dayton, Ohio and the surrounding environs, for making my time there both vicarious and expedient. There's something to be said about the solidity of the Midwest, which as someone who grew up in Michigan, resonates in me with leaden stupefaction and the mute nothingness of intergalactic dark matter. When Dorothy said, "There's no place like home!" she really meant Dayton, Ohio.

Next I want to thank my best friend and wife, Masumi Nishida, for her encouragement and faith in me, and her magnificent ongoing role as my teacher and guide in discovering the wonders of Japan and Japanese culture, despite my resistance to achieving even a rudimentary grasp of the Japanese language.

For their inestimable contributions to my literary and intellectual development, and my tentative, fleeting grasp on reality, I also wish to express my appreciation and awe shucks to: Tom Robbins, Kurt Vonnegut, John Irving, Stanislaw Lem, Studs Terkel, E. L. Doctorow, Jerzy Kosinski, Ken Kesey, Sinclair Lewis, Ralph Ellison, Bertrand Russell, Ludwig Wittgenstein, Ralph Nader, Noam Chomsky, Naomi Klein, Chris Hedges, Howard Zinn, Bill Moyers, Malcolm X, Martin Luther King, Buddha, Jesus of Nazareth, the Dalai Lama, Nelson Mandela, Mahatma Gandhi, George Carlin, Cornell West, Thomas Kuhn, Aldous Huxley, Neil Postman, and Jared Diamond.

For their continuing friendship, support, unsolicited and often unspoken words of bewildered praise, I extend my heartfelt gratitude to Randy Calligan, Mickey Eres Finn, Ron Ruiz, Nic Penrake, Judy Rachel, Gary Clark, Jan-Louise Haller, Gilly Adkins, Oliver Lamm, Alex Malherbe, Russell Swider, Jermaine Inoue, and Helen Paterson. Special thanks to Travis Rood for his editorial suggestions and proofing my initial manuscript.

Lastly, for their belief in me and their unwavering enthusiasm, thanks and butterfly kisses go out to my new publisher Literary Vagabond Books, specifically the svelte and droll head of that organization, Sybil Fairbanks, and my editor there, Porterhouse Thames. Both of you are studies in and witness to the irrepressible power of the human imagination.

Prologue

When Josef and Pavlína Trůžičkot sat down before the immigration officer at Ellis Island, they spoke only their native Czech. Nodding is universal. So they nodded. Their excitement and desire to begin a new life in the land of opportunity was likewise mirrored among the others being processed that day. There naturally was apprehension, and the fear of the unknown, but the stomach butterflies manifested themselves on the outside as quick smiles, wide eyes, and a lot of nodding heads.

"We'll Americanize the spelling of your surname to make things easier for you. T-R-U-T-H. Are you okay with that?"

Josef and Pavlína nodded.

It was 1891. They rented a flat in New Jersey, where Josef worked long hours as a common laborer on the docks in Newark. Pavlína kept the household running smoothly and took care of their four children. Ten years later they moved 450 miles due west and bought their own modest home in Cleveland, Ohio. Their proudest achievement was being able to send their oldest son, Luther, to Case Western Reserve University.

Luther Truth graduated magna cum laude with a B.A. in Finance and Accounting, married an Irish girl right out of college, and spent the next ten years amassing a fortune, which all disappeared in the few nightmare days of the great stock market crash in October 1929. Luther remained unemployed until finally in 1936, he joined the ranks of Roosevelt's Works Progress Administration (the WPA) building roads.

By then he and his wife Esther had five children. They eventually lost four of them in a rooming house fire which claimed over one hundred other equally poor and desperate residents. The one survivor was their second child, Winston, who had the good fortune, or perhaps augury, to have run away from home a year earlier.

Winston Truth, who never went back to visit, or ever even saw his parents again, lived by his own guile and gift for petty crime until he was 20. Then unable to avoid the call of patriotic duty by an America suddenly at war, he joined the army and was sent overseas as an infantryman for the duration of World War II. After participating in the brutal liberation of France and final ground invasion of Germany, he returned to a deliriously victorious America.

Winston, much sobered by two years in the trenches, moved to Akron, Ohio and became a truck driver. In 1947, he married Veronique, a Swiss-French girl who had just finished her nursing studies. She never became a nurse. Nine months later they had their only child, Aaron.

Determined that he not end up a common, working-class cuss like his father, for his entire childhood Aaron's doting parents stressed the value of a college education. Unfortunately, before he could enter university, Aaron Truth's number came up in the draft lottery and he was shipped off to fight in Vietnam. He never saw any action himself but learned well the lessons of war. Men all around him were being destroyed physically and psychologically. Vietnam proved to be a pointless war and a pointless squandering of human lives. Now Aaron couldn't even imagine a war which had any point.

He eventually kept true to his parents' hopes for him. Shortly after America was driven out of Southeast Asia and the last few soldiers and diplomats were lifted off the roof of the abandoned Saigon embassy, he returned to Akron. A few months later he set off to attend Kent State University. Kent State, of course, had its own tragedies associated with the war. Students had been gunned down in cold blood while demonstrating for an end to the bloody, disgraceful conflict. Aaron felt right at home there. He got a degree in Fine Arts and after four years was ready to embrace the world with his idealistic visions of a world living in harmony.

Aaron joined the Peace Corps and was shipped off to Africa. While in Tanzania, he met an equally idealistic Polish-American girl, Susan Zaleski, who had studied social work in college. It was love at first sight. Both knew they were perfect for one another. After three years of farming and teaching eager young minds in the Serengeti town of Moshi, with its breathtaking view of Mount Kilimanjaro, they returned to the U.S. and immediately got married. They settled back in Akron.

Susan was fragile. At least her reproductive system was. After four miscarriages, in what doctors warned would be an unwise and risky attempt, she managed a full-term pregnancy.

Martin Truth was born.

They knew Martin was special. The doctors had deemed it highly unlikely that Susan would give birth. What more of a sign did they need! They held their new infant, certain that he had a unique and special place in the world. He was destined to do great things. They would do their part. The mobile hovering over Martin's crib consisted of planetary objects and peace signs.

Though he was a mere yawning, sleeping, nursing, burping, crying prototype and promise of a fully functioning human, from his first day home from the hospital, Susan read to him. Following suit, Aaron after a full day of work as a graphic designer, spent hours explaining to their baby boy how peace in the world was paramount, love was the chosen path to perfection, beauty was the universal language, and ascending above all other a priori principles, truth reigned supreme.

As an infant and then as a child, Martin was a great listener. Even when those around him spouted nonsense, he listened quietly, deciding what he would have said instead. He was very discerning, even at times harshly judgmental, but no really one knew. Everyone loved him.

Life was suburban perfection for Martin and his parents until he turned seven. They moved from a one-bedroom family-starter in the Kenmore area of industrial Akron to a three-bedroom colonial in chic North Hill. Father got a promotion. Mother joined the Polish-American Club. Martin started the second grade.

Then everything horribly changed.

His father was diagnosed with pancreatic cancer. Six months later he was dead.

There was a modest life insurance policy. The money quickly ran out. Susan tried to get a job. She had no experience and her formal training in social work was past its expiration date.

Despondent and down to their last few dollars, she and Martin moved in with her in-laws. That was a disaster. They had their own financial problems and were deeply bitter about the loss of their only son. Somehow they seemed to hold Susan responsible for his death. Plus they were now too old and set in their ways to have a grown woman and a young boy around. Every day they let her know that they expected her to move out and start living like a responsible adult. Weeks, then months passed. Susan became desperate.

Then she met Lt. Colonel Bruce Dietrich.

Lt. Colonel Bruce Dietrich — he always let people know he should be addressed in this manner — was literally just passing through. He was on his way back to Dayton, after visiting his parents in Youngstown. He pulled off the freeway when he spotted the troubled-looking Susan, standing next to the car she had borrowed from her in-laws to run errands. It had a flat.

After he changed the tire, Lt. Colonel Bruce Dietrich offered to take the grateful Susan and her "handsome young boy" for a bite to eat.

Lt. Colonel Bruce Dietrich was a striking sight to behold. His uniform, his commanding posture, his angular carved-of-courage jaw, high cheekbones, slick swept-back jet black hair.

Over the next month, one thing led to another. Susan was finally able to accommodate the increasingly insistent pestering of her in-laws. She moved out. In fact she moved out of Akron entirely and into the protective custody of Lt. Colonel Bruce Dietrich. He owned a substantial house in Springboro, a suburb of Dayton. They were promptly married.

The real facts of her new situation now gradually unfolded.

Lt. Colonel Bruce Dietrich was not a Lt. Colonel anymore. He was retired from the army but unable to let go of the halcyon days of his military glory, most of which were products of his imagination and hyper-inflated ego. He currently worked as a program manager for Lockheed Martin, a military contractor attached to Wright-Patterson AFB. When he wasn't managing programs, he was drinking. When he drank, he was mentally and physically abusive to everyone around him. Three marriages had already been reduced to rubble by the man's temper-fueled fists.

Susan took the abuse. She felt she had no choice. She became a double victim as she also took the abuse which was intended for Martin, who she did everything in her power to protect.

Martin spent the next eleven years avoiding his step-father. Tragically this meant minimum contact with his mother as well, who never seemed out of the paranoid and incarcerative clutches of Lt. Colonel Bruce Dietrich. She lived those years under house arrest, in solitary confinement of both the body and the mind.

As Martin progressed through grade school, then junior high, he never let on that his home was a cage-fighting battleground for two grossly mismatched opponents — his dear mother who struggled just to survive, and a drunk pugilistic beast who was never seen in public without his medal-bedecked uniform. Martin withdrew and became increasingly stoic and fiercely independent. He buried himself in his books, repressed the guilty anguish of not being able to do anything to help his mom, and often wondered why the peace, love, beauty and truth his real father once spoke of, had entirely skipped over his household, leaving them at the mercy of such a violent and hateful man as Lt. Colonel Bruce Dietrich.

By high school, Martin had become even more withdrawn. Nevertheless at any given time, he managed to have two to three close friends. Of course, he never invited them to his house. He spent as much time as he could out and about, as little time as possible at home. He became an anonymous boarder there, ducking in and out of his room like a church mouse.

Martin was extremely good-looking. But if he in fact had any idea, he never let on that he knew how frequently he was on the short list for the saccharine daydreams of girls in his school. Lost in his own world, he was soft-spoken if not entirely mute, as he roamed the halls of Springboro H.S., seemingly oblivious to — yet quietly taking in — everything and everyone around him. His ghostlike and solitary persona was further reinforced by his reputation as the smartest kid in the school. Some of the lesser gifted called him the Bionic Brain. In this age of television, computer games and Napster, smart kids were, of course, to be avoided at all costs. Doing well at academics was considered a contagious, perhaps lethal form of weirdness.

He maintained his near invisibility and complete lack of celebrity until an incident at the very beginning of his senior year.

Martin had just begun a part-time job at a Circle K convenience store in nearby Franklin. There was a loud crash. He looked up from stocking the freezer compartment with ice cream bars to see a white Ford passenger van had just plowed into the utility pole at the entrance to their lot. The pole was bent over forty-five degrees and at least one electrical wire had been severed and dangled behind the vehicle, sparking and twisting like a giant electrified anaconda. The van was filling with smoke and the driver could be seen slumped over the steering wheel.

The vehicle was painted with a logo and name — Theresa Pierce Retirement Community — and was full of elderly residents out on some excursion. The smoke was causing confusion and panic. Several appeared to be choking. By the time Martin got to the van, someone had managed to open one of the rear passenger doors from the inside. But no one was exiting.

Martin started pulling people out as fast as he could. Finally, he reached inside for the last passenger, an old woman who was hunched over in the rear seat gasping for breath. Flames were bursting up right behind her, nearly setting her hair ablaze. The fire was quickly spreading into the seats and up across the fabric lining of the roof. Moving as quickly as possible and now nearly blinded himself by the smoke, he picked her up and out, then quickly ran to deposit her among the rest of the passengers, who fearing an explosion had retreated to the opposite side of the parking lot.

When he turned back around, he could see the driver still behind the wheel unconscious. Martin sprinted back. The heat of the fire intensified as he approached.

When he reached the driver, though the man's face already had a layer of soot on it, Martin could see that his lips were blue. He had apparently stopped breathing. The guy was a huge African-American man, probably in his late 40s or early 50s. Martin struggled to unfasten his seat belt. Then lacking a firm grip on the bulky dead weight of his enormous torso, it was all Martin could do to unwedge him from behind the steering wheel and out of the driver's seat. Suddenly another pair of arms were there to help. The two of them struggled but managed to carry and drag the gentleman to a small patch of grass between the curb and sidewalk, a safe distance from the vehicle, now almost entirely engulfed in flames and thick black smoke.

Martin had never had any formal training in CPR. But perhaps fearing that one day his battered mother would need it, he had read up on it extensively.

He bent down over the man, pinched his nose with one hand, with the other reached with his fingers inside the man's mouth to make sure he hadn't swallowed his tongue, then put his own mouth over the man's now purple lips and started forcefully breathing air into his lungs. He continued this for almost ten minutes, when he was finally relieved by emergency responders from the Fire Department, which included a paramedic who did have the required formal training.

Relieved of his emergency duties, Martin stumbled back into the store. He felt light-headed and drained. For a while, he could barely move. After sitting slumped in the storage room for a short while, he recovered and completed his shift. Things were eventually restored to normal in the Circle K parking lot. He finally got around to restocking the ice cream freezer chest.

Next day, the phone started ringing. That afternoon alone he was interviewed by not less than five reporters. One was even from CNN.

Someone had taken some photos with an Instamatic. One was featured on the front page of the Dayton Daily News and in just about every television broadcast covering the incident.

It was the feel-good story of the week.

There was Martin Truth, straddling the huge mound of a dying black man, giving him mouth-to-mouth resuscitation. A typical headline read:

Area Teen Rescues Retirees
from Burning Vehicle!
Saves Man's Life!

It turned out that Martin had indeed saved the driver's life. The man had suffered some sort of embolism and his lungs were drowning in their own fluids. Martin had kept him alive until the paramedics were able to properly take over. And he had solely been responsible for pulling fourteen very old, seriously feeble, and relatively helpless people out of a burning vehicle.

He was a hero.

A few clueless, perhaps envious fellow classmates — mostly jocks and other less-than-zero narcissists — sneered behind his back and called him a "suck face fag" or muttered in passing, "Give that boy some nigger lips!" But word of his display of courage and selflessness spread, and he was eventually awarded a Presidential Citizens Medal For Community Service, by then-president Bill Clinton. This later became instrumental in obtaining the scholarship he would need to attend college.

Because of his drinking, Lt. Colonel Bruce Dietrich had been relieved of his duties at the air force base and now could barely feed the family, much less consider paying for Martin's college. Not that he would have anyway. He openly resented the attention and praise Martin received. Fortunately, Martin ended up with a generous National Merit Scholarship which covered all of his tuition, books and educational fees. With his 3.98 GPA in high school and dazzling SAT scores, upon graduating he had six major universities vying for him.

When he arrived for freshman orientation at Cornell University in Ithaca, NY, for the first time in a very long time he felt like he had a home. He took to university life as a dolphin does to the open seas. He loved attending class, devoured textbooks with an insatiable hunger for all there was to know, and always went the extra mile. He would hand in seven pages for a two-page assignment. Martin made the library his second home, eschewing the convenience of online research using a computer in his dorm room, just to be in the midst of all those books.

Even more important, in terms of delivering him from the cocoon of isolation and shyness which had enveloped him for over a decade, was his involvement in campus political and community organizations. Every semester after his freshman year, he volunteered for special community service work, first at a homeless shelter, then at a special school for the disabled, finally at a local AIDS hospice. One summer saw him doing eight weeks with Habitat For Humanity in Georgia, the following one a research internship for the renowned Southern Poverty Law Center in Montgomery, Alabama.

He was a busy young man.

Martin had tried to keep in touch with his mom. She rarely was available to talk. When he said he wanted to come home for a holiday visit, she discouraged it. Slowly, they drifted further and further apart. She eventually stopped calling. Her silence marginalized his genuine concerns for her safety. Martin's dwindling thoughts about life in suburban Dayton, Ohio slowly dispersed in the background noise, as campus life, academics, and volunteer work increasingly monopolized his time and attention. Feelings about home then more manifested themselves as rare prickles of guilt about not feeling much of anything at all about the situation there. At least now he was spared the immediate fear and constant hatred he felt for his step-father. His former frustration and sense of helplessness had now evolved into an inert resignation and a vague if unfounded assumption, that things must be alright if he hadn't heard otherwise.

The wake-up call finally came a few years later when he was in the second semester of his masters program at University of Chicago.

One call. He would never get another.

It was from a homicide detective with the City of Dayton Police Department.

Susan Maria Truth had earlier that day endured her worst beating ever. There was a struggle over a gun and Lt. Colonel Bruce Dietrich shot her at point blank range in the face.

Martin returned to Dayton for the closed casket funeral. He gave statements to the authorities regarding his step-father's history of domestic abuse. Hopefully they would put him away forever.

He dropped his classes at University of Chicago for the current semester and stayed home. Both of his parents were gone now. It didn't seem possible. They were both so young.

But his grief couldn't go on forever. What's the point of lamenting death if life is wasted?

He returned to his studies at U of C, and a year-and-a-half later graduated with highest honors, earning an MA in political science.

By some convoluted logic prompted by the murder, Martin arrived at a decision which would shape the rest of his life. Wracked by guilt and blaming himself for abandoning his mom, haunted by a sense of hopelessness and frustration fomented by memories of his home life, yet buoyed by the fundamental belief that irrespective of the Lt. Colonel Bruce Dietrichs of the world, peace, love, beauty and truth still had a fighting chance, he vowed he would devote himself to making a difference — a positive difference.

From the day he graduated from University of Chicago, Martin Truth decided to commit his life to public service. Conjoined with a naïve but certain faith in democracy — the noble experiment in self-government that *was* America — that meant serving his country by seeking elected office.

Chapter One

Martin had never seen Alison this angry.

"But you promised. You lying bastard! Why didn't you tell me?"

"Come on, Alison. I can't just quit. Not yet. I was going to say some—"

"Right. When? You are a total wimp-ass. Why did I trust you?"

"It's just this one last go at it. I think I have a chance this—"

"You are delusional! Completely and totally delusional. Why do I listen to you? Why did I ever listen to you? You're a fool. A complete idiot. I'm sure glad we don't have kids. They'd be retarded!"

"Okay okay. I knew you'd be upset. But let's not go saying things you'll regret later."

"Now that's something we agree on. So I'm not going to. In fact right now I'm going to say something which I will *never* regret. In fact, it's something I should've said long time ago. GOOD-BYE!!"

Martin sat there listening to her pack her bags. Not ten minutes later, she was out the door.

Is this really happening? Would she change her mind? Would she be back? Maybe later this evening? In the morning?

He was in shock.

Shock but…

There was something else.

Relief?

Closure?

A bittersweetness?

A self-affirming martyrdom?

Was there a *giddiness* lurking behind the surface pain and incipient tears?

Giddiness? Hardly!…

But something. He couldn't quite grab it.

It? It?

His head was spinning.

He stared but his gaze just floated, unfocused and inert.

There was one thing he *did* know for certain.

He had screwed up.

Martin had gotten held up in traffic and arrived home a little late. The mail was sitting there waiting, as always. Alison got to it first. And right on top sat…

The letter from the Registrar of Voters Office, approving his fourth run for Congress.

His fourth! Was it possible? Who would've thought? This all started over six years ago!

Astonishing and exhilarating as that might be, he had to face the facts.

So far it wasn't going very well.

First time, he only got 27 votes. Second time a barely measurable .3% of the whole district. Last election he came roaring into whole digits and then some, at a whopping 1.7% of the vote.

Progress. But not exactly the stuff of victory laps.

Doing some rough calculation, at this rate he might finally get a majority around his 37th attempt. He'd be 103 years old.

At the same time, winning was not the point. It was about conviction. About taking a stand.

If there was no one out there representing a real choice, what did that say about democracy? It said it was a big joke!

Then again, wasn't it? The two major parties both stood for the same things: More military, more war, more destruction of the environment, more money for the rich, more attacks on individual rights, more invasion of personal privacy, more of all the things which Martin was certain was taking the country down the road of ruin. More more more. And less of the core essential things which made it great: Equality, opportunity, peace, sense of community, compassion for the less fortunate, a good quality of life for everyone, a confident healthy citizenry, shared prosperity, clean air, clean water, nutritious food, a thriving eco-friendly economy, national pride, things to be genuinely proud of — all of the chest-thumping stuff of the American Dream.

Every day Martin reminded himself of the promise he made the day he left university life. He would try to make a difference. He would devote his life to doing things which made a positive contribution, to his community, to his country.

Alison knew this. That's why she loved him. At least that's what she used to say.

Of course, things change with time. As people themselves change.

Martin could see her side of the story. This had been building for some time now. They had had their share of up-all-night discussions, then as time went on, full-blown fights, followed by droughts of deaf-mute silence and avoiding one another. Lately these often lasted for days.

More and more they argued about what they were doing with their lives, what choices they were making, whether how they were going about things made any sense — all of which inevitably ended up pointing at his involvement in politics: Is this how we want to spend the best days of our youth? Is there any future in this? Isn't it time to grow up and be realistic? Ideals are a wonderful thing but what's the point of ideals if they never come into play? What's the point of playing the game if you know you're going to lose?

Yes, she had a point. And that point for her apparently now trumped whatever romanticized view they'd thus far shared of living a life of commitment, of sacrifice, of dedication to a set of core values come hell or high water. Of course he would lose. Regardless, he would stand tall. They would feel proud. They would stay true to what they believed in. It was Socrates and the hemlock.

How noble.

Alison had moved on. The posturing of a principled loser just wasn't worth it to her anymore. She was finally fed up with the futility of it all.

In his lowest moments, he knew how she felt. It got to him too.

He wasn't kidding himself. He knew how this latest run for Congress was going to end. He wasn't *delusional*, one of Alison's favorite words these days.

At the same time, he knew what he had to do. Standing on the sidelines was not an option. It's like that quote by the Scottish clergyman Peter Marshall: *"A different world cannot be built by indifferent people."*

And he had to be honest with himself. That's not where he had screwed up so badly here. Remaining true to his ideals, half-baked or not, was not the problem. The screw-up was making a promise to Alison that he couldn't possibly keep. Telling her that he would get a decent job and start making enough money to support a family, buy a house, make babies, try to live a normal life.

Had he really said that?

She must have drugged him.

• • •

Martin lit up a joint. Not so unusual. Over the past few years, at least twice a week, he and Alison had toked up, then went through their mechanized routine of lovemaking. The marijuana made what had become totally predictable at least hedonistically engaging, as each individually got lost inside the deep chambers of carnal rapture. The participation of the other made it a cut above masturbating. Even on the off nights, they often would still share at least a couple drags, then watch mindless television or vegetate on the internet. Each had their own laptop. They had all of the modern conveniences to make it easier to ignore one another.

He took his third hit off the joint. A blissful fog descended upon him.

It was time for some honesty. Some clarity.

He couldn't say with absolute conviction he would miss her. Sure, with her gone there would be something askew. But it would be more the feeling that some regular element or feature was unaccounted for or out of service. Like the fridge had stopped making ice cubes. The arts and entertainment section was missing from the Sunday newspaper. Or his favorite internet music site wouldn't let him download tunes anymore.

What a sad note. They had been together almost eight years. Admittedly, the last two had shown signs of wear and tear. Alison had been talking more and more about wanting to start a family. It got to be quite annoying. She kept saying her biological clock was ticking. Right. Like being 27 was peering into the moribund abyss of menopause.

Her disenchantment with him — or was it disengagement — really started much before that. He noticed that once she got that awful job with the bank four years ago, almost immediately her whole world view started to get skewed. As a couple they looked more and more like a random match, then a complete mismatch, him still dressing like he was a nerdy grad student and her going for Prada.

Their fiery passion for discussing politics and what was going on in the world became more forced, less frequent, almost certain to result in them 'agreeing to disagree', if not screaming at one another. Even their agreement on things seemed tentative and artificial. Eventually they both avoided bringing up anything controversial. The critical issues of the day gave way to small talk and harmless trivia.

What *did* they talk about? Not much. Not much that Martin could actually remember. Basically he stopped trying to discuss anything he truly thought important, and quit paying attention to 99% of what Alison had to say. It seemed like whatever it was she babbled on about either had to do with banking, the lame people she worked with, the petty in-fighting and backbiting of office politics, or … babies. Babies her friends were having. Babies her friends had just had. Babies spit out by celebrity couples. Someone at work taking maternity leave. Anonymous babies in the park, at the mall, in a passing car. *Baby On Board!*

It had to be what they called *baby fever*. A function of her hormones kicking in, or perhaps society's not-so-subtle programming for her to procreate and play her part in perpetuating the species. Whatever caused this cerebral malfunction was no excuse. Bringing children into this terrifying world, which lately seemed bent on destroying every living thing on the planet, was a monumental decision. Seven billion and counting. Let's pop another one into the pile. For what? Maybe it was time for people to stop and think about this whole making babies business.

"But they're so cute and cuddly, I want one of my own."

Get a kitten!

"It's the perfect expression of love, a couple creating and bringing new life into the world."

The perfect expression of love is to get along and to stop nagging!

"But, Martin!…"

Okay okay. He got it. That's why she left.

Now she could go look for another sperm donor.

Martin kicked off his shoes and leaned back. A thin filament of smoke still rose from the glowing ember of weed at the bottom of the bowl. He took another hit, closed his eyes. He could hear the rhythm of his blood as it pulsed through the capillaries of his ears. Warm bubbles spread through his body. His fingertips lightly tingled. He felt like he was suspended in jelly. Or was it styrofoam?

He surrendered to it, diffusing into the gelatinous limbo.

A pleasant dispassion now displaced the anxiety he had been feeling. In the ambient pool of the softly undulating void, an epiphany floated to the surface like a translucent mermaid from mysterious, secretive depths.

He imagined himself smiling. A Buddha-like apparition floated in his mind's eye.

The analgesic calm of reason had indeed come to the rescue…

Alison was gone. It actually made sense. In fact it was good. Even if he hadn't handled things the way he should have, Martin now felt certain what had happened was.the right thing. Breaking up was inevitable. The writing had been on the wall for quite some time now. Frankly, it was hard to think of a time when they had really gotten along. Nearly impossible.

Nearly. Impossible. To think of a time …

Actually … at this point it was impossible to think at all.

What was he trying to think of?

Usually Martin only took one or two hits, just enough to relax and enjoy a mild buzz. But tonight, lost in his deliberations and not really paying attention, he had smoked a joint and an entire bowl. His head felt like a hot air balloon. The sound coming from the television was *extremely* grating and he couldn't make sense out of *anything* anyone was saying. Was that Conan O'Brien? He was leering at some babe's cleavage like he was getting ready to bungee jump. She was trying to act indignant — or was it coy? — as in, *"Hey, what's the deal? You're not at all interested in this fascinating story I'm telling, you BAD BOY!"*

Fuck this! Television. What a wasteland. Enough brain damage for one night.

Martin crawled into bed. Before the cannabis coma overpowered him, he reached over to Alison's side of the bed.

Alright! He had two pillows.

Now that's living!

• • •

Things took a turn for the worse after that first night.

He was having nightmares.

Well, more accurately he was having *one* nightmare. The same nightmare over and over. Nightly for almost three weeks now.

It was to be expected. Guilt. Regret. Blowback.

The nightmare started innocently and pleasantly enough. He and Alison were on campus. Which campus wasn't certain. It was sort of a hybrid of Cornell and the University of Chicago. Trees and flowers in spring. Sunny skies. Things were good back then. They would meet at lunch or late afternoon after classes. Thrilled at the prospect of seeing one another. Just being together. It was rainbows and balloons as they strolled hand in hand, smiling so much it hurt.

Then two strange men came up behind them. They grabbed Alison and pulled her between them. At first, Martin refused to believe they meant any harm. In fact, he seemed to feel a peculiar camaraderie with them. He joked in his typical unassuming, cordial manner. But they brazenly mocked his attempt to be friendly, and glaring at him with spitefulness, started backing away. Alison now fiercely struggled to get free. Martin took a tentative step toward her, reaching out to take her hand. One of the assailants suddenly pulled a knife and swiped it at Martin's face, just missing his nose. Alison now became even more horrified and started screaming, though in the haunting null of the dream, no sound issued from her. Martin felt the raw anguish of her desperation, as she pleaded for his help. But he retreated like a pathetic coward, more frightened than he'd ever been in life. Martin suddenly turned and ran to save himself. When he briefly glanced over his shoulder, he caught the horror and loathing in Alison's eyes as the two thugs wrestled her to the ground. One of them held her flailing body, the other stood over her, unzipping his fly. Martin just kept running, through a viscous sludge of dread and despair, running and gasping for breath, tormented by having just abandoned his beloved Alison. Moments later, wracked with guilt and shaking uncontrollably, he found himself in a dark room, a restaurant in a musty cavern no less, lit only by the candles on the tables. Before him sat two glasses of wine. Who was he there with? He kept looking around anxiously and waiting. Finally his mother appeared in the doorway, then walked over to the table. There was a bullet hole in her forehead with blood trickling out of it, though she seemed unfazed by it. "Alison's dead. It's your fault." Martin burst into tears. It was a horrible, painful crying that hurt so deep it felt like he was being disemboweled. He cried so hard he couldn't breathe. Asphyxiation ripped at his lungs and his mother just stood there shaking her bleeding head, offering no comfort or support. "You let Alison die. You let me die." She scowled at him with contempt, then turned to leave. He would start to plead. "Mother, no. Come back!"

Abruptly the nightmare would end.

Martin woke up choking, crying, trembling, covered in sweat.

There was no way he could go back to sleep, so he always got up and got dressed.

He paced. Sucked down cup after cup of coffee. Watched bland early morning television.

He had no appetite and couldn't force himself to eat breakfast. He dragged himself to work. He was so tired it was all he could do to just show up. By lunch he was dizzy from lack of nourishment. By the end of the day he was sure his life signs had all disappeared.

Martin drove a delivery van for Future Perfect, a local courier service. Nothing like putting his college education to good use. Not surprisingly, when he finally left the comfort zone of university life, there weren't any listings in the Dayton Daily News classifieds for someone with a BA in Philosophy (minor in Peace Studies and Peace Science) and an MA in Political Science. Not in Springboro, Ohio anyway.

It was a job. Mindless. No pressure. Even being at his worst — and after nearly twenty reruns of the Alison-mom nightmare, he was physically and psychologically at his rock bottom worst — was no obstacle to his performing his simple duties.

Only one person commented on his deteriorating condition. It was the dispatcher, Evelyn. Heart of gold, face of stone, body of a rhinoceros, Evvie single-handedly kept the tobacco industry in the black. Martin could not recall ever seeing her without a lit cigarette in her hand. The inside of her index and middle fingers were the color of saddle leather. Her voice sounded like a Harley Davidson on a cold morning.

"Here are fourteen deliveries. They all should've been there half an hour ago. You look like your cat died, turned into a vampire and sucked out all of your blood. What gives? If you need a bone marrow transplant, I'll put a notice in the employee newsletter."

"I'm on a hunger strike. I'm protesting 7-11 jacking up the price of their corn dogs."

"Well damn, Marty. Good for you. Taking a stand on an issue I personally can get behind. Seriously. It's this political stuff, isn't it? Politics is poison. It attracts the worst and kills off the best. But don't forget: If you do go to Washington, I'll be your executive secretary *and* your body guard. Two for the price of one."

Which reminded him — not that he forgot, since it was something he couldn't help but think about despite his compromised state — he had an important meeting tonight. Well, important as they ever were. Which admittedly wasn't very important in the grand scheme of things. In any case, the entire brain-heavy campaign planning committee would be there. They had supposedly been quite busy whipping up a whole new approach for his upcoming courtship of the voting public. This time around, they were hoping to get things started as early as possible, in order to get a leg up on the incumbent, who not only had the advantage of being an incumbent but had a ton of cash in his re-election coffers.

They couldn't match his opponent's 10,000 to 1 monetary advantage. Time was all they had going for them. Hit the streets early and come out swinging. At least their version of swinging, which would appear to the impartial observer more like a quadriplegic attacking a piñata with a pea shooter than a street fight.

In the past, Martin had always been right in the thick of the initial planning and there until every last detail was in place. After all, it was his campaign. It was his ass on the line. Important as it was that the campaign appeal to the public, it also had to be comfortable for him. It had to feel right, set the correct tone, be like an old familiar sweat shirt or sweater, one that felt natural and familiar. Otherwise, he couldn't sell it. He would come off as phony as ... as ... as well, the typical phony politician.

Unfortunately this time around, at least for now, Martin was clearly missing-in-action. For what seemed like forever, he had been mostly useless at these strategy brainstorming sessions. After Alison left him, he had thoroughly fallen apart. He couldn't concentrate. He was tired beyond words. He constantly hovered between a paralytic agitation and a somnolent stupor. He felt more numb than alive. The difference between awake and asleep was purely academic.

Everyone at party headquarters was sympathetic. They agreed he should take some time. Get his head straight. Not to worry. They would crank out some ideas and when he felt ready to come back and dig in his heels, he could fine tune things to his liking.

It was going on a month now.

His head still wasn't straight. Not by a long shot. From the looks of things, it might not be for a long time.

But life goes on. There was work to do. He'd show up tonight and see if he could pull himself out of the mental quicksand. He'd try anyway. Sink or swim, as they say.

For him it felt like swim ... and sink anyway.

• • •

So.

Here he was.

But who was he kidding?

As he sat there listening to the six members of the officially titled Executive Committee and Election Strategy Council, it was all Martin could do to keep awake. His eyelids were made of lead and his brain was pure mush.

He truly respected these people. No … he loved these people!

But he still couldn't get it together to focus on what was going on.

Phyllis Wagner, executive director for this chapter of the Green Party, ran the show. Boy, did she ever! She put the 'charge' in 'in charge'. Then there was Bill Townsend, officially his campaign manager, always there with a joke and a smile. Imogene Kurtz and Bob Phelps, who both worked for the Ohio Department of Job and Family Services, were the links to all of the local progressive community organizations. The brilliant Lincoln Haskell, an associate professor and political activist at University of Dayton, rallied the youth vote and provided phenomenal insights into the political process. Least but certainly not last was Helen Bueller, secretary and gofer, responsible more than anyone else for actually getting things done.

All of them had been with him for his last two campaigns. Phyllis, Bill and Helen had been there from the very beginning, when a few months out of college he wandered into their modest office in Phyllis's home, and announced he was available as a candidate for U.S. Congress. They must have thought he was crazy! Whether they did or not, they put him on the ballot, at twenty-three the youngest person to ever run for the Ohio 3rd District U.S. House of Representatives congressional seat. If he had gotten elected, he would just be turning twenty-five — by law the minimum age for a congressman — only a few days before assuming office.

"What do you think, Martin?"

He heard his name. It punctured the slinky scrim of his disjointed reverie.

Phyllis had said something. He looked up. All eyes were on him.

"I'm sorry. I was someplace else. Think of what?"

"We're talking about going for broke. Hiring a bona fide heavy-hitter. You know, a big league consultant who knows exactly how to play the game."

"Expensive, I imagine. Can we afford that?"

"We don't know. We're just talking about it. All along we've had good ideas. Three times running, we've given this our best shot. But it's not coming together. Something's not clicking. Last election even that Libertarian Potts guy got 5,000 more votes than you. That bozo can't even utter a coherent sentence."

"Don't remind me. Anyway, do what you think is best. I trust you guys."

Trust them he would have to. At least for now. Campaigning nine months before election day was a thankless enough task. But with Alison gone, his heart wasn't in it. And he had no idea where his head was at.

If only I had a brain.

• • •

Alison.

Nine months.

He had foolishly promised her that in nine months he'd be in the delivery room at her side for their long-awaited first child, not sitting in front of a television watching election returns. Yes, he had broken his word.

Big time.

He felt like a real shithead. Alison had stuck by him for almost eight years. He probably wouldn't find anyone like her again ever. Not even close. She was just about perfect for him. So it had seemed at the outset. Until failure moved in and became a permanent fixture in their lives. His failure, not hers. She kept moving forward. Maybe not the forward he would have preferred. But by any normal, accepted standards, everything for her kept getting better.

Even when she was in college, she was a winner. Incredibly attractive. Kind of a Sandra Bullock attractive. So smart. Everybody liked her. Other guys were always salivating like dogs. They would try to hit on her even when Martin was right there standing next to her.

Hmm. What did that say about him?

He and Alison left university at the same time, him with his masters in political science, her with her bachelors in business and banking. For two years she did a stint with a online stock brokerage. The guys that ran it were in their early-30s and viewed themselves as dot com dissidents. They prided themselves in not being sucked in by all of the corporate bullshit. Alison thrived on the informality. She contributed much more than what they gave her credit for or was reflected in her modest salary. But she was happy. When they unexpectedly sold their firm to a hedge fund out of Texas, she found herself out of a job.

That was when things changed.

It was right after the big crash of 2008 and the job market was tight. They couldn't live decently on what he was making as a courier, that is, without pinching pennies and obsessing over money all of the time. Finally, she landed a great entry level executive position which promised a lot of upward mobility with Bank of America.

Martin begged her not to take it. Bank of America was one of the worst of the country's mega-banks. It represented everything Martin hated about corporate America. It was implicated in all sorts of corrupt practices, it ripped off investors and customers alike, scammed the disabled and the poor, sleazed out of paying their taxes at all levels, sidestepped fees to the local communities where they did business, aggressively and illegally threw homeowners out on the street using unsavory procedures to foreclose, on and on. Against the revulsion that Martin felt in every fiber of his body…

She took the job.

She never blinked. She never looked back.

Martin tried to forgive her. He tried to ignore the changes he was seeing in her.

He was sure he hid the contempt he was increasingly feeling for her.

Probably not.

Okay. Definitely not. He was a lousy actor.

It surely was all a moot point now anyway.

She was history. Gone for good.

And that was that.

Maybe that's the only way it could be: An inevitable ending to a flawed romance. He probably should have seen it coming. But he didn't want to. Rationalization is love's best ally. Maybe she was perfect for him. Maybe not. Whatever. But *he* definitely was not perfect for *her*. Meaning their relationship had from the beginning been a time-bomb ticking.

Okay. He could accept that. He'd have to accept that. It wasn't like he had a choice.

Mercifully, against the random, sometime brutal realities of life, Martin now came prepared. He had the ultimate contingency plan. There's nothing like standing over your mother's grave, looking into the cold silence and immutability of death, to shotgun a new paradigm into the frontal lobes of the cerebral cortex.

So it now was and always would be for Martin…

Even if he was a total fuck-up in his personal life, he would make up for it in public life. Even if as in the present circumstance, he couldn't keep his word to Alison, he would make absolute certain on the remote chance he actually got elected, that unlike 99% of the politicians in office nowadays, he would keep his word to the voting public. He would keep every last one of his campaign promises. No ambivalence. No excuses. No compromises.

Which left only one critical question to be answered.

What did Martin Truth stand for? Besides keeping campaign promises.

As the Green Party candidate he obviously believed in protecting the environment. Something had to be done to stop global warming, if it wasn't too late already. We had to end our addiction to fossil fuels, especially oil. There should be huge private and public investments in renewable alternative energy sources: wind, ocean, solar. We had to reverse deforestation. End desertification. Halt the privatization of water and other basic necessities. Encourage local food production, promote organic agriculture, and reduce the use of pesticides and GMO seeds. In general, the world needed to back off corporatizing everything and return to local production and control. With bold and determined political leaders on the front lines, it needed to confront and defeat the multinational corporate juggernaut that was polluting and destroying the Earth.

As might be expected, Martin's progressivism extended broadly from his commitment to environmental causes to a number of co-related social issues. He categorically took exception to the every-man-for-himself madness of the right wing and believed that all of us through representative government should take a greater role in helping others, especially those who were less able to fend for themselves. This included the old, the infirm, victims of racism and other forms of discrimination. And those who had lost their jobs and fallen on hard times. The poor. The undereducated. Children. Most definitely children! Without a doubt, Martin would be labeled as a bleeding-heart liberal by the crass law-of-the-jungle conservatives, who he thought lacked both compassion and common decency, people who called themselves Christians but somehow missed the most obvious and critical aspects of Christ's teachings: Feed the hungry, clothe the poor, heal the sick, tend to the needs of the less fortunate.

> "For I was hungry, and you gave Me *something* to eat; I was thirsty, and you gave Me *something* to drink; I was a stranger, and you invited Me in; naked, and you clothed Me; I was sick, and you visited Me; I was in prison, and you came to Me ... Truly I say to you, to the extent that you did it to one of these brothers of Mine, *even* the least *of them,* you did it to Me." – Matthew 25:35/36/40

Hardly what could be called a Bible-thumper, questionably even a Christian at all by any conventional standards, Martin had used that passage in his campaign literature last election season. Very few voters seemed to appreciate its relevance to the progressive ideals he espoused. If they did, they still managed to forget about him when it came time to vote.

Martin was also deeply committed to human rights, under relentless assault long before humankind even recognized what they were. It was ironic that now in many countries which had long had an onerous record of human rights abuses, there were significant improvements, while in America itself, allegedly champion of humane and just treatment, fairness, and respect for all, human rights was suffering dismal setbacks every day.

He was especially concerned about the intrusive levels of officially unacknowledged surveillance, and the constant push for locking up more and more citizens. There seemed to be a new mentality taking over which destroyed any sense of proportion and reason with respect to incarceration. It certainly was destroying justice and equality before the law. The operating principle was: *If we build it, they will come*. Or more to the point: *We've built a helluva lot of these prisons, now we've got to fill them!* They were filling the prisons all right. Mostly with people of color.

Admittedly, there was a lot on his wish list, a substantial catalog of action items which embraced the things Martin thought had to be done immediately to reverse the downward, self-sabotaging course of the country. It was a daunting set of tasks requiring the energy of the whole nation working together, unified and determined in their dedication to rebuild a great America.

Daunting or not, these were the things which drove him to seek a seat in Congress.

These were the things he thought crucial for a better world.

These were the things he felt passionate about.

Even if right now he felt no passion.

Right now Martin didn't feel much of anything. He was ambling aimlessly through each featureless day like some malfunctioning automaton or decaying zombie.

Life right now sadly lacked an urgent and profound sense of purpose.

Six days a week he reported to Future Perfect and rush-delivered everything from legal documents to machine parts, gift packages to electronic devices, butterfly collections to family photo albums. Once he picked up at a home then dropped off at the airport some forgetful university professor's passport. Another time when a medivac transport vehicle experienced mechanical problems, he delivered a kidney packed in ice and locked in a thermal carrier. Then there was the time he rushed some sexy lingerie from Victoria's Secret to an upscale hotel near the business center of town.

Whatever the cargo, every day was pretty much like every other as he crisscrossed the 250 square miles of metro Dayton. At least before, weaving through endless traffic and piling up more parking tickets, he used to daydream about how all this would change if he somehow miraculously won the coming election. But now his daydreams felt like stale reruns. He was feeling like an old man on life support.

One of the few positive things he could say about his job was that they used environmentally-friendly natural gas powered vans. Otherwise, it was nothing much to write home about. The pay was pretty bad. He had no benefits to speak of — no health insurance, no paid vacation, only a handful of sick days, the minimum number of paid holidays.

He couldn't relate to anyone who worked there. He had nothing in common with the line employees, the drivers, maintenance guys, office help. It was a strain trying to keep up his end of conversations on television shows he never had seen, sports teams he couldn't care less about, and celebrities whose names he recognized but wouldn't know if they knocked on his door and offered their autographs.

Of course, he glad-handed everyone and put on his best smile, mostly because he generally liked people and tried to get along with most everyone in any situation. But he also was holding out for the unlikely prospect that at some point he might get to share with them what was truly important to him and what he spent his *quality* time on, which of course were his political ideas and his candidacy for the district's congressional seat.

Fat chance.

No one there took him seriously.

No one seem capable of registering, much less grasping his deep commitment to politics. When he tried to explain that he was the Green Party candidate for the district's congressional seat, from the looks he got he wondered if he had inadvertently started speaking in some obscure Chinese dialect. His fellow workers typically got a glazed look of bewilderment, as if he were telling them what life was like for him and his pet octopus on the fourth moon of Neptune. The management team, which because it was a small company of only thirty-seven employees consisted of three executives, a line manager and an accountant, all looked at him with undisguised disdain and mistrust. Martin assumed they were politically ultra-conservative and just the mention of the Green Party got their hackles doing a St. Vitus dance. They probably thought he was Che Guevara.

As a result of the indifference, if not outright antipathy there, it had been quite some time since he mentioned anything remotely related to politics or public policy. No sense adding anxiety to confusion. He showed up, did his job, smiled, collected a paycheck.

From another perspective, he really had no right to complain. It covered the bills. And because he lived so minimally, his salary even left over a decent surplus for his two "luxuries", his addiction to buying books and his support for a number of charitable non-profits. He bought a couple new books each week, then contributed what he could afford to causes. He sent modest but regular sums to a few environmental groups, Doctors Without Borders, Southern Poverty Law Center, and participated in two child sponsorship programs, one in Africa and the other Central America.

The truly laudable aspect of the job was that it only occupied forty hours of his week. Exactly forty hours. Future Perfect was too cheap to pay overtime. He did have to report six days. He worked seven hours Monday through Friday, then five hours Saturday. Regardless, this still left him plenty of time to work on his campaign. Every weekday he was free from 4 pm on, then had a fair chunk of the weekend, since on Saturday he was done at noon.

"He said he can meet with us on Saturday, Martin. Martin? Are you with us?"

Phyllis pulled him out of his trance. What was she saying?

"Uh yes … Saturday. What about Saturday?"

"While you've been channeling Helen Keller, Bill got hold of a campaign consultant who comes highly recommended. His name is Charles Montgomery and he's out of Cincinnati."

"Wow. Cincinnati."

"He'll be here at 4:30 on Saturday. I promise we won't commit to anything until everyone is completely satisfied he's right for you. But he's got a great track record."

"Wow. Great track record."

"Okay. See you then."

"4:30 Saturday."

"Splendid."

• • •

He hated him immediately. The guy was wearing suspenders. Suspenders!

Martin had arrived on time. In fact, he was there at 4:25. Then he sat and waited until the self-important dickweed blew in at 5:05.

Not that the rude son-of-a-bitch showed one iota of embarrassment or remorse.

As soon as he stepped in the door, Martin wanted to cut his losses and run. The guy dumped his briefcase and a pile of file folders on the table like he was body slamming Hulk Hogan. Then, smiling a rapturous 'America's Next Male Supermodel' smile, his salon-tanned face beaming as if this was the greatest day of his life, his hand shot out like he was breaking cement blocks with the tips of his fingers.

"Well well! Martin Truth. The man of the hour. Boy, am I glad I finally get to meet you! Charles Montgomery. But everyone calls me Monty."

Martin hesitated. He knew what was coming. He tentatively extended his hand.

Yup. As expected, it ended up on the wrong end of a metacarpal bone crushing. *Monty*, eh? What a typical Type A-personality raging asshole!

"I'm Martin Truth. But everyone calls me a liar."

"Ha ha ha. That's priceless. I love a good sense of humor. Unfortunately, Martin, others before you have tarnished your noble profession. In terms of public confidence, politicians rank somewhere below the Mafia and slightly above child pornographers. But I gotta tell you, in it's offbeat own way, Martin Truth is perfect. I like it!"

Martin Truth. Monty *liked* it. Wonderful. Martin wanted to think of it as just another name but no one ever would leave it alone. It started in elementary school and never slowed up.

He was sick of it. Now that he had been commodified for public consumption, the word plays had reached truly annoying new heights. He had never thought puns were especially clever or fun. Being assaulted on a personal level confirmed his worst suspicions. As campaign slogans, they seemed to guarantee that no one would take him or his candidacy seriously.

We hold <u>*this*</u> *Truth to be self-evident* . . . it had a nice ring to it but the only thing that soon became self-evident was that no one was going to vote for him.

The whole Truth and nothing but the Truth . . . as if he was being sworn in to testify in his own insanity trial. What else could explain his running for office on a third-party ticket?

Truth in politics! — which morphed into — *Truth in government!* . . . certainly had promise except no one figured out it had anything to do with him. His brand recognition was zero.

Nothing but the Truth! . . . turned out to be anybody but Martin Truth.

Truth will triumph! . . . proved to be not accurate in any sense.

Honesty + honor = Truth . . . what is this? New math?

He was sick of gimmicks.

Hopefully this bozo would have some amazing new ideas. After all, he supposedly got the big bucks. He *was* from Cincinnati. *And* he had a great track record.

"So, Martin, I don't know if you've ever thought about doing something with your name, but I was thinking of something along the lines of, *The Truth will set you free!* Whaddya think? I mean just for starters."

OMG! What an idiot! If this joker was working for free, they were paying him too much.

"Well gosh, Monty. It's certainly original. I think if this were 1856, we'd have a real winner."

"1856? I'm not following you."

"No problem. I entirely understand. I got this from a program on Comedy Central. Do you get satellite? Anyway, 1856 was before they abolished slavery. So, you know ... *set you free.* As in give the slaves their freedom. But hey! Maybe it would still work now. You're the expert here. You *are* from Cincinnati."

Martin winked at Monty, then glanced over at Phyllis to see how she was taking this. She wasn't easy to read. It wasn't clear whether her face was the color of Red Bull because of the humiliation she was feeling for having brought in this Slick Willy to spew this kind of drivel, or furious at Martin for wasting no time yanking Monty's chain.

The rest of the meeting was a blur. Everything Monty said was a blur or caused blurring in the eyes of everyone in the room. One thing could be said for sure. His enthusiasm was beyond question. The guy was in a perpetual state of hosting *Deal Or No Deal.*

It dragged on for nearly three hours. It seemed like months.

Monty had the final word, which wasn't much of a surprise, since up to this point he had done 99.9% of the talking.

"Okay! Gotta go. But I have to tell ya, I'm very excited. *Very* excited. We got a lot done tonight. A *lot* done! A good beginning. A *damn* good beginning. Alright now. See ya!"

Monty's head was still bouncing up and down like a dashboard bobble head doll, as he retreated out the door with the strut of a gladiator who had just slaughtered everything in sight.

Martin wearily looked over at Phyllis. She was ready for him.

"Listen, Martin, don't start."

"What? I was just going to tell you how brilliant I think Monty is. How perfectly he fits in with our team."

"Give me a break. You don't cut anyone any slack. Like you've got something better? Where's *your* plan? He was just … just a little nervous."

"You have to be human to be nervous. The guy was a hologram."

"Enough, Martin. You've said your piece. Your obvious disdain hardly comes as a surprise. You're becoming so predictable. All I'm going to say is give the guy a chance. We have a lot of money tied up in this gentleman. Let's see what he's got. Everyone raves about him. Everyone I've talked to anyway."

"Money? I thought this was just an audition."

Phyllis, never at a loss for words … was at a loss for words. Solid, forthright, implacable, unshakeable, she actually looked a bit sheepish.

Apparently two days ago, she had cut a check. Monty had talked her into a sizable retainer. It was non-refundable.

The conversation had gone something like this: *"I've been checking out your Martin Truth. Excellent candidate. We've really got something here. Let me tell you, Phyllis, this type of campaign is exactly my cup of tea. I don't give a damn what happened before. I can take your Truth guy over the top. This is absolutely a match made in Heaven. So let's not waste any time. I'll be there Saturday. I'm bringing my whole bag of secret weapons. No reason to hold back anything at all. We'll hit the ground running. Phyllis, I'm feeling really good about this. I mean really good!"*

Monty was such a cyclone of bullshit, he was so insistent and obnoxious, even Phyllis's carefully crafted fortress of defenses crumbled in the onslaught. She agreed to a tidy sum.

"How much, Phyllis? What's left in the bank?"

"He assured me that the retainer was small change. It was pennies on the dollar compared to what we'll be hauling in once his fundraising kicks into full swing. Martin, it was only a tenth of what he usually charges!"

"Do we have *any* money left?"

"Actually I had to go into my own savings."

"Your savings? How much did you personally put into this?"

"$5000. But don't worry about it. If this doesn't work out, I'll … it'll be my problem."

So that's where it stood. They were broke *and* they were stuck with Monty Motor Mouth.

Martin spent every evening for the next week meeting with Charles 'Monty' Montgomery. He did exactly as he was told. He forced himself to keep an open mind and gave Monty every opportunity to show his stuff. Martin did it, for lack of a better reason, to make Phyllis happy. Then too, there was the remote possibility some good would come of it.

It was easy to see what Monty was up to. There was a method to his madness. But it was still madness. The very same madness that had turned politics into a big game and emptied it of any substance. It was the sound bite and bumper sticker insipidness that had made unlikely, if not entirely impossible, any meaningful communication between a candidate and the people he would be representing.

Beyond constantly wrestling with the feeling that he was being manipulated and sucked into a mind set that was craven, mercenary, irresponsible, and lacking in any semblance of intelligence, there were personality issues.

Monty certainly had a way with words. He was like Howard Stern but without the polish.

"I've been looking at your stump speeches. We need to hone them a bit. Trim the fat. People want things cut and dried. Clean and easy."

Actually, Martin in principle agreed with the idea. He did prefer simple and straightforward, within reasonable limits.

"As long as I don't end up spouting empty platitudes, I'm fine with that. And, of course, I refuse to misrepresent my position on anything."

"Right. Whatever. Listen, Truth. I don't think you get it. It doesn't matter what the voters *think* you believe in. It doesn't even matter what *you* think you believe in."

What I think I believe in?

"All that matters is getting elected. Then you can go in there and do whatever turns your crank. Fuck yes! Do the right thing. Take whatever holier-than-thou stance you want. Mother Theresa and all that shit."

Martin froze.

He couldn't say anything.

He couldn't *let* himself say anything. Because one thing would lead to another and then he'd have to *kill* the guy!

He just sat there. Biting his tongue. Was there steam blasting out of his ears like he was one of the Three Stooges?

That exchange, unfortunately, pretty much set the tone for everything that went down for all of the subsequent evenings.

Monty kept telling Martin it's all about winning. If he didn't win, end of story. Game over. No chance of doing all of those wonderful high-minded things he wanted to do. He'd be swept under the carpet. Forgotten. Losers don't just lose. They vanish into thin air.

If Martin had to venture a guess, he decided that if Monty had ever been to college, he had studied at the Joseph Stalin School of Diplomacy.

Miraculously, the evenings passed without Martin committing a homicide. The week with Charles Montgomery constituted the greatest exercise in self-control in Martin's entire life, greater than he could have *ever* imagined himself capable of.

Of course, he knew that present-day politics was a lot of PR blather at the expense of substance. But Monty's ideas were appalling. Crude. They were so ruthless, so unprincipled, so baldly rapacious, so detached from and anathema to institutional democracy, Martin felt like he was being dragged through a Franz Kafka story. At one point, Monty even hinted — take that back, he outright said — that since a substantial number of voting places in the district were using the Diebold electronic voting machines, as soon as the campaign came up with enough money, he'd hire a hacker to switch a number of votes their way.

"We'll win this goddamn thing by hook or crook! Are you with me?"

Phyllis was there when Monty proposed the voting machine fraud and was so mortified by the underhandedness of the idea, she couldn't even respond. She'd gotten them into this mess. Now all she could think about was how to get rid of this barbarian and get their money back.

Then the inconceivable happened.

Monty tendered his resignation.

Actually, it wasn't so much a tendering as having a hysterical tantrum and mental breakdown, seemingly provoked by nothing more than the lock on his briefcase jamming.

Martin again was early. Monty again was late. This had become the drill.

When Monty finally bolted through the door, something was different. The guy looked like he had just been impaled with Dante's vision of Hell. Again he dumped a giant stack of folders on the table, peculiar in itself because he had never referred to any of the reams of material in them, at least not so far.

Then he tried to open his briefcase. He seemed a bit frantic about it. The briefcase wouldn't cooperate. Monty started pounding it with his fist and yelling.

"Open up, you motherfucker!"

For the first time since these meetings started, Martin smiled. Then he burst out laughing.

Monty picked up the briefcase and threw it against the wall. It still wouldn't open. Then he noticed Martin laughing, joined by Phyllis doing her own bit of smirking. At that moment, Bill arrived and poked his head in the door. He had been wanting to sit in on one of the sessions. From what he had been hearing, they were too good to miss.

"What's going on, guys?"

Monty went ballistic. With one sweeping motion of his arm, he pushed all of the file folders off the table onto the floor. Papers and pamphlets went flying. Then he picked up the briefcase with both hands as if to clobber Bill with it.

"I'll tell you what's going on. I'm outta here. This is a waste of time." He looked at Martin. "You're a fucking loser. You don't stand a chance in China." He turned to Bill, then to Phyllis. "I don't want my name on this. I don't want to be anywhere near this when it goes down in flames. 'A' is for asshole. 'Z' is for Zanzibar. I *hope* the polar caps melt. Fuck you very much!"

He was out the door before anyone had time to take a breath.

Martin looked at Phyllis doing his best to look serious.

"How are we polling in China?"

The three of them spent the next fifteen minutes in hysterical laughter, as they recounted not just what had happened this evening, but the ridiculousness of the entire six days Martin had spent trying to work with this lunatic.

Phyllis was not usually one for knee-slapping belly-laughing. Tonight was an exception.

But soon a sobering reality reared its ugly head.

The money.

Over the next few days, Phyllis repeatedly called Monty's office but only got an answering machine. Eventually she resigned herself to the fact that the retainer was gone. This meant the war chest for Martin's campaign was down to nickels and her $5000 had just gone up in smoke.

The more they talked about it, the more they agreed that Charles Montgomery had hustled them and probably had done so right from the beginning. He never had any intention to follow through till the end of the campaign. He was likely between jobs and saw an opportunity for some easy cash from some desperate and gullible people.

Phyllis just couldn't believe it. Not that she was naïve. But she found it inconceivable that someone like Monty could sit across the table from decent human beings like themselves, knowing full well that it was all just a show and that he was intentionally ripping them off.

Smarting from the callous assault on her faith in her fellow human beings, she turned to Martin for comfort, for his validation of her core belief that people were essentially good.

"Can you believe this kind of behavior, Martin?"

"Yes. You saw how he was acting."

"Which means what?"

"Bath salts."

CHAPTER TWO

Matt Gardner was a legend.

He'd successfully run for Congress five times. The coming election seemed to be in the bag. Gardner as a candidate and as a political icon seemed invulnerable. His public career had started more than twenty years ago when practically unknown he successfully ran for mayor of Dayton. Coming from way behind, he had squeaked by his opponent, who conveniently one month before the election was unexpectedly plagued by scandals involving payoffs from local contractors, then just days before the election was caught in bed with an escort during a high roller political junket in Las Vegas.

Not that Gardner's time as mayor and in the House of Representatives itself was free of its own scandals and mishaps. But nothing seemed to be able to knock him off course or slow him down. If the phrase 'Teflon politician' wasn't invented for Matt Gardner, it should have been.

Every year it was something. As mayor, he was accused of misusing campaign funds and accepting questionable contributions. At one point, rumors of his sexual harassment of two young hotties in his secretarial pool surfaced. The pastor of his church even refused to endorse him for re-election, hinting that he was less than exemplary with respect to a couple unspecified commandments.

All of this naturally was dredged up when he first ran for the district's congressional seat. But it seemed to make no difference. Gardner won by a respectable margin, approaching a landslide.

He had now been in Congress for almost ten years. The unflattering aspersions and incriminating accusations continued to be a steady drumbeat.

His name would be mentioned in connection to kick-backs from defense contractors — he currently sat on the Armed Services and Homeland Security committees — or as a prime target for investigation by the House Committee on Ethics. Some whistleblower would talk about misallocation of government funds and campaign donations, everything from elaborate improvements to his already ultra-plush home in Washington Township, to personal trips for him and his family to Hawaii and the Bahamas. An embittered campaign worker — female and usually very young and attractive — would accuse him of groping. Speaking fees arranged by powerful lobbyists would come up missing on his tax returns.

But nothing would stick. Gardner could be dropped head first in a huge vat of crude oil and crawl out looking like he was on his way to his wedding.

His most famous blunder was a doozy. A few years ago when North Korea was doing more than its usual amount of saber-rattling, Gardner introduced a bill in Congress to build a multi-billion dollar missile defense system on the East Coast to guard against the anticipated volley of missiles from Kim Jong-il and the rest of the commie nutcases running things there. The bill made it all the way to the floor of the House before someone finally pointed out that North Korea was west of the U.S. and the anticipated volley of missiles would arrive on the West Coast.

Not that the proposed system actually had anything to do with safeguarding America. Its real purpose was creating more billions of dollars in business for the defense industry. Not coincidentally, corporations like Lockheed Martin, Northrop Grumman, and Boeing — the top three involved in ground-based missile defense system development — were major contributors to Gardner's campaign coffers. He was just taking care of those who took care of him at election time.

No one seemed to care about any of this. Or those who cared were silenced or ignored.

In terms of the media, something might be mentioned in passing but most stories implicating Gardner in any untoward or even blatantly stupid behavior just got buried in the blather. Either blather in the form of celebrity gossip, or blather about whatever the latest hot political topic of the week was. Sometimes it was just dumb luck and serendipitous timing, but often enough it could be attributed to savvy and shrewdness on Gardner's part. If Woody Allen wasn't marrying his grand daughter or one of the Kardashians getting pregnant by some beefcake, Gardner would himself create a stir by calling a press conference and making some dramatic announcement, full of patriotic grandiloquence and kettle drum clichés. One way or the other, in terms of anything serious enough to damage his public persona or political career, the bad stuff always got pushed off the radar.

This tactic generally was becoming more and more business-as-usual across the political landscape. Hot topics of the moment were more frequently than not, diversions and distractions designed to keep the media dialogue and therefore public awareness from focusing on the real issues. Most of the alleged "major crises" of the country seemed to fit this mold. They were introduced and promulgated with catchy slogans and gross oversimplifications — carefully crafted talking points — which served a political agenda having little to do with making America a decent place for the majority of citizens and a lot to do with making a few connected people very rich. People that were already incomprehensibly rich.

The last decade had seen the frequent and skillful deployment of these weapons of mass disinformation. Politics was becoming George Orwell on acid and a double espresso.

Raising the national debt limit was evidence that welfare cheats and the idle poor expected the country to borrow money from those damn Chinese so that they could live high off the dole. Reforming health care showed that the pinko Marxists who had infiltrated the country wanted to turn America into another

Godless orgiastic socialist Sweden. Any talk of the slightest increase in taxes on the rich was class warfare, a spiteful and thankless attack on the wonderful people who created all the good jobs for working Americans. Any attempt to reduce the defense budget, even the elimination of pork barrel boondoggles which had no demonstrable purpose in defending the country, was a treasonous surrender to al-Qaeda and the other Muslim towelheads who hated our freedom and who would not sleep until America was a pile of rubble. Government funding for *any* women's health services — even breast cancer screening and Pap smears — was a vile, poorly disguised attempt by a small minority of oversexed sluts to get the government to subsidize their whorish ways so they could have irresponsible boffing whenever their hyperactive libidos demanded.

Matt Gardner was a genius at this type of obfuscation. Whether he had behind-the-scenes help from right wing think tanks like the Heritage Foundation, and political hatchet men like Karl Rove and Grover Norquist, or came up with it on his own, one thing couldn't be denied. He was good at it!

His genius lay in making the most inane, ill-informed and poorly-conceived propositions sound plausible, even appealing, then delivering these polished turds and non-sequiturs with the poise and conviction of a Nobel laureate. He was a one-man weapon of mass distraction.

When asked by a reporter why he voted to repeal health care reform, he replied…

"If you don't think America is the greatest country in the
world, well then, you just haven't been looking.
Maybe you should send your resume to
the Beijing Daily Gazette."

On his missile defense system boondoggle…

"I can't stand by while a bunch of hippie peace-freaks
disarm this country. How could I sleep at night
thinking missiles could be raining down
on my children right here in Ohio?"

He defended his opposition to allocating research funds for green energy technology…

"Did Thomas Edison come pleading for an allowance from
his rich Uncle Sam? I don't think so. My youngest
kid loves her hula hoop. Did this great little
toy require a Department of Energy
grant? There's your answer."

Gardner apparently didn't detect any irony in his remarks on world peace, in an address delivered at a summer youth camp sponsored by the YMCA of Greater Dayton…

"Yes, I'm all for it! We just need to do a little mopping up, get rid of some troublemakers. You can't have world peace when there's a bunch of bullies running around."

He had a simple, straightforward approach to international relations...

"I'm not aware of any bickering that a nice Predator Drone can't resolve."

Someone once asked Gardner if America was still competitive in the world economy...

"They talk about China. Ever looked at China's money, the won-ton or the one-hung-lo or whatever it is? It looks like bubble gum wrappers. So I say maybe they should feed that to their billions of starving people."

On a guest editorial in the New York Times about cutting unnecessary weapons systems and putting the money to work rebuilding America's infrastructure...

"Personally, I'd rather see a little paint peeling on a bridge than a big hole in the ground where the bridge used to be, because some jeehodderist walked into town with a H-bomb strapped to his bellybutton."

Predictably, he had his own special take on the Department of Defense liberalizing its policies about gays in the military. He shared them at a luncheon picnic for all fourteen of the Dayton area Veterans of Foreign Wars posts...

"Listen. I've been in the military. I know exactly how the military works. And that's why as far as having gays in the military, I see no problem. Someone's got to tidy up the barracks and do the ironing."

Recently, this appeared on his website...

"If God wanted America to be under the Shari'ah Law of Islam, then I guarantee you, the Bible would have been written in Arabic, not in English."

And the truth was, his audiences and loyal supporters *did* constantly yuck it up like the chef put magic mushrooms in the oyster dip. Such a funny guy, that Matt Gardner. What a great congressman!

Could the voting public possibly be that stupid?

As Martin himself put it: "I don't even know where to begin."

• • •

After the fiasco with Monty Montgomery, everyone at Green Party headquarters doubled down. True, they had only lost a week. But because expectations were high that having a heavy hitter on their team was going to rev the campaign into some previously unachievable high gear, it now felt like they were going backwards.

They scrambled. But there wasn't much to work with.

There were a few dozen generic *Martin Truth For Congress* posters and fliers left over from the last campaign. They got those up in the few places where they were allowed. Rock bands and raves had prompted the area city councils to clamp down harshly on public postering. At least Martin was getting exposure in convenience stores and on community bulletin boards. Posters trumpeting his bid for public office hung next to fliers advertising yard sales and rooms for rent. His loyal campaign staff were doing the best they could with no budget. They could honestly claim *Martin Truth For Congress* owned the laundromats and car washes in southeast Dayton!

This kind of busywork — the "details" of implementing a campaign, irksome but essential as they were — wasn't something Martin worried or even thought about. Phyllis, with Helen at her side, always managed to get the job done and get it done right. To the extent he took notice, he suspected it was mainly high school students, kids not even old enough to vote, who were the core of the "street teams" working on his behalf.

By nature and by default, Martin concentrated his energy on being an effective candidate and imagining himself in the role of a congressman, on the off chance that he actually became one. Sometimes it took a lot of imagination.

In some twisted way, it was probably good to have a straight job so completely unrelated to politics. There was no conflict of interest, and certainly what little brainpower he used driving around town and getting people to sign delivery receipts in no way competed with the higher cerebral functions needed to formulate policy positions, write speeches and position papers, strategize, attend and often conduct private meetings and public meet-and-greets, and generally present himself as credibly and convincingly as he could as a candidate for Congress.

He did his job and lived in his head. Mindlessly sitting at the wheel of a delivery van allowed him the freedom, mental space, and privacy to be working on his campaign most of his waking hours. Martin was back to being the quiet, detached young man he had been in high school.

There was, of course, one person at Future Perfect who he regularly interacted with and occasionally confided in, though usually not about his political career, as on a more personal level. That was Evelyn Castenegas. As dispatcher, Evelyn passed along a steady stream of assignments to Martin while he was on duty, so it was inevitable that they developed a comfortable familiarity, superficial as it was. Evelyn was one of those tough-as-nails heart-of-gold types, easy to misjudge and dislike at first, but ultimately someone to grow respectfully fond of. Despite her chain-smoking, battle-hardened, and prison-warden persona, her built-for-grueling-terrain body contained the deep caring soul of a person who had experienced enough tragedy and hard times of her own, to charge her with a deep sensitivity and compassion for others.

"Marty, I'm worried about you."

"No need to worry, Evelyn. I'm doing okay."

"Then why do you look like an autopsy would be an improvement?"

"You're right. I meant to do something about that. I'm having a bad hair day, for sure."

"Come here, young man."

Martin came over and sat on the corner of Evelyn's desk — not an easy maneuver in view of the many piles of paperwork, at least a dozen regulatory manuals, bottles of fingernail polish, hair brushes, a make-up mirror and numerous other grooming implements, three pictures of her grandchildren, a giant multi-line telephone workstation, a huge flat-panel monitor, two ashtrays overflowing with gum wrappers and cigarette butts, and a computer keyboard that somehow still functioned despite evidence of massive coffee spills, dried gobs of sandwich condiments, bread crumbs, Krispy Kreme donut droppings, and tobacco ashes clogging its keys.

"Yes?"

"You've got beautiful eyes. I wish my daughter-in-law had your eyes."

"You wanted to tell me I have beautiful eyes?"

"No, I just want you to know you can always talk to me."

"Thanks, Evelyn. I appreciate that."

She handed him a large bubble-padded envelope.

"This needs to go out immediately. West side industrial park."

"I feel better already. Is my hair okay for this delivery?"

She picked up one of her brushes and with her other hand turned his head side to side.

"I don't think we have time for this. Just wear this."

She handed him a baseball cap. Martin started to put it on, then noticed what it said.

Congressman Matt Gardner.
For a safe and secure America!

"Thanks anyway. I think I'll pass."

Suddenly Evelyn rolled her eyes and looked sheepish.

"Sorry, Marty. I forgot."

"It's okay. Even I forget sometimes."

"Really? You forget that you're not a Republican?"

"Uh … no. I forget how bad I look in hats."

Obviously, *Martin Truth For Congress* had a lot of work to do.

• • •

Martin was back at Norton's. This was the fourth time this week. It was becoming a regular thing. He wasn't sure why. It definitely wasn't his kind of place. A sports bar?

Not a typical sports bar, however. Or what Martin thought a typical sports bar might be.

There was a strange mixture of people. Working class heroes and quasi-professionals. They looked like they either drove a tow truck or sold the cars that got towed.

It was fine. It served its purpose. He wasn't looking for company or conversation. He was looking for oblivion. He was avoiding going home as long as he could put it off. Unfortunately, no matter how late he got home, the *nightmare* would be waiting up for him. Lately, however, he found if he had six or seven beers when he hit the sack, he could at least get a few hours sleep. He was still a zombie next day, but a slightly better rested one.

He looked up from his third Heineken and noticed a decent-looking brunette smiling at him from across the bar. Maybe late 20s early 30s. A few extra pounds. Big hair. Not his type. Especially with the bulbous boobs pushed up and in, lunging over the top of her tight camisole. Much too available. Too flagrantly looking to be picked up.

She started walking around the bar, never taking her eyes off of him. Now she was sitting on the next stool.

"I don't like to beat around the bush. If you have $100 and want some company, let's go."

A prostitute.

This was not the kind of place he would've expected to find a working girl, whatever kind of place that was.

"Aren't you worried I'm a cop?"

"I gave a cop a handjob last night. In his patrol car. Maybe you know him."

"I'm not a cop. I was just curious. It seems like it might be an occupational hazard."

"Everything involves risk. I guess I like to live dangerously. How about you?"

"Do I like to live dangerously? Oh yeah, that's definitely me. I'm a real Indiana Jones."

"Okay then. Let's have some fun. I promise to put a smile on that *very* sad face of yours."

"I'm … I don't … I think you might have better luck with one of the other patrons here. How about that guy over there?" He nodded toward a burly dude in a Cincinnati Reds pullover and cowboy hat, who was sizing up his next shot at the pool table.

"But I like you."

"Right. I'm sure I'd like you too. It's just a bit sudden. Listen, how about if I buy you a drink?"

"I'll take what I can get."

He bought her a drink. And five more.

In return he got an earful.

She was 32, had two kids and a deadbeat husband who left and refused to pay child support. She lived in a small, shabby two-bedroom house that was being foreclosed on because of a sub-prime loan she had been talked into by the bank. She had a sister living with her who had recently been laid off by a local construction company which went bankrupt.

"So my sister watches my kids while I'm out here spreading my legs to make ends meet."

The alcohol had loosened her tongue a bit.

"If you don't mind me asking, what happened to your husband? And why isn't he paying child support? He could end up in jail."

"Not this slick asshole. He's an attorney and is always coming up with a ton of outrageous shit. I get more summons than everyone else in this state combined. He knows I can't afford an attorney. Plus he's got pull. He's one of the partners at Fennwick, Gardner, Steele & Baldwin. Heard of them?"

He'd heard of them alright. Gardner. His opponent. That was *his* law firm. They had clout. They were the biggest bullies on the block.

"Yeah. I know them. Gardner's our congressman."

"What a creep that guy is too! He's a Barnie Stinson Bobble Head with Chucky's brain. Anyway, no money from the old man. He started sleeping with some secretary that works there who's half his age. Out the door he went. I hope she gives him herpes."

"That won't pay the bills."

"If I had anyone, anyone at all to turn to. My parents want to help. They love the kids. They're great grandparents. But they're worse off than me. My dad? They forced him to retire early. The guy is only 57 and the company where he worked for over thirty years kicks him out on the street. Nobody will hire him at his age. Now he's been diagnosed with colon cancer. My mother's been diabetic all her life. They have no health insurance anymore. They're fighting it but I can see they're going to have to declare bankruptcy. There's no way they can pay all those medical bills. Then what? The house they've worked all their lives to buy, the bill collectors will get that. It's fucked. Totally fucked! ... I'm sorry. I shouldn't be dumping all of this on you."

"No no. It's fine. I'm just... I'm amazed. I mean, most people would give up."

"Give up and what?"

Martin pulled out his wallet. He had a fifty dollar bill and a few singles. He handed her the fifty.

"Just take this. I'm not expecting you to do anything. But you need this more than me."

"I can give you a blow job."

"No, no thanks. I appreciate it. But I'd better go. Take care of yourself. And be careful."

"I'm always careful. But it's never enough, is it? Anything can happen. You're a sweet guy. Thanks for the fifty."

On the way back to his car, it hit him. He never mentioned he was running for Congress. Maybe she would have voted for him.

• • •

The next day at work he couldn't shake it.

It kept replaying over and over.

The girl.

The prostitute.

Well, she wasn't really a prostitute. She was just someone driven by desperation. It certainly wasn't her first choice. It was a last resort. How many out there were just like her? This fucked up economy. The shredding of the safety net for so many people. Factories closing. Jobs going to China and India. People overwhelmed by debt. Losing their homes. Declaring bankruptcy. Those guys in the Washington bubble with their power lunches, always being seduced and suckered by the crony capitalists, relentlessly courted by influence peddlers, being handed buckets of money by investment banks and the pharmaceutical companies, were totally out of touch with what the average citizen had to do to survive. The lobbyists. The corporate donors. Round and round go the revolving doors. What a sham. What a total mess.

Suddenly he felt ashamed.

Here he was: Crybaby Marty feeling all sorry for himself. Acting like a spoiled brat because his girlfriend left. Moping, drinking, wasting time when there was work to be done. How pathetic. Woe is me says the pitiful teary-eyed drama queen.

It made him sick. *He* made him sick! What a pathetic loser!

It was going to stop right now. Not to make light of a tragic situation, but meeting that poor girl was just what he needed. This was a wake up call. Talking to — damn! he didn't even know her name — talking to whoever she was, really put things in perspective. It made him realize how trite and paltry his own silly problems were and how he needed to get his head screwed on right again. There were thousands of people out there just like her, miserable and without hope through no fault of their own. What kind of society intentionally ignores the ones among them who are most in need? What kind of men and women were these selfish blowhards currently in Congress who could only talk about more tax breaks for their rich friends and not even give passing thought to the less fortunate in America? — except maybe to mock them and threaten to make their lives even more miserable.

Okay. He had gotten sidetracked. But that was about to change.

Back to work. Back on track. Back on the attack.

Martin Truth for U.S. Congress.

Time to kick some ass!

• • •

Martin had just delivered a box of antiseptic latex gloves to Garden of the Goddess, a psychic based in mondo-chic Kettering. Latex gloves? What the hell was that all about?

He found himself in the immediate proximity of campaign headquarters. It was lunch time. Of course, lunch time was subject to being instantly nullified if an important delivery came up. Mercifully, he had not heard from Evelyn for the last twenty minutes.

He stopped at Potbelly Sandwich Works to grab a grilled vegetable and mozzarella hoagie, then popped in to the campaign office. Three young ladies who looked like they should be selling girl scout cookies were stuffing envelopes in the front work area. They giggled when they saw Martin. He felt like a rock star.

He headed for the back room. Phyllis was at her desk just finishing a phone call.

"Are you getting these volunteers from the orphanage?"

"Kettering Fairmont H. S. loaned them to us. They're experiencing the savage battleground of contemporary politics first hand. Hey, Martin! I've got some news. We have an intern coming. She's from Rutgers University and she's just finishing up her masters program in political science. If I understood correctly, she'll be here within the next couple days."

"The more the merrier. As the captain of the Titanic said, 'Next round's on me. How do—"

"How do you like your seawater? You're repeating yourself. Tsk tsk. So young for senility to be setting in. You'll be at the meeting tomorrow night?"

"Does a bald eagle need hair transplants? Of course, Frau Wagner. I'm totally fired up now. Wouldn't miss it for all of the WMDs in Iraq."

CHAPTER THREE

Martin was in mid-sentence when she appeared in the doorway of the conference room in back, where they always held their meetings. No one had heard her come in.

"It's that moment of transitioning into the fundraising part that I—"

He stopped.

Everything stopped.

If Jamila Parks wasn't the most stunning human being to set foot in greater Dayton, Ohio, then the million dollar question was, who was?

Either accustomed to or oblivious of the impression she made on people, she just looked up from her iPhone and smiled. It was an agreeable smile with just a smidgen of prankishness.

"According to Google maps, this is the right place. Green Party, 3rd Congressional District. Martin Truth for Congress."

They still didn't have signage for their office space. Though it was street front property, it wasn't like they were running a bakery or a dry cleaners. They weren't encouraging pedestrians to drop in.

Phyllis stood up and went over to her.

"You must be … from Rutgers?"

"Jamila Parks. I talked to you on the phone. You're Phyllis, right?"

They shook hands and Phyllis pointed to the only vacant seat in the room. Against the wall slightly behind Helen and Lincoln.

Martin realized his mouth was still hanging open, halfway through the last syllable he had uttered. He closed it. That was about all he was capable of. All motor function was on pause. He sat there frozen and stared. He couldn't feel his body, his limbs, his hands. He did feel his face. It was flushed, as if he were bending over a pan of boiling water.

When Phyllis said an intern was coming, this was not at all what he was expecting. 'Intern' for some reason called to mind a mousy creature, with bad posture, maybe dental braces, dull hair pulled up in a bun, horn-rim glasses with thick bottle lenses, standard issue librarian attire, and a face that had never ventured into even pre-adolescent experiments with makeup.

Jamila was tall, slender, lithe and graceful. She moved with the certainty of a highly trained athlete but the ethereal fluidity of a ballerina. She was wearing a simple black pullover tee, platform ankle boots, a camouflage jacket, tight low cut jeans accessorized with a jeweled silver chain, and had a large heavy-duty denim handbag slung over one shoulder. Somehow she made it all look like she was doing the celebrity walk at the Grammys.

But it was her face that truly pulled focus. Framed by beaded mini-braids which fell from the precise cornrowing of her entire head, her face seemed to light from within. Jamila — as her name would suggest — was African-American. Her skin was flawless, the color and texture of a delicious caramel syrup.

Martin studied her more intently. He suddenly realized she looked like someone he knew. How could that be? He didn't know *anyone* who looked anything like her. But she was so incredibly familiar.

Then the light suddenly came on!

Martin was not much of a fan of pop music. But there had been a billboard he passed about a hundred times, maybe a year ago. It was for some mega-star who was doing a concert in Cincinnati. *That* was who this young beauty looked like!

He remembered! Rihanna. Her name was Rihanna.

The resemblance was uncanny.

At the same time, this girl — what was her name? Jalala? Jehovah? Jemima? — went way beyond the pop singer. There was this intelligence, this intensity, this depth, purposefulness …

"Normally, the candidate himself is here at these meetings. But when he can't make it, we just put this inflatable doll here in his place. I think it's an incredible likeness. What do you think, Miss Parks?"

"I guess. I mean, I'd have to see Martin Truth in person to really make a final call. But this does indeed seem to be a remarkable likeness."

They were making fun of him.

"I … what was I saying?"

"Oh, goodness! I'm sorry, Martin. It *is* you after all."

At least his mouth seemed to be working again.

"Very funny, Phyllis. It's all that hypnosis I've been doing to stop me eating the hair on my arms. Sometimes it just takes over."

Martin felt like an idiot. It must have been obvious to everyone. Then again, it couldn't have just been him that noticed how incredibly *stunning* this young lady was. He tried his best to regroup and look matter-of-fact.

"I'm Martin Truth."

They were all in hysterics. Now everyone was a comedian.

"No. I'm Martin Truth."

"Excuse me. *I'm* Martin Truth."

"You were Martin Truth yesterday. It's my turn."

"This is a major breakthrough, Martin. For three years you've been telling everyone you're Barry Manilow."

Jamila came to the rescue. Sort of.

"Mr. Truth. It's an honor to be here and to work with you. Some people have trouble with my name. It's Jamila. Jamila Parks. I'm here to observe and help. This is an official assignment arranged by my university. It's not, contrary to the rumors floating around, the result of a deal I made with a prosecuting attorney. If I had to plea bargain, I would've taken the prison time."

More easy laughter at his expense. Well, at least she had a sense of humor.

"Just call me Martin."

"Or DJ Truth, King of the Turn-the-Tables."

Bill winked. But the fun was over. It was back to business.

They went on for another thirty minutes or so. The main topic was money.

Wasn't it always?

When the meeting adjourned, Jamila talked briefly with each of them. They all welcomed her and made themselves available if she needed any help getting around or adjusting to her new temporary home in Dayton.

Martin hung back and was last in line. But Jamila was out the door before he got another opportunity to make a fool of himself.

Over the next few weeks, Martin slowly began to adjust to Jamila's constant and mesmerizing presence. It wasn't easy by any stretch. Then again, as she was learning the ropes and adjusting to her new surroundings, she pretty much stayed in the background, so he didn't have to deal much with her one-on-one. Eventually, some sort of sangfroid seemed to take hold and he was able to be himself, or something approximating it.

Yet whenever he really looked at her — something he found himself doing more than he thought was prudent or appropriate — or on those few occasions she addressed him directly, his stomach flipped, his throat went dry, he felt a gnawing sensation in those places where gnawing typically gnawed in a man who was turned on by a beautiful woman. He was confident he was keeping his reaction sufficiently contained that no one else noticed. At the very least, he wasn't turning into a drooling hunchback the way he had that first encounter.

It was understood that as an intern Jamila was there to both do research for her masters thesis, and to actively participate in the campaign itself. Employing her recent educational tools and her fresh perspective as an outsider — for what novelty and objectivity that might confer — she was expected during her stay with them to offer what insights she might have towards improving his chances of winning, or at least making a respectable showing.

Her masters program included a focused study of the impact, or more accurate the lack of it, by minor political parties in the electoral process. The two major parties historically had been very effective at shutting out any upstart threats to their duopoly. Teddy Roosevelt's Progressive Party, nicknamed the Bull Moose Party, had been strangled by a lack of financial support when his previous supporters stuck with the tried and true Republican political machine. More recently, challengers Ross Perot in 1992 and 1996, then Ralph Nader in four successive runs starting in 1996, were mocked and derided by the press, effectively marginalized by being excluded from forums and debates critical for any kind of public awareness and voting traction. Shutting out the shrill voices of these third-party intruders, often the only worthy contributions to the political dialogue, was the one thing Republicans and Democrats could agree on.

Now, more than ever, there was a crying need for serious third-party contenders at all levels. The two major parties were migrating more and more to the safe, unimaginative and largely unproductive center-right of the political spectrum, their positions on most key issues becoming increasingly indistinguishable. The disparities in their programs and legislative agendas were marginal. They were differences that made no difference. Lacking a third-party challenge meant that there wasn't much choice at all at the polls. Jamila's thesis would explore the encouraging premise that the current anemia in the political environment might provide a unique opportunity for a minor party like the Libertarians, the Greens, or even the Socialist Party, to finally achieve a foothold and evolve into a credible force in U.S. politics.

Beyond the prospects of her making positive technical contributions to Martin's campaign, Jamila brought some pleasant surprises to the mix. She got along great with everyone. She had a sharp, perceptive sense of humor, combining the flippant irreverence of academia with a street-smart edginess that was characteristically African-American. Phyllis made it obvious she was especially pleased to have her around, and spent the first couple weeks after Jamila's arrival elucidating the history of the local Green Party and how Martin's campaigns for the congressional seat had played out so far. Jamila listened attentively, took a lot of notes, but for the present didn't have a lot to say. Jamila explained that she liked to have as much information as possible before she made any judgments or volunteered her ideas.

"You don't have to worry about me, Phyllis. I'm definitely not shy. Enjoy the peace and quiet for now. Once I get started, you'll look back on these days and wonder if someone slipped me the yakkety-yak pill. You'll be scrambling to find the mute button."

How dead-on that turned out to be.

• • •

Martin would be delivering his campaign spiel at three different functions this weekend.

There was the Catholic Order of Foresters, followed by the Homestar Safe Haven YWCA. Then he would wrap up his triumphant tour sipping tea at the Dayton Women's Club.

He was on his way home from work when his cell phone rang.

It was Jamila! How did she get his number?

"Martin. I want to come with you this weekend. You know, to your campaign thingies."

"Uh, sure. Just talk to Phyllis. I'm sure it's fine. Personally, I think it's an excellent idea. Are you sure you can handle the excitement though?"

"I'll meditate for the next few days and build up my alpha waves."

It went pretty much as expected. No one was quite sure who this politician was and why he was there. Then again, Martin wasn't always sure himself. These sorts of functions were more social than educational. He hated to spoil everyone's fun by bringing up politics.

Fortunately, he was polished in the art of making the best of a pointless exercise. At each gathering, he gave a short stump speech, during which he poked fun at himself, engaged in some light interaction with a few people in the audience, and managed at minimum to walk out the door with everyone liking him. There was maybe even a slim chance they would remember he was running for Congress.

Jamila was impressed. Martin was good. When he gave his prepared speech, he sounded personable and sincere. It didn't sound canned. He had a strong, even, warm speaking voice. He managed to cover a lot of ground but kept it engaging by using interesting anecdotes to illustrate his points.

She certainly had no problem agreeing with everything she was hearing. Martin said all the right things, at least in terms of her own political biases and appreciation of the critical issues of the times. Even if she had been inclined to disagree with his positions, she would have felt quite at ease with the man. He was affable and charming in a homey Midwestern way.

Martin was even better after the formal presentation, just talking one-on-one with people.

She stood off to the side as he took a moment with each person. Rather than watch him, she studied them. She noticed how their eyes would glaze over when he brought up certain topics. She noted their body language. How as Martin emphasized certain points, they would lean back and inch away, regardless of how personally charming they found him.

It confirmed what she suspected all along.

Even when people respected his ideas and appreciated his commitment, they didn't entirely resonate with him or share his passion. Even if they liked him personally, he definitely wasn't reaching their hearts. Thus his political views never stood a chance. They were just words.

Jamila knew exactly what was wrong. More importantly, she felt she knew how to fix it.

She decided to hold off. Timing and the right approach were crucial.

She was positive none of them were ready, at least not yet. Plus she herself needed some time to prepare. Never known for her diplomatic skills, Jamila suspected that what she had to say in all likelihood would land more like a cluster bomb than a soap bubble and she would be greeted more as a raging rhinoceros than a fairy princess.

She would bite her tongue for now and bring it up when the time was right.

• • •

Two weeks later the time was right.

They had been having strategy meeting after strategy meeting and had nothing to show for it except for that bruised look people get when they've been beating their heads against a wall.

Jamila came out with both barrels blazing, the meek fly-on-the-wall spectator metamorphosed into a self-assured and assertive firebrand.

She laid out the plan.

It was built around candidate pledges, notoriously made famous by Grover Norquist, who with his no-new-taxes pledge had eviscerated government and caused massive gridlock in the legislative branch.

These pledges would go much further than even Norquist's. These would be impregnable, steel-reinforced, bulletproof cages. They would effectively be legally-enforceable contracts which brooked no compromise and left no room for ambiguity or interpretation.

It was fighting fire with fire, only hopefully this fire would undo the damage that Norquist's and similar tactics by the fanatic right — the Tea Party and ultra conservative wing of the Republican Party — had done. It was a hard ball strategy to get government working again by singling out one-by-one the saboteurs of representative democracy and giving them an ultimatum …

Shape up or ship out.

The success of the strategy entirely hinged on reaching out to voters on hot button issues, those things which they *already* felt passionate about — matters which already had set the fire in their bellies ablaze.

To get the ball rolling, the campaign committee's job would be to identify the unique vulnerabilities of Martin's Republican opponent here in Ohio's 3rd District, the congressional incumbent, Matt Gardner. They would look at the campaign promises contained in his speeches, his press materials, his campaign materials, and on his web site, comparing them with his voting record. Pledges, targeting those specific issues that the voting public felt most adamant about, would then be shaped around Gardner's performance in Congress, literally to confront him with his own words and his own broken promises.

While this preparatory work was undertaken, and then the pledge strategy actually implemented, Martin himself could continue to address voters in broad strokes, offering his vision for America. The pledge strategy would be working away quietly in the background. Just before the election, however, there would be a showdown. Presumably Martin would triumph. The pledges would destroy Gardner's credibility by hammering him on his treacherous voting record in Congress, nailing him to the cross with his own duplicity.

Jamila summed it up.

"This is war. We dress for battle. And we arm ourselves sufficient to the task. We know what we're up against. We can't take on Gardner and his huge campaign chest any other way. We'll call him out on his broken promises, his lies, his blatant hypocrisy. The pledge is a line in the sand, an ultimatum. Either he comes around or we take him out."

After a stunned silence, symptomatic of the serious soul-searching going on in the room, Phyllis finally spoke up.

"So we're going to stoop their level, is that it?"

"Cowering is better than stooping? Wringing our hands is better than letting them have it between eyes? People like Gardner have stolen our democracy, they've looted the treasury, they're ruining lives, marginalizing people like you and I. You want to be all pleasant and nice? History is littered with the bodies of nice people who said the same thing. They held their heads high only to get them chopped off."

Jamila was *not* one for mincing words.

Lincoln had some qualms.

"I don't know. Something just doesn't feel right. Are these enforceable pledges even legal? Aren't they unconstitutional?"

"This approach grew out a workshop I participated in at Rutgers for six months. They've been analyzing this concept from every possible angle for three years, looking at legal precedents, studying every single ruling pertaining to the voting process. We've even gone so far as looking at local and state election regulations. We haven't turned up a single thing that says these pledges are any different than any other civil contract. There's nothing that says we as citizens can't put in writing exactly what we expect from our elected representatives. In fact, I'll take it a step further. An ironclad pledge actually underscores the very relationship that constituents have with their elected representatives in a democratic system of government. Implied when the voting public chooses someone to go to Washington is that the individual will go there and represent the interests of those people. They're supposed to do our bidding. Maybe it hasn't ever been put down in writing before but we certainly have it in their own words. *'If elected I will blah blah blah ... '* A verbal promise is in a sense a contract."

Always willing to error on the side of civility, perhaps reflecting some deep-seated if impossible to validate belief that people were basically good and deserved a minimum level of courtesy and respect, Bill was having a gosh-golly moment.

"Hmm. Well ... okay. I'm sure you're right. Even so ... I don't know ... I guess ... it seems almost insulting to require ..."

Jamila snipped that in the bud. She had zero patience for talk of graciousness under duress.

"Insulting? *Insulting?* I'll tell you what's insulting. It's to listen to all their blather about how much they care about us, about all the good things they will do for us, then have them disappear inside the beltway bubble and rake in the money from lobbyists and campaign donors, then vote *not* for the good of the people, but so that the corporations, Wall Street, mega-banks, and military contractors can pile up even more money to bribe them with. It's made a sham of our whole system and a shambles of our once-great country. Now *that's* insulting!"

Everyone retreated into more soul-searching.

Phyllis, normally the picture of iron composure and military discipline, looked bruised. Demoralized. She seemed to be hanging on by her fingertips, mindful of some closely held prayer for civility and grace. She sat staring at her hands, talking under her breath to no one in particular.

"Has it come to this? Has it really come to this?"

Martin had been conspicuously silent. He cleared his throat and looked directly at Phyllis.

"With all due respect, I think you know as well as everybody in this room where we're at. It's not very difficult to see the writing on the wall. It may be noble but it's not very satisfying. Losing I mean. There's a lot at stake in this country. Ours is one tiny battle in a larger war. Democracy is on the chopping block. So far the imperial corporatists have done a good job of making mincemeat of our noble experiment. But we haven't lost. At least I hope it's not too late. I guess my only hesitation … actually I don't know why I'm hesitating."

Jamila's voice was even and her words now tempered by a genuine humility.

"Martin. Phyllis. Everyone here. I know I'm young. I'm probably out of line. But I speak out of concern and real conviction. I don't think it's too late. But time is running out. Our only hope is to get as many of these bastards out of office as we can, and get some good people like Martin here to take their place. I don't at all believe the ends justify the means. I just don't think the means here are outside the boundaries. Time is running out. This is playing for keeps. It's batter up and we're in the last inning. We need to step up to the plate and hit a home run."

A faint smile worked itself from behind Phyllis's wizened eyes.

"Sports metaphors don't exactly turn my crank, Jamila."

"What kind of metaphor would you like? Cooking? Biblical? Disney?"

"No no. It's fine. You're right. Last inning. Swing for the stands."

"So … can I take that as a yes?"

"Jamila. You're either a bargain with the Devil or a blessing directly from the Lord on high. I can't decide. But yes … if everyone agrees, it's a yes. I won't stand in the way. Let's give it a try."

• • •

There was no doubt now. Jamila Parks, Version 2.0 had descended upon them.

Wrapped in scrolls of wisdom and twists of barbwire, as she had promised Phyllis would eventually happen, her tranquil, meditative, fact-finding phase and concomitant vow of silence had abruptly ended and had been supplanted by an assertive, hyper-creative, talkative, raucous, relentless frenzy which might be compared to a natural disaster of the good kind — maybe the violent eruption of a volcano leaving in its wake a majestic new tropical island of unparalleled splendor.

Her being there definitely was a good thing, even if at times it caused turbulence and not a little gnashing of teeth. Everything had dramatically improved. The glaring contrast between *before* and *after* was proof positive that Martin's campaign had over three grueling and irksome election cycles slowly drifted into the doldrums, a process which had crept up so gradually and so stealthily that no one had noticed.

If Jamila had a fault — and arguably it was a virtue — it was her directness. No one could ever accuse her of beating around the bush. She was decisive, unambiguous, determined, and always ready for battle. She had no patience for niggling or half-way measures. Nothing worth doing was worth doing any less than full out, whatever the matter at hand.

Martin had a dedicated website for his campaign — martintruthforcongress.com — which offered a comprehensive and painfully accurate overview of him, his history, his credentials, his political philosophy, his position on key issues, and his vision for America. It was clean and professional, informative, pleasant on the eyes, easy to navigate, and overall very wholesome.

Jamila wasn't exactly impressed.

"This is so boring I'd rather stare at the back of my monitor!"

Martin looked puzzled.

"What's wrong with it?"

"That would take more time than we have. We'd miss the election. I can tell you what's right with it."

"What's that?"

"Nothing."

"Could you maybe be a *little* more specific?"

"Martin. You're a fascinating guy. You say all the right things. You're intelligent. Funny. Maybe I'd go as far as to say that you're charming. Your website looks like a government page for Singapore, only not that exciting. Plus, it's about as entertaining as reading the ingredients label on a package of frozen waffles."

"Entertaining? Why should it be entertaining? It's not World of Warcraft or Game of Thrones. People don't come to my site looking for a good time."

"That's for sure."

They were looking at his home page on Phyllis's desktop Dell. Jamila pointed at the screen.

"Is that the stat counter in the corner? What does it say?"

They could both see it read 391.

"How long has this been up? What does that tell you? No one wants to look at this snooze fest. Let me tell you about viral. If a website's got some genuine appeal, you don't have to advertise, do search engine optimization, or play any of those games with Google and Yahoo. Word spreads over the internet faster than ice crystals at the North Pole."

"Exactly what do you want to do? Make it look like a Ken doll fan site?"

"That would be an improvement. At least you could lock down the Barbie vote."

Martin sensed Jamila was right. Pride never got in his way.

"So you think we should redesign it? Give it some sex appeal?"

Her reply pretty much summed up her approach to politics and life in general.

"Are you gonna fuss with your hair and tie your shoelaces again … or you gonna *dance?*"

They went to work.

First, they shot some new photos. It turned out that Bob Phelps was excellent with a camera and had a top-of-the-line Pentax. He also had just bought the best Sony HD camcorder on the market. So in addition to getting some great still photos, they shot over two hours of video showing Martin in action. They filmed one of his public speeches — actually one of the best he had delivered to date. Luck was with them. The audience was enthusiastic to the point of almost being rowdy, though this was more a function of how much beer they had had before Martin took the podium. It looked like he had generated this enormous groundswell of support. They also did footage of him just being himself.

Walking in the park. At home on his computer. Riding his mountain bike. Talking to some children at an elementary school.

Next, Phyllis contacted Kettering Fairmont H.S. and talked to a close friend there who was a counselor. Sure enough, there were two students, one a junior and the other a senior, who were self-taught website experts. They had even done some work for the school itself with phenomenal results.

Two weeks later, the photos had been optimized, the videos edited and enhanced with a host of professional looking titles and effects, and the high school students, working close with Martin, Bob and Jamila, put the finishing touches on the new dazzling design of the Martin Truth For Congress website. The whole production was uploaded and now live.

They all gathered around the main office computer that evening to appraise their work.

Jamila was grinning from ear to ear.

"Now that looks hot!"

Soon, they were like kids, fighting for the mouse, clicking on various pull down menus, bouncing from one page to the next, flipping through the slide shows, playing the videos.

It did look hot! Especially for a campaign website. Somehow, however, the bright colors, the flashy graphics, the overlays, pop-up windows, and the dynamic interaction with the visitor which the site now invited, served by contrast to make Martin himself more natural and real. There was no doubt that he was a "modern kind of guy", unafraid to employ the latest technology to push his message. At the same time, the actual images offered of him avoided the stiffness, formality and self-importance that plagued many political figures. He came across as a real human being, a decent and competent fellow with a solid message and most importantly, a heart.

By the end of the week, Jamila was able to point to their success in simplest terms.

"Wow! Check out the stat counter at the bottom of the page."

It read 7,418.

• • •

Martin as usual was a few minutes early. He was surprised to find Jamila already sitting at the conference table. She was looking at some handwritten notes, making little notations in the margins.

He relished these one-on-one sessions with her.

He could sit and look at her for hours. Not that there was ever any silence between them. Sometimes they sounded like two auctioneers trying to reach the top row in a football stadium.

He felt ridiculous. Since she first walked in the door that evening a few weeks ago, he'd had this raging crush on her. He hadn't felt anything like this since junior high school. Maybe he should write her name a thousand times in his notebook. Doodle hearts on the cover.

He knew better than to say anything about his feelings, but he wished he could at least tell her that she was absolutely the most beautiful woman in the world. She probably already knew.

He wondered if he was becoming a full-blown, card-carrying masochist. The obvious prerequisites were there.

First off, there was the certain, wholly frustrating impossibility of the situation. Despite the frequency of their contact — sometimes just the two of them as was the case this evening, more often in planning meetings with his whole contingent of campaign staffers — he couldn't even begin to think about breaching the official, professional, and mutually-respected barrier which had to hold firm between them, he as a congressional candidate and she as volunteer intern. As if some Midwestern rube as pathetically inept with the opposite sex as he was, could take advantage of this East Coast warrior woman, as sophisticated and strong-willed as they come.

But the real potential for branding him a masochist came from the amount of abuse he took from her. Granted, it was constructive abuse. In fact her ideas seemed to be turning his whole candidacy on its head.

But it was still abuse.

Which he frankly found charming.

Which he in point of fact seemed to be thriving on.

And there it boldly stood. The text book definition of masochism.

In preparation for tonight's get together, he had steeled himself for the worst. Jamila just recently insisted they immediately start working on his public persona. It wasn't something he had given much thought. He assumed he had one. But he also assumed a persona was a given. You had what you had. Like brown hair. Or blue eyes. He had never stood in front of a mirror and practiced looking studly, like a lot of boys used to do in high school. He didn't have attitude or cool dance moves or swagger. What ridiculous demands was she going to subject him to?

After an atypical few minutes of silence, she came roaring out of the gate.

"Your image."

"Image is everything."

"For starters, Truth, that beard makes you look like a janitor at a community college."

"It's not a beard. It's a goatee."

"What was Lenin's? A goatee?"

"John Lennon?"

"Very funny. You can't take chances with facial hair. Unless you're George Clooney."

"I can get rid of it. Can I borrow your Lady Schick?"

"Do you own a decent tie? One that you didn't pick up at an estate sale?"

"I don't have to wear ties."

"You mean 'tie' singular. Do you have more than just that one with the seagulls?"

"My ex-girlfriend loved that tie."

"Is she from Bulgaria? Anyway, if she's your *ex*-girlfriend, there's no better reason to put it in the memorabilia trunk with the box of snowflake contact lenses she left behind and the baggie of her toenail clippings."

"How do you know about those?"

"Another thing, your name is a fucking liability. It's a gigantic distraction. A huge ear sore. You might as well have a banana growing out of your forehead."

"It's not as bad as Buster Hymen."

"Have you ever tried to talk to someone with a banana growing out of their forehead?

"Can't say I have."

"Whatever. It's fine. We'll just work around it. But we definitely shouldn't turn your campaign into a slobbering pun fest."

Alright! Now *that* he definitely could go along with. Martin had always hated those stupid slogans about truth this and truth that. At the same time, there was something about Jamila's take-no-prisoners approach that made him defensive and brought out the urge to fight back.

"Hey, Parks. What makes you the big expert here? You haven't even finished your degree. Where's your impressive record of victory laps?"

"I don't have any. But I have something which apparently is sorely lacking around here."

"What's that?"

"Common sense."

She had a point. Sometimes things got pretty far off track. Or not even close to the track in the first place. Like that Monty Spumante high-roller consultant guy.

"Just for argument's sake, let's assume for a minute you know what you're talking about."

"For argument's sake? Martin, let me put it to you straight. We need each other. I need you because nobody around here, despite all their liberal chic open-mindedness and egalitarian yada yada, is going to take seriously some 22-year-old niggah chick—"

"Just stop right there! That's not—"

"Hear me out! I need you because if you can see the merit of my ideas, these other sheeple here will go along with the program. And you need me because if something doesn't change dramatically, the only votes you're gonna get are your grandmother and your kissing cousins."

"My grandmother is dead. Both of them."

"I like you, Martin. I think you would be a phenomenal congressman. I really mean that. You stand for the right things and I know you always fight for what you believe in. But even though you'd be a great congressman, from what I'm seeing, you'll never get that chance."

"I appreciate your vote of confidence."

"I'm telling it like it is. Unless you're completely out of your skull, with the way things are going you can't possibly think that you're going to win this election. You might even come in again behind that ... that wacko. What's his name?"

"Peter Potts, the People's One-Man Political Posse. He's definitely a wacko. He even misspelled 'Libertarian' on one of his campaign posters. Alright. I'll just sit here and lick my wounds, while you tell me your plan to conquer the world."

"Your sarcasm is causing you points."

"I feel like I've been in the penalty box since I walked in the door."

"If you can't take the heat, stay out of the kitchen."

"I can take some heat. But I'm allergic to having starter cables attached to my genitals."

"Martin, look. I'm just trying to figure you out. There's a lot of ways we could go with this. I don't want to beat my head against the wall. It messes up my cornrows. But I'll tell you what. If you're absolutely serious about making changes, we'll kick this into high gear. But I need to organize my thoughts. This is Wednesday. We'll talk over dinner, say Friday or Saturday."

"Of course, I'm serious. I'm in or I wouldn't be sitting here talking to you."

"Yes, you would. You look like a dog waiting for a bone."

Okay. She had his number. However, he knew better than acknowledge it.

"Saturday works for me. Eight o'clock?"

"Okay. 8:00 it is. We'll go to my second favorite restaurant."

Jamila winked at him just before she disappeared out the door.

Dinner? Hmm. Was she coming on to him? Was it possible? She must have some notion of the effect she had on him. She basically said so with that dog bone comment. Maybe …

Then he came to his senses.

A rose by any other name is a rose.

Martin was pretty sure it was the same with masochism.

When was Jamila's birthday?

Maybe he could buy her a whip.

• • •

Martin was surprised that Jamila had chosen Olive Garden. It seemed too yuppie for her. Though he wasn't quite sure what exactly would be her kind of place.

"Olive Garden is easy. I don't have to think. Besides, I like their breadsticks."

What was easy for Martin was to just sit there and stare. God, she was beautiful! He wasn't sure if this was love or lust. But whatever it was, it certainly was intense.

Her lips were moving. Was she saying something?

"Martin. With food they recommend opening your mouth, and then using that fork you're holding to put bite-size morsels into said mouth, placing them on the center of your tongue. Chewing, then swallowing comes next. This may be a *chichi* restaurant with the best service this side of Palermo, but the food still doesn't float up off the plate."

He was making a fool of himself. Again! There was no excuse for being a drooling lump. But Jamila was a real dish, certainly far more interesting than the plate of food in front of him. Did he look as guilty as he felt?

“Linguine is like fine wine. You have to let it breathe to bring out its rich essential flavors.”

“Right.”

Too bad they were here to discuss business. He certainly would much prefer to have this be a purely social affair. Relax, talk, laugh. Enjoy this sassy, enigmatic, brilliant young lady. Maybe try to do some repair work on the *total idiot* opinion she must have of him.

Martin leaned forward to take his first bite. Jamila had already finished eating in what had to be Guinness World Record time. She wiped her mouth, and nudged her plate aside. She wasn’t going to wait for dessert to get started on the business at hand.

“Like I said the other night, we’ve got to work on your image.”

“What’s wrong with my image?”

“Everything. But let me correct that. It’s not just image. I actually mean persona.”

“Image? Persona? What’s the difference?”

“Design versus function.”

“Are you dropping acid?”

“Martin, I like you. You have the right ideas. But I still probably wouldn’t vote for you.”

“That’s crazy.”

“Not as crazy as the typical voter. Don’t take it personally. I wouldn’t intentionally *not* vote for you. I would just forget.”

“Forget?”

“Martin. You’re boring.”

“Really? Boring? Hmm. Let me think. What should I say to that? I know. *Fuck you!*”

“That’s more passion than I’ve seen out of you since I dragged myself into this doomed enterprise you call a campaign.”

“What about my website? That was a big leap forward.”

“It’s a start. But it’s just the internet. Your persona is more than a URL.”

Martin twisted some linguine onto his fork, took his second bite, then as per Jamila’s instructions, chewed and swallowed. All of which gave him a precious moment to think.

“I think I give off an image of responsibility. Control. Concern. Caring. Intelligence.”

“That’s great for a veterinarian. I’d take my cat to you.”

“I had a cat when I was a kid. It got run over by a truck. Her name was Pop Tart.”

“*That’s* more interesting than anything in your campaign literature.”

“I can’t put that in my campaign literature. A lot of people hate cats. I’d lose the dog lover vote. What are you thinking?”

“I feel like I’m talking to a third grader. Martin! Wake up! This is show business.”

“Oh, I see. You want me to become a carnival hawker like those other bozos.”

"Not quite. But I do expect you to be interesting. Engaging. Exciting!"

"I thought you said you liked the way I handle my public appearances."

"You do fine. But remember, that public *you* is only seen by a small percentage of voters. Just the ones you get to talk to. Not to belittle anyone's efforts but almost all of your speaking engagements are small potatoes. I understand it goes with the territory. Third party. Green ticket. You're on the C circuit, with an occasional B gig thrown in when someone fucks up. But it's not just physical. I'm talking about your persona, that image that immediately comes to mind when someone hears your name. If I say Johnny Depp, *bam!* Immediately you get an image. A *very cool* image, thanks to his great looks and a lot of outstanding movies."

"Should I dress up as Captain Jack Sparrow?"

"I was thinking Edward Scissorhands."

"Willy Wonka?"

"At least you wouldn't be boring."

"Show business, eh? What's with that anyway? When did the hugely important enterprise of running the most powerful country in the world become American Idol?"

"I can't give you an exact date. But it is what it is. Don't get yourself all worked up here. I'm just trying to help. No one expects you to dance like Danny Kaye. I just want you to come across."

"Danny Kaye? You know who Danny Kaye is?"

"Oh! Because I'm a *negro*, eh? I couldn't *possibly* know about Danny Kaye. Okay, let's go with one of my black brothers. How about Sammy Davis, Jr.? Or the Nicholas Brothers?"

Damn! She was so good at bludgeoning him into a full-on retreat. Tapping holes in his skull so she could hammer her message home.

Is this what she was up to? Breaking him down? Is that why she always came out swinging? And right now. Did she really think he was being childish? Stubborn? Impossible?

"I didn't mean—"

"Look. Television changed everything. It's just what happened. It started with Kennedy. Now politics is a sitcom. My point is simple. People used to go to movies with Johnny Depp in them purely by accident. They went to a movie and there he was. Then they started to dig *him*. He developed a recognizable and highly attractive persona. Now they go to a movie *just* to see Johnny Depp. He's the draw. Same with you. We develop a highly recognizable and appealing image. Then they'll come to you. Or at least they'll pay attention to you."

"How about we get a beer?"

"Don't change the subject! Are you down with this or not?"

"I'm fed up with failure. As long as you promise I won't have to do Sammy Davis Jr.'s greatest hits."

"You might have to do some Jim Carrey."

"Sure. The 'Eternal Sunshine of the Spotless Mind'? I could manage that."

"So far you seem to have 'Dumb and Dumber' down pat."

"Do I have to take this abuse?"

"You're in politics. It's the first line in the job description."

Good point. And proof positive *again* that he was indeed a masochist.

At the same time, in this particular moment, he was becoming a *testy* masochist.

"You know, it's all so easy for you. You sit there like you're playing with a department store mannikin, trying on different clothes, changing hair styles. Do you know what this feels like?"

"I know what it feels like to pout. Poor baby!"

"You're unbelievable! You really enjoy this, don't you?"

Jamila tried her best but she couldn't keep herself from momentarily breaking out in a fit of laughter. She finally managed to get herself under control but was still smiling sheepishly. She actually appeared to be slightly embarrassed. Was she blushing?

"Evidence to the contrary, no. I don't enjoy this. I mean, I don't enjoy embarrassing you. Or emasculating you."

"Emasculating! Perfect word."

"Just work with me, okay? All I'm trying to get at is, there's this side of you which quite honestly is wonderful. But it doesn't play well. Not with the public. It makes you an easy target. If anyone even bothers to target you in the first place."

"See! You always have to twist the knife, don't you?"

"It's very simple. You've got to counter the perception that you're some stuffy academic. That you're a bookish wimp."

"I *am* a bookish wimp."

"Martin, you're a great guy. A good person. A *very* good person. But people want heroes. Even if you haven't done anything heroic, we have to somehow make it look like you have. Make it look like you've got the right stuff. That when push comes to shove, you'll always be out in front leading the charge. What did Bill Clinton say? In today's world, people will go with strong and wrong any day over weak and right."

"How about we make me strong and right?"

"We've definitely had way too much of strong and wrong, that's for sure."

"Tyranny is always better organized than freedom."

"Who's that?"

"Jay Z."

"You're a dork."

"Charles Peguy, French poet."

"I overheard Phyllis mention something about your step-father being an ex-military guy. Maybe we could do something with that. This is a military town. Martin Truth, self-made man cut from the sinews of a high ranking warrior."

"Jamila. My step-father murdered my mother. He shot her in the face. He's not exactly the kind of guy you want to build my campaign around."

"I'm sorry. That's fucked-up. Really fucked up!"

"You don't have to remind me."

"Then give me something. Give the niggah girl *something* to work with, Martin Truth!"

He put his fork down, pushed his plate aside, and leaned as far forward as he could without tipping the table over.

"You want something? I'll give you something. You love to throw around that … you love saying niggah this and niggah that. You just love to see how uncomfortable it makes people. Okay. Let's talk about some of your niggah friends. How about Martin Luther King? How about Malcolm X? Or Jesse Jackson?"

She could see he was pissed but didn't back down. She returned his cold steely stare with her own.

"What's your point?"

"There's a principle involved here."

"What principle? What the fuck are you talking about?"

"Would you be sitting here telling Martin Luther King he needed to beef it up a bit, throw in some crowd-pleasing one-liners? Buff up his image a bit for prime-time TV?"

Martin started doing his own lousy imitation of Jamila. It was a pathetic impersonation which bore no resemblance to her, but still was very effective at mocking her attitude and essential blackness.

"Now Dr. King, we're really not getting through to the southern rednecks. You need to maybe work a little hillbilly into your persona. Maybe a cowboy hat and a nice suede leather vest with some fringe would do the trick. And you, Malcolm. I just don't know where to start. You're so goddamn brainy and articulate. A lot of people resent having that know-it-all shit-eating solemnity shoved in their faces. For starters, that taqiyah has to go. Makes you look like some freak show camel jockey. Ahab the Arab, sheik of the burning ghetto. Honestly, Malcolm? I don't see why you don't just go with a fro, bro'. It works for Sly Stone. He sells records like they was honey-chitlins and black-eyed bean dip."

Nothing was said for what seemed like an eternity. Jamila just stared at Martin. There was no visible hostility. It was hard to imagine what she was thinking. Then she just nodded.

"Okay. Got it. You've said what you have to say."

Martin couldn't let it go. She had really gotten to him. He dug in.

"No. I've got more. Where's this coming from anyway? Is this something you only reserve for us pitiful white folk? Or maybe you just like toying with a bookish wimp like me? You didn't answer my question. Would you really be pulling this crap with Malcolm X and Dr. King? Would you try to spit-shine their personas to a media-friendly high gloss? Then again, maybe you would. Maybe you've got no respect for anyone. Even those good old black legendaries couldn't cut it in Jamila's world."

"This isn't *my* world, any more than it's *your* world. Or Martin Luther King's world. *That's* the point! I don't know what kind of world we live in anymore."

"Well, I do. You, of all people, a woman of color, should know. Your people have been sold down the river so many times, what do you have to show for it? What good did all that 'uh yes, massah' and 'uh no, massah' do? What did it get you? I'll tell you what. You got nothing. All you have now, all you ever had, all you in the end held onto, is the only thing that gives a human being dignity and worth. You held onto your identity. You held on to your souls. But now you want me to sell mine."

"Are you finished with your incoherent rant?"

"No! I'm just getting warmed up."

"Martin! You are so difficult. And so out of touch. This is simple. You want people to vote for you. People don't vote for someone they don't understand. Or don't like. Or don't notice. This is a big nasty indifferent world. You've got to meet people halfway. You're got to give them a Martin Truth they can identify with, appreciate, learn to trust. It's about laying a foundation."

He started shouting. People at other tables turned to look, gazing on with quickly mounting unease.

"I HAVE A FOUNDATION! It's called … MY PRINCIPLES. MY IDEAS. MY IDEALS. WHAT I STAND FOR. MY VISION FOR THE COUNTRY I LOVE. IF THAT'S NOT GOOD ENOUGH—"

"ALRIGHT! Alright! It's good enough, Martin! Yes. I think it's good enough …"

People were staring. Martin forced himself to calm down.

Jamila started crying. She quickly grabbed tissue from her handbag and tried to wipe her eyes.

"… I really do."

The tears kept coming. She wouldn't look at him. Keeping her head down and turned to the side, slowly and unsteadily she stood up.

"I'll be right back."

She sobbed as she weaved her way across the restaurant. Martin watched her the whole way. Finally she slipped into the ladies room.

She was gone nearly ten minutes. When she returned, she appeared completely calm and collected. There was no sign of tears. But no sign of mirth either. She sat down with almost a prim air about her. For a moment, her typically erect posture seemed even more pronounced and perfect.

Then Jamila reached across the table, took each of Martin's hands in hers, and looked him squarely in the eyes. She looked like she was about to decree a death sentence.

"Forget everything I've been saying tonight."

"You're giving up on me?"

"Hardly. I just know when I'm wrong."

"First I'm wrong and you're right. Then I accept the fact I'm probably wrong. Now you say you were wrong. How am I supposed to make sense of this?"

"Martin. You're fine. It's not you. Forget all that persona bullshit. You're not boring. Not terminally boring anyway. It took me a minute. But I realized I'm just taking out my own frustrations on you. I'm … I'm sorry. I didn't mean—"

"Stop! Let's just not say anything for a couple minutes. I need to shift gears. Do something. Anything. This is so ... so ... *thoroughly confusing*."

Jamila reached for another bread stick. She was sticking to her love affair with the breadsticks, if not anything else. This had to be her eighth or ninth. How did she stay so thin?

They sat in silence for the next ten minutes. Martin ordered two coffees. He looked at the dessert menu, then decided to pass. Jamila was staring off in space, her gaze pointed in the general direction of the bottles of spirits on the upper shelves behind the bar in the center of the restaurant. Martin noticed.

"Do you want a drink?"

Jamila didn't answer.

Then she spoke.

"Martin, this has to be between us and only us. I don't want the others to know about this. It's no big deal. I just don't want it bandied about like cheap gossip."

"I'm really not in the mood for any more big surprises right now. But I guess we're good. So yes, I'll play along. I'm sworn to secrecy. Should I raise my right hand?"

"What's my last name?"

"Your last name? Parks. Jamila Parks. Did I win something?"

"Do you know who my great aunt is?"

This was getting weirder by the minute. Maybe this seemingly brilliant young lady was one of those bipolar types. The roller coaster carrying her psyche had reached the top and now it was in the midst of the big plunge.

"Aretha Franklin? Department of Parks and Recreation? I don't know. Who?"

"Rosa Parks."

Rosa Parks! The civil rights heroine! Martin immediately regretted that he tried to joke about it.

"I'm sorry I … sometimes my sense of humor—"

"She was a great lady, Martin. Greater than people will ever know. I spent a great deal of time with her before she passed away."

"I'm in total awe. I mean that. You're so lucky! Now I see where all your—"

"What people don't know is that at the end of her life, there were things she was very bitter about. You see, everything she did, starting with the day back in 1955 when she refused to give up her seat to that white person and got arrested, bore a deep message that resonated with the thousands of black folks who still lived under the oppressive fist of racism, nearly a century after they had allegedly been freed from the chains of slavery. But what was the end result? Now they live with a different set of chains. Racism is illegal. But in fact, it's still going strong. In some ways, it's more virulent than ever."

"But that's not her fault. How could she be bitter? What she did was courageous and noble. That one act inspired a whole movement. Wasn't she called the 'first lady of civil rights'? Something along those lines?"

"You know your history. Yes, she became a symbol. A symbol for all of the amazing things to be done in the name of freedom and equality and justice. But symbols are just that. Sometimes symbols actually substitute for reality. What's changed? Look at our country now. Technically, we're the land of the free. A nation of equal opportunity, regardless of skin color."

She suddenly started shaking her head.

"No! Let's get off that topic. How about this? Allegedly we're the beacon of democracy throughout the world. But what's the reality? We prop up dictators, as long as they buy our weapons. We support some of the most vicious and autocratic regimes, as long as they play ball, play by our rules. We send our own young men and women into battle to die defending monarchs, as long as they keep shipping us oil. We send innocent people who without evidence we label as terrorists to anti-democratic countries to lock up indefinitely and torture."

"What's this got to do with your great aunt?"

"It's all the same game. I should say the *gaming* of reality. My great aunt got sick of being used as part of a storybook version of history. Everything gets turned into a Hollywood script. Everyone shouts for joy in the big climactic final scene, the orchestra fires up, the sky fills with fireworks, the hero is hoisted on the shoulders of the crowd, they all dance off into the sunset. Problem solved. They lived happily ever after."

"That's just human nature. People need that."

"You're right. That's how people process information. They need a narrative. The problem is who writes and controls the narrative. And that's the big problem now *period.* It's your problem. It's my problem. And for the public, for the 99% of them who aren't even aware of it, it's *their* problem."

"How is it your problem, Jamila? You seem to be on top of all of this. You're the one who came up with the pledge idea. You're the one who we're hoping can look at my campaign with fresh eyes, look at me objectively, tell me what's going to play well in the eyes of the public, help me get some perspective on what I've got going for me in terms of presentation, what my personal strengths and weaknesses are. This is valuable stuff. I don't expect you to have all of the answers but every little bit helps. And you're helping a lot."

"I'm of two minds on this. It's like what you said about having a foundation. That struck a chord. A big thunderous chord. Maybe I was naïve but that's what I used to believe. I didn't get into the poly-sci program at Rutgers to play these kinds of games. To go out and tell someone like you the very things I've been spewing. Politics *should* be about principles, ideas, values. But we don't talk about those things anymore. The narrative has been stolen by the right and mutilated by the media. It's who's up and who's down, who are the winners and the losers. But I can tell you who the losers really are. It's the people. They always get fucked. Of course, that's not the narrative. It's all become Super Bowl. Jersey Shore. America's Next Supermodel. We're so concerned about which side a candidate parts his hair on, whether he smoked weed with his fraternity brothers in college, or whether Donald Trump invited him for lunch, there's no room anymore for ideas. There's no room for people like you, Martin."

"I feel like a dog left out in the rain."

"Whether we like it or not, we're all in this together. A helpless bunch of niggahs at a slave auction."

“So what’s the solution? What do we do? So far what you’ve been saying to me, to all of us with the campaign has been: We didn’t make the rules but they’re the rules. We play to win.”

“There is no solution. No real solution. Not yet. The only possible solution is getting rid of the current crop of corporation-owned lackeys and start kicking some ass in the halls of Congress. Make some changes. Big changes! Get money out of politics. Take down Citizens United. Run the corporate lobbyists out. Kick-start democracy by having legislators who represent the people and not big money. It’s either that or the only alternative is revolution. That certainly ain’t gonna happen. The general public is so brainwashed, they don’t even see a problem, not on a systemic level. But if we go issue by issue, we have some slim chance of getting in their heads and swapping out the crooks and liars in office for some good legislators. Hopefully before it’s too late.”

“Your great-aunt would be proud of what you’re trying to do.”

“My great-aunt would be more appalled now than ever. She knows what it’s like to be trivialized, iconized, marginalized. To be used. But what happened to her was silly child’s play compared to what’s going on now. Guys like Karl Rove, these vicious phony citizens groups like the Swift Boaters and Special Operations Opsec Education Fund, and of course, this whole Tea Party thing. She couldn’t have imagined any of this stuff. She was a woman of ideas, principles, and most of all ideals. From the seed of that one act of rebellion, and her association with Martin Luther King and all of the courageous people that stood toe-to-toe with the brutal bigots in uniform, taking their insults and beatings, she fashioned in her imagination the world she wanted her children, her nieces and nephews, her great-nieces like me, to grow up in. And she fought for what she believed in. They didn’t poll focus groups or have people texting ‘1’ for yes and ‘2’ for no, to decide what was right and wrong.”

“You know all this. I don’t understand what argument you are having with yourself. You seem so conflicted. Now it’s like you want to throw me to the wolves. Is that it? I really don’t understand where this is going or what it means.”

“It means that I hate the fucking world I live in! It means I wake up in the middle of the night wondering if this is all a waste of time. Tonight it means that you’re right. Having you do the soft shoe and some magic tricks is not the way the win this election. It means that we aren’t going to do a Martin Truth makeover. All of that, as necessary and important as it’s made out to be — and yes it does have a place but it’s not the main thing — is a big distraction, and intentionally so. You, Martin Truth with the banana growing out of your head, are *not* boring. It’s *them* who are boring. So stick to it, and stick it to them. Give ‘em what you think is right. Wake them up. Speak your mind loud and clear. We’ll lob the bombs and clear a path into town for your victory parade. That’s all we can do.”

“I love it when you talk war talk. I get this intense visceral reaction. Maybe I should dress in camouflage for all of my speeches from now on.”

“Just be sure to wear the tie with the seagulls.”

“I do think it works well with the goatee.”

“Uh, sorry. The goatee still has to go.”

"How about snowflake contacts?"

"Way too gay for this district. You'd be better off keeping the goatee but sprinkling it with toenail clippings, preferably female."

• • •

As they started to wrestle with the mechanics of implementing Jamila's pledge strategy, Martin still wasn't 100% sold. Though he usually was a beacon of thoughtful optimism, his unborn Siamese twin was a shadow of vexing skepticism.

"Pledges schmedges. I'm still not understanding how they can make a difference."

"That's because you hear 'pledges' and you go stupid on me."

"Jamila, you're a pit bull."

"Did I say stupid? I'm sorry I meant to say that it's much too easy to hear the term 'pledge' and then in reference to the particular strategy we are discussing, to predictably lose sight of the larger enterprise."

"Now I feel patronized. Is it just me? Or do you completely piss off everybody?"

Of course, this was a white lie. He wasn't pissed off. He loved her toughness. He was totally enamored with her energy and take-no-prisoners attitude.

"Martin. Focus. Yes, we're talking pledges. Everybody knows of them from Überfuehrer Norquist and from the 2011 Iowa caucuses when the Republican candidates were asked to sign all sorts of nonsense. But *our* pledges are different. These are not pretty-please promises. They're designed to kick the candidate where it really hurts, then when he's bent over, give him a big swift boot out of office."

"Nice."

"Hardly. But these guys don't play nice. So fuck them! Anyway, the thing is not the pledge. The thing is the poisoning of the bait. It's the tactic of forcing the guy between a rock and a hard place. The rock is what the voting public wants and the hard place is the guy's sell-out voting record. We're just performing a public service by putting a spotlight on the gaping discrepancy between the two. Using the pledge."

"Nobody's going to sign these things. Especially numb nuts Gardner. He may be an asshole but he's a shrewd asshole."

"Exactly! I don't expect him to. But when he refuses, he faces a shitstorm of voter backlash. Courtesy of us."

"We'll never get the cooperation of the media. TV will never run with this. They'll stick with stories about hot dog eating contests and crippled roller bladers trying to make it an Olympic event. Or the usual blood-and-guts at six with freeway decapitations and exploding barbecue pits."

"You're probably right. But there are other ways to get people's attention."

"You're not going to have a Buddhist monk set himself on fire, are you?"

"Wow! Martin. What a great idea! Why didn't I think of that. Is there a Buddhist monastery in Dayton?"

"Yeah, it's right between the Yeti encampment and the crashed UFO. You still haven't answered my question."

"No."

"No, what?"

"No, I'm not going to have a Buddhist monk set himself on fire."

Jamila had the courtesy to wait for him to laugh first. She could wrap him around her little finger twice, twirl him in the air, then toss him into a dumpster full of turkey stuffing. He was helpless. Beyond being the hottest babe on either side of the international date line, she was genuinely funny. Not just what she said, but the way she would say it, then just look at you, defying you to keep a straight face.

Again she won. Martin tried unsuccessfully to keep from laughing as he rolled his eyes and threw his hands in the air in mock frustration.

"Okay okay. Scratch one Buddhist monk flambé. What's the plan?"

"We'll make it up as we go. Trust me, there are lots of opportunities to make news and grab people's attention."

"You don't have a clue, do you?"

"Festivals, carnivals, dog shows, flea markets, farmers markets, bake sales. I don't know. Let me think. Can you ride a horse? We'll enter you in a rodeo."

"That's real cute. You're grasping at straws. Desperation has set in."

"Well, I may not know your particular community here. But I do know that wherever there are people, there's a way to grab their attention. You're right. You caught me off guard. But I know this can work. For starters, we can use the social networks. Facebook. Twitter. Google+. Blogger. Pinterest. Create some rumbles. Then it's just a matter of picking and choosing the right events. Or creating our own. I was serious about flea markets and festivals. But we also need to visit organizations and clubs in the community. It'll be issue-focused, and which ones we target and what we say will depend on what the pledges themselves say. We're still early in the process. We've got all that stuff ahead of us still."

"You try to make it seem so easy. It's sounds like an uphill battle to me."

"Duh! Tell me your last three campaigns weren't an uphill battle. Like straight up! Nothing new there. It's like climbing a difficult mountain. You choose your route carefully, don't waste energy or fritter away time on dead ends, keep a clear head, and just keep forging ahead."

"Rah rah rah, siss coom bah."

"I'll tell you something else. If it's handled right, the confrontation itself will be big news."

"Confrontation? What confrontation?"

"Handing him the pledges, bozo. He won't see it coming. We just have make sure it's done right. Very publicly. Lots of eyes on him. One way or another, make sure the press is there. That way he's got to say 'yes' or 'no'. Of course, he'll refuse to sign them. Then we take him down for being a blowhard."

"Why hasn't anyone else tried this pledge idea? Other than the ruthless bastards on the right, who seem to never run out of ways to cripple the country and suck up to their kleptomaniac rich friends."

"There's a first time for everything."

"The first dog they put into earth orbit never came back."

"And the first sheep they cloned used to hop like a bunny and hoot like an owl. But seriously, Martin. I *do* know why progressives haven't tried it."

"Do I want to hear this?"

"I don't know. Do you?"

"I guess … maybe … sort of."

"It's because they're a bunch of self-righteous pussies."

"Isn't that a little harsh?"

"That's the PC version. I didn't want to upset you."

"Actually, I'm already upset. Very upset. But not because of what you just said."

"Why are you upset then?"

"Because … because this is something that's been bothering me for a long time. Left wing wimpiness. Because … the truth is, I guess I'm wondering if I'm just another one of those self-righteous pussies. And now I'm upset because *I* never had the balls to say what you just said! Because you know? You are. You're absolutely right."

"Martin. Neither you or I made these rules. It's not the way it's supposed to be. At the same time, you jumped into the arena. Maybe you were up for a pleasant game of badminton. Instead you find yourself surrounded by a bunch of gladiators. That's the whole problem with the left. They keep looking for the shuttlecock and hoping the blood and guts will go away. They hold their heads high and get them lopped off. But it's not a choice. Either you play the game to win, or you lose. There are things which I don't believe in doing. I don't believe in lying. These vile, slanderous commercials the ruthless wing nuts on the right put out are disgusting. Off limits as far as I'm concerned. But keep in mind exactly what we're doing here. We're not making stuff up. We're taking the candidate's own rope, the one he made himself by being a treacherous, lying, two-faced hypocrite, and letting him hang himself with it."

Jamila stopped talking. She just sat there and let it sink in. Several minutes passed.

Then the light of comprehension in Martin's eyes began to flicker. Slowly his gaze became steady, relaxed. He leaned forward, riveted, mesmerized. His lips were compressed and he was nodding.

She *was* right.

Absolutely right.

"Okay. I want to be perfectly clear about all of this. I hate to have to ask you. But please run the whole thing by me one more time."

"The whole thing? Beginning to end?"

"Yes. Beginning to end."

And she did.

Chapter Four

For the next ten days, Martin's campaign committee keyed in on the things that were really important to the voters in the district. The hotbuttons. The wedge issues.

Jamila had done her homework.

"Okay, here's where we need to be looking. I'll just go down the list. Nationally 74% of Americans are in favor of ending oil subsidies to companies like Exxon-Mobil and Chevron."

Bill shaking his head.

"Somebody cares. But not enough. No way."

Lincoln doodling on a note pad.

"It's a non-starter. Next."

"Good numbers on reducing the defense budget. 76% of the American voting public are sick of the Pentagon spending tax dollars on military systems it doesn't need."

This provoked a minor uproar, mostly outright laughter. Bill winked at her.

"Whew! Nice try. But that's not going to fly here."

Lincoln just shook his head. He even stopped doodling.

"Look around you, young lady. This is buzz cut central. It's a military town. You've got Wright-Patterson Air Force Base. Defense contracts are the life blood. Without them Dayton would look like Detroit."

Even if it was a non-starter, this touched a raw nerve in Martin.

"I'd personally like to cut the defense budget in half. But as ashamed as I am to admit it, I never *ever* bring up defense. Not in my speeches. Not in the press kit. It'd be like going to the Vatican and yelling, 'The Pope is butt buddies with Pat Robertson.' Maybe worse."

"Catholics are so touchy that way."

"Martin, you've been watching way too much Geraldo Rivera."

Jamila forged ahead.

"How about this? A CNN poll on what has been termed the Buffett Rule showed that 72% of Americans favored its passage. As you know, the Buffett Rule raised the prospects of a more equitable tax rate on the rich. This is not an anomaly. Other more recent polls show huge public support for higher taxes on the top 1%. We're talking a minimum of 65% in the most conservative survey. There was a New York Times-CBS News poll which said that 72% of those queried agreed that federal taxes should be raised for households making more than $250,000. That figure included 55% of Republicans, 74% of Independents and 83% of all Democrats. And here's a shocker. A poll by The Harrison Group found that 67% of people earning $450,000 per year or more — which *is* the 1% — favored increased taxes. On themselves!"

Phyllis was beaming ... well, as much as she ever beamed.

"Absolutely! Fair taxation's a real winner. It's on everyone's mind. Even in this smarmy end of town. It's become apparent even to the dull-witted that any talk by the Republicans about tax reform is just cover for less taxes on the wealthy."

Bill with his chic little coffee house *in* this smarmy end of town was the ears of the street.

"Yup! This is a hot topic. My customers are smart, informed. They *don't* watch Fox News. They're doing well enough to afford to be responsible. Most say they would even pay a little more if the rich paid their fair share. It ain't going to happen under this administration and this tight fisted Congress."

Normally rather quiet, Imogene piped up. She was the perfect archetype of a social worker. Gray slacks. White blouse. Frumpy granny glasses hanging around her neck on a silver chain. Prematurely gray hair pulled back in a pony tail. She was 52 but carried the weight of several lifetimes on her shoulders and the pain of knowing too much human suffering.

"I've got over 120 in my caseload now and I don't know but maybe three or four of them who doesn't seriously want to work. Everybody keeps talking about making life easier on the 'job creators' so they can put people back to work. What a fraud. Gardner was on the front lines trying to pull down tax rates even more. Back in 2012, he voted for both versions of the Ryan budget."

Bob Phelps worked in the same capacity as Imogene, a veteran social worker for the Ohio Department of Job and Family Services. He was five or six years younger, balding, carried a few extra pounds, dressed like an off-duty police officer, and was a widower.

He was shaking his head and had a look of intense disgust on his face.

"Brutal, inhumane plans which cut everything to the bone and give even more tax breaks to the caviar and country club set. I read that on top of the Bush cuts, on average the Ryan bill stuffs another $265,000 into the bulging pockets of the millionaires. I honestly couldn't believe it. Cuts to food stamps, school lunch programs, women's health care, child care, heating oil assistance. Literally every single program now in place to help poor people would get a major haircut. And the rich get showered with more money from Daddy Warbucks, our U.S. Treasury. Fox News called it courageous. It's the courage of Charles Manson."

Jamila had been writing furiously.

"Which brings up two more goldmines: Social Security and Medicare. Despite vicious and hugely misleading ads by the ultra right, imposing majorities of Americans do *not* want Congress screwing around with these programs. The polls come in at high 70s, low 80s on this. One poll even reported that 75% of Americans are in favor of *increasing* Social Security benefits. So what about the folks around here? Wow, Phyllis. You look pretty psyched!"

"Winners both. Social security and Medicare. Even Medicaid. I don't know anyone who wants them tampered with. Except a few anarchists."

Bill raised his coffee mug in a mock toast.

"That nut job Libertarian, Peter Potts."

Phyllis's face was a portrait of contempt.

"Yeah, him and Rand Paul." She looked up and gave Jamila her penetrating iron horse stare. "Jamila. This one is hay for the making. Gardner is always schmoozing senior citizens, talking about how we owe it to them to keep them healthy and make their retirement years comfortable. There was one speech I remember where the guy actually got all teary-eyed, talking about his grandmother."

"What a hypocrite! He was probably teary-eyed because she wouldn't sign her social security checks over to him."

They could always count on Martin. Behind his innocent, boyish good looks lurked a grizzled, sardonic George Carlin.

Jamila finished writing on her legal pad.

"Okay, we've got taxes on the rich, Social Security and Medicare. I've got four more hotbutton issues. On health care reform, during the big debates before Obama's health care initiative passed, 72% of Americans favored the inclusion of the public option. Health care still a huge concern with people, and rightfully so. With the messy launch of Obamacare and the incessant attempts by Republicans to repeal it, tensions are still high and the yelling never stops. The public option and even single-payer always get decent polling percentages."

Martin was particularly knowledgeable about health care reform. He had made it a major focus for his last two campaigns.

"You guys know where I stand. But I'll sum it up for Jamila. Obamacare is a pig with a lot of lipstick. It was a huge giveaway to the health care industry and insurance companies, and didn't solve the real problems. Most people supported it and opposed it for the wrong reasons. Like most everybody in this country, I think people here are confused. There's been so much back and forth. Plus the Republicans have done an effective job making up their own facts and statistics. It should be cut and dry but I still don't think voters have any clear picture of it. Gardner, of course, came out against any kind of reform. That was knee jerk. Unfortunately, in terms of Obamacare he was right for the wrong reasons."

Phyllis and the rest were all nodding in agreement.

"It's a touchy topic in this town. The health care industry is the second biggest employer behind the military. Everyone is paranoid. They're afraid that any more attempts to fix it will muck it up even more."

Jamila looked at her laptop.

"Food labeling. Genetically modified veggies and the like. Not much buzz about this in the media but the interesting thing is that there are some very strong opinions out there. And it's very one-sided across the political spectrum. This is all from a very recent ABC poll. First off, I was surprised to find out that barely a third of Americans think GMO foods are safe to eat. And more than half believe they are actually unsafe. The result is, 93% believe that foods containing GMOs should be clearly labeled as such. But the food industry lobbies are hugely powerful. And persuasive. Nothing gets done. In fact, local initiatives almost always go down in defeat because so much money is pumped into ads opposing them. Is this worth pursuing?"

Bill jumped in.

"93%! That's impressive. Normally you can't get that many people to agree that the sun will come up tomorrow. Martin? Lincoln? Anyone? What's Gardner's record on this?"

Martin and Lincoln started talking at the same time.

"Just as you'd expect—"

"He gets a lot of money from—"

"Go ahead, Lincoln. I'm sure you're more up to speed on this."

Lincoln pulled a well-worn sheaf of papers out of his briefcase.

"Voted lockstep with the food industry in the last two congressional sessions. As I believe Martin was about to say, he votes his pocketbook. He gets sizeable campaign contributions from the big corporations. Pepsico, Tyson, Nestle, General Mills, Coca-Cola."

Phyllis had been lost in her own thoughts but finally spoke up.

"I've been trying to think how to put this. I mean, 93% dictates that we take this issue seriously. But there's something that bothers me about it. I think people are *in principle* very concerned about purity of food. No one wants to feed themselves and their families anything which might be risky. On the other hand, I don't think it's a burning issue with most folks. Meaning, it's not something they've had to deal with on a personal level, as a personal crisis. Despite the risk they perceive in GMOs, no one — at least no one that anyone knows of — has died from them. It's not like cancer where everyone has someone in their family or among their friends who's had to deal with it."

"So what do we do with this?"

"I say we go with it but at a lower priority. We should keep it on the back burner, unless of course, something comes up in the next few months which pushes it out front as a campaign issue. We've got Gardner dead to rights on this, but GMOs still are a bit of an abstraction in the public's mind. Social Security and Medicare, taxes on the wealthy are hot topics right now. Important as food labeling is, it's not getting people stirred up."

Jamila was already moving on.

"This one is interesting. Well, it's interesting to most kids my age. But it's something that especially affects all of the working poor. Minimum wage. The current federal minimum wage of $7.25 is in equivalent dollars the same as it was in 1956. There is a huge groundswell of public sentiment about this. Over 70% are behind raising it to above $10 per hour. That's 84% Democrats, 66% Independents, and 52% Republicans."

Bob looked at Imogene, which she took as a cue.

"That's all we hear. Poor people work full-time jobs and still can't make ends meet. If they work, they lose their benefits from us. Getting a minimum wage job actually sets them back. Talk about a reverse incentive."

Lincoln looked puzzled.

"Jamila, you said $7.25 was the equivalent to minimum wage in 1956. I have always seen it being equated with 1997."

"That's true. In the intervening years, people actually made a bit more. Adjusted for inflation, wages in today's dollars went up and peaked in 1967, then slowly came back down. By 1997, they were back at 1956 levels. The point is, despite the vast, widely-touted increases in worker productivity, wages have basically been stagnant for over four decades. People work harder and more effectively but see no reward for their efforts. It all goes toward increased profits and executive bonuses."

"And buttplug voted every time against an increase. He's consistent. Always on the wrong side of any issue affecting the working class."

"He's a card-carrying sadist."

"He's for a safety net … one made out of barb wire."

"That's a bit disrepectful. You should probably say *Congressman* Buttplug."

Phyllis offered her imprimatur.

"This is a big issue affecting a lot of people. Even here in Kettering, there are a lot of low wage jobs. Everyone knows someone working at minimum wage. Even if it's a high school student working part-time at Mickey D's. Whenever Gardner discusses the minimum wage, he gets this pained expression of mock concern. Like he's got an impacted wisdom tooth or is in the final stage of a breach birth. It's pathetic!"

"My my, Phyllis."

"Breach birth?"

"Aaagh! I didn't need that image."

Phyllis seemed rather proud of herself.

Lincoln had his own informed take on the issue.

"This used to be a third rail for politicians and would provoke a lot of backlash from the so-called job creators. But it has certainly leaped into the limelight recently. You've got California raising the state minimum wage to $10 and the little city of SeaTac, Washington raising theirs to $15 per hour, which got a lot of news coverage. What do you say, Martin? You're out there talking to people."

"This galls me. Expecting anyone, especially someone who's married and has a family, to live on $7.25 an hour is ridiculous. The right wing has traditionally been effective at keeping this off the table and out of the public eye. But I think that's rapidly changing. I say we go with it. Hey, Jamila. How many do we need?"

"Four at the most. Otherwise, it fragments the public's attention. Four might be pushing it."

"What else you got?"

Jamila held up her notes.

"Actually, one more and I'm done. And this one's a biggie. According to a recent New York Times/CBS News poll on the war in Afghanistan, 76% of the public clearly opposes it and favors an immediate withdrawal. The vast majority of Americans see it as a gigantic waste of money and lives. They're sick of the dilly-dallying around. They want out."

This was Bill's area of expertise, if not his entire raison d'être. He had been a peace activist in college and was always front and center at rallies and marches against the wars — all wars — traveling regularly to Cincinnati and Columbus, even Washington DC, for demonstrations.

"Even with all of the flag-waving that goes on around here, I think your percentage would hold up well here in this district. The farmers are a bunch of isolationists. But more importantly, the defense industry itself opposes this kind of misadventure. The more money the country spends on soldiers in the field, meaning bombs-and-bullets warfare, the less there is for research and development, which here is their real bread and butter. I guess you could say, they live in a science-fiction comic book bubble at Wright-Patterson. Iraq and Afghanistan, and any other forays by troops and operational weapons on the ground, cuts into the money they want to make their futuristic high-tech gadgets. The only possible boon has been the drones. They do a lot of drone testing and development, so the War on Terror has been a great boost to business. But again, once a piece of machinery is battlefield proven and ready, it actually works against their interests locally for the defense department to be shelling out to use it in actual wars. So the simple answer is, Jamila, that you'll find a lot of support here for bringing the boys home."

"From what I've read, our buddy Mr. Gardner hasn't found a weapon system or a war he wouldn't do cartwheels over. He's Romeo, and Juliet is anything to do with bombs and bullets."

"The guy's record is abysmal. He's Dick Cheney on steroids. The guy has stars-and-stripes underwear for his entire family."

Martin acted like he was offended.

"Excuse me! You have a problem with red, white and blue boxers?"

"Only that you never wash them."

"Issues of personal hygiene aside, I refuse to pose for a press photo in my undies."

"Is that a pipe bomb in your pocket or are you just glad I'm thinking of voting for you?"

Jamila tried to keep a straight face. She finally starting laughing. Not at what they had said. She was laughing because they seemed to find their idiotic jokes so *funny*.

"Okay, children. It looks like we've got five solid issues to address with the pledges, and one on stand-by. We should keep it at four, so here's what we do. Let's combine Medicare and Social Security. Functionally the programs are linked anyway. Plus they're equally popular with the public. Anybody have a problem with that? Phyllis?"

"Makes sense."

"So the four are increasing taxes on the rich, leaving Social Security and Medicare alone, raising the minimum wage, and finally, ending the war in Afghanistan."

Nodding assent from everyone.

"Anticipating that Social Security would be one of them — and quite honestly that was an easy call — I have here a sample pledge. I threw this together last night at home. Of course, we'll have to fine-tune it a bit and include Medicare in the final version. But the idea is there. It's based on the template my seminar study group at Rutgers formulated while prototyping this strategy. This was only a few months ago. It's way ahead of the curve."

She passed copies to everyone. They read in silence for several minutes.

> I, Matthew Gardner, if re-elected to my seat in the U.S. House of Representatives, hereby commit to co-sponsor and vote in favor of legislation to establish a 10-year moratorium on any reductions to social security benefits, increasing the eligibility age, or making any other alteration in the program as it is now configured, such as might negatively impact eligible recipients of such benefits. I will not resist, discourage, or in any manner put up an impediment to, and in fact will publicly and on the floor of Congress actively promote, any and all legislation in support of this measure. If no other legislator comes forth to offer such a moratorium, I will create and introduce by my own initiative, within 90 days of taking office, such a legislative act for consideration by Congress.
>
> I further understand and fully agree to the following: If I violate the above-stated terms of this pledge, I will tender on the 91st day after taking the oath of office for my legislative seat, my full and unqualified resignation from this elected position. Moreover, within one year of my resignation, I will refund all contributions made by individual donors in support of my candidacy for this office.
>
> This entire pledge constitutes a legally binding contract between myself and that class of citizens who will be my constituents, should I win the upcoming election. In the event that I fail to perform the above-required actions, redress may be sought by those same citizens in the form of a class-action suit in a civil court of law, and I will be liable for a minimum of $10,000,000 damages for breach of contract. If I fail to resign from office due to my failure to fulfill the other requirements of this contract, I may be liable for an additional class-action settlement for an amount not less than $50,000,000. No portion of these specified settlements may be paid from campaign donations, PACs or SuperPACs.
>
> I take this pledge voluntarily and with full appreciation of my responsibility to the citizens of the 3rd U.S. Congressional District of Ohio as their elected representative. I accept the terms of this pledge as legally binding, and with a thorough and lucid understanding of its requirements and consequences.

Signed: ________________

Date: _________________

When they were done, no one actually spoke. At least no one uttered a coherent sentence.

What was heard were mumbled exclamations and spontaneous gasps, addressed to no one in particular, expressing a host of reactions: Surprise. Awe. Shock. Astonishment. Appreciation. These utterances seemed to float in the room, fluttering rhetorical wisps, invisible little gusts and whirls, stunned butterflies dancing around the edges of human speech.

"Unh."

"Wuuh."

"Ssshvu."

"Mmmm!"

"Phwoooh!"

Phyllis finally injected some actual content into the eddies of air hovering among them.

"Whew! I remember the time back when, Jamila, you said that the pledges would be ironclad, bulletproof. But I never imagined anything as powerful as this. You keep your promises."

"I try."

For the next half-hour, they went over the text of the pledge line-by-line.

Each had some unnecessary question about what this or that meant. Jamila replied with the requisite superfluous answer. It was all very polite, a lot of chin scratching and nodding.

The truth was, everyone in this tight little group was very perceptive, quick, informed, intelligent. The wording of the pledge was entirely straightforward, the legal implications easy to grasp. What was really going on now was more group therapy than actually dealing with the language and technicalities of the document. The fierce no-nonsense terms of the pledge had blindsided them. All of the chatter was just them collectively trying to get comfortable with something they clearly could see was a weapon of awesome power, a fearsome device for seriously challenging the incumbent Gardner, putting him on the defensive, and getting him to shape up. Or even possibly destroying him.

Finally, there was no more to be said.

Phyllis yawned. It was contagious and spread around the room.

"Martin, do you have anything to add before we adjourn?"

"Does anyone know where I can buy a Kevlar body suit?"

Jamila didn't know much about body armor. But she was sure about her politics.

"You've nothing to fear. This is going to make you look good. Real good!"

"Great. My image is very important to me. I've always wanted an open-casket funeral."

Jamila smiled and played along.

"And refuse the hood at the hanging. Or do they use firing squads here in Ohio?"

"You're not providing much comfort."

"It'll be over quick."

• • •

Two days later — just enough time for the dust to settle in everyone's mind with respect to the wording of the pledges — they all met again.

Phyllis seemed resigned to the idea that she would at least for a while be sharing her traditional role as matriarchal sovereign and resident taskmaster with the upstart intern from Rutgers.

Jamila dropped another bombshell.

But to her credit, she eased into it very tactfully this time.

"Bob and Imogene. Maybe you can help me here. You're in a good position to judge this."

She handed them each a document, then distributed copies to Phyllis, Martin, Lincoln, Bill, and Helen. The text was brief and everyone read it at least twice over the next 25 seconds.

PETITION: Citizen Public Policy Poll and
Endorsement – *Social Security and Medicare*

> I am a registered voter and will only vote for a candidate who will leave Social Security and Medicare alone. If a candidate for public office guarantees unequivocally to fight for keeping Social Security and Medicare as they currently stand, I will give that candidate my unqualified support.

Beneath the text were lines, each offering a place for a signature, printed name, home address, telephone number, and email address.

"So Bob and Imogene. You're in regular contact with the public. How many of the people you normally talk to would sign this?"

"I can't speak for Bob. But probably most, if not all of my clients would gladly sign this. If they aren't themselves receiving Social Security or getting assistance from Medicare, someone close to them is. Their parents or their grandparents. An aunt or uncle."

Bob was nodding enthusiastically.

"Precisely. Medicare and Medicaid are huge concerns. Obviously, by the time they come to us, our clients don't have any health insurance. The majority of my caseload has every problem you can imagine. All of the typical diseases plus alcoholism, substance abuse. Their eating habits are poor. Some of it is ignorance. Typically they just can't afford to eat right. It's a closed feedback loop. Malnutrition plays a huge factor. Kids grow up poorly nourished, making them more vulnerable later in life. What health services they get are the worst. I can't imagine this is different for any of the other caseworkers in our department. Health care, or I should say the lack of it, is a big chunk of what we deal with at Family Services."

Lincoln was as always soft-spoken but certain of his words.

"I've seen the numbers on this. I can bring them in next time. And you were right, Jamila. We all were right. The five issues we identified in our last meeting are *the* wedge issues in this town, this whole region. Medicare and Social Security top the list. They should be Gardner's Achilles heel. But as you know, the guy's like the Energizer Bunny."

Bill held up his copy. He was obviously quite enthused.

"People are usually reluctant to sign petitions. But I can see them climbing all over this. It's not so much a demand for action — which for some reason scares people — as it is a simple straightforward statement of what they believe in. This would get a lot of support. And I'm assuming there would be similar petitions for the other issues."

"Exactly."

Jamila looked around the table.

"Admittedly, I only gave you half of the story the other night."

Martin grinned at her but still was being serious.

"Didn't think we could handle it, eh?"

"I didn't want to dilute in anyone's mind the importance or the incredible power of the candidate pledges. They're the silver bullet here. At the same time, we are trying to get you elected, Martin. The pledges alone won't make the necessary connection."

"I don't follow."

"Okay. We've got Gardner dead to rights on five issues, with one more in the bullpen. The public sees things one way but Gardner votes another. Yet they still keep on voting for the jerk. This, by the way, keeps happening all over the country, over and over at all levels. There's a complete disconnect."

"People are disconnected all right. They're all over the map."

"This one works directly against *you*. People do not make the connection that Gardner is not representing them, therefore they should stop voting for him. Sounds strange. But it's true. Look at the percentages. 75% of the people in this district want the war in Afghanistan over, 62% of them vote for a guy who is thumbs up not only for that war but for every conceivable abuse of America's military power around the world. More than 70% want the top 1% to pay their fair share in taxes, 62% of them vote for a guy that has voted for every single tax cut for the wealthy since he took office, *and* voted for both versions of the Ryan budget, which gives even more tax breaks for the filthy rich."

"So what do we do?"

"We make it simple. We make it so simple that they can't miss it."

"They?"

"The voting public. We go to them. That's where these petitions come in. The one I gave you is for Social Security and Medicare. But as Bill pointed out, there's a similar petition for each of the four pledges we'll be confronting Gardner with."

"We're going to show him these petitions?"

"The idea is to raise public awareness, to get people thinking … *'I will only vote for a candidate who blah blah blah. I will give that candidate my full support.'* But the short answer is yes. Eventually, we will show these to Gardner. That's the whole idea of doing any of this."

Both Martin and Phyllis both looked very concerned. Phyllis spoke up first.

"Am I missing something? I'm not sure I see the merits in that."

"There aren't any merits directly in terms of this campaign per se. But they give the pledges punching power and legitimacy. It's really very straightforward. Say we get 20,000 signatures on at least one of the petitions. That's 20,000 people standing behind the associated pledge. Theoretically, Gardner should feel the heat and sign the pledge, recognizing that the possibility of losing 20,000 votes could cost him the election. *'I will only vote for a candidate who ... '* The pledge backed by 20,000 signatures on the petition draws a clear line in the sand. Either he crosses it or he doesn't. It's a gamble. We have to keep our fingers crossed that he doesn't sign the pledge."

"So this is a very risky strategy. It's very possible that we will be handing Gardner another landslide."

"Only if he signs the pledges."

Martin tried to come off as casual as he could. He cleared his throat and took a sip of water.

"But the simple fact is, we lose this game of chicken and we're back to zero."

"Actually, Martin — and I'm not meaning to be rude here — you *are* at zero with the likely prospect of remaining at zero. In essence, you have nothing to lose here because without divine intervention, you're going to lose this election. But with what we're setting up here, Gardner *does* stand to lose, and lose big time. We're putting all of the risk in his court."

"What makes you think he won't sign?"

"Because he's a short-sighted, over-confident, arrogant dickweed."

"That may be true. But if they were staring at a pile of 20,000 signatures, someone working his campaign would tell him he should take it seriously. They're not stupid."

"He won't sign. He can't sign."

"That doesn't make sense."

"As they always say, follow the money. He's bought and paid for. If he signs any of the four pledges, there will be major hell to pay. He'll lose all of his serious donors and be a pariah. Trust me, he won't sign."

"I hope you're right."

"I'm not Nostradamus. But look at the big picture. Let's assume I'm right. He brushes aside the petitions, refuses to sign the pledges, goes on with business as usual. Look at what he's handed you on a silver platter: 20,000 pissed off voters."

"Why will they be pissed off? They haven't been so far. They just keep sucking up to this photogenic puppet like he's their favorite Hannah Montana doll."

"Because they've never had it laid out in black and white. Gardner's been incredibly good at obfuscation. His speeches are full of vague, ambiguous claims, pretty promises, and justifications. He plays the patriotism card well. He's unflappable and has a marvelous smile. The guy should be on Dancing With The Stars."

"And that's what he'll keep on doing. That's what all of these doublespeak Republicans do. Talk one game and walk another."

"But like I said, Martin, Phyllis, all of you. If — or I should say — *when* he blows off the petitions, he's handing us 20,000 voters, ripe for some serious education. It's our job to educate them and get them angry. People need it spelled out for them. They need to feel it, personally. There's no way — and again I'm not denigrating the competence or good intentions of anyone in this room — there's no way you're going to get 20,000 people to pay attention otherwise. Especially the way this campaign is going. Especially because you're the Green Party and frankly not on the radar screen of 99% of the public. That's the beauty of using petitions. The document you're holding is *the* petition we'll use, plain and simple. There's no affiliation. There's no mention of any political party. It's a citizen's action survey. Grass roots."

Phyllis looked indignant. Her moral compass was spinning wildly.

"Grass roots? Hardly. This is our baby. And now that you've explained it thoroughly, the whole thing seems highly deceptive."

Jamila at first looked at her like she was crazy. Then judgment got the better of impatience.

"Phyllis, I can kind of understand your … your queasiness. But objectively, there's nothing to be uncomfortable about. It's straightforward. We're polling the voting public using a petition. The voting public takes a stand. We've given them a voice. We make sure the incumbent hears that voice by presenting the petition and a corresponding pledge committing him to go to Washington and vote the way the public wants. The incumbent says, 'Fuck off!' We go back to the voting public and give them his reply. Then separately, doing just what we're doing anyway with this campaign, we spell out in big letters that there *is* a candidate who not only agrees with them, but has willingly signed the pledge. If elected, this particular candidate *will* go to Washington and *do* the right thing."

"You make it sound like a fairy tale."

"If we can get Martin elected, it will be a fairy tale! One with a great ending, that's for sure. Hey, Bill, Martin, Lincoln. You're so quiet, it's scary!"

Bill shrugged and winced slightly.

"It seems pretty straightforward. Perhaps it's a little borderline. A touch of chicanery. But there's no blatant deception."

Lincoln seemed deep in thought.

"It's like nuclear energy. It has both positive and negative applications. I most definitely wouldn't want this to get in the wrong hands. Like Bill says, the ethical implications are a gray zone. But it's impact is very black and white."

Martin typically was torn between his ideals and realpolitik.

"I'd like to think this is noble. In its brutish way, it does give voice to the citizen. Actually, just on its own terms it gives them a voice. The brutishness comes in because we're using it to gain advantage. If it works, I can live with having to use strong-arm tactics. It's not like we're marching around town in brown shirts with billy clubs. We're providing a valuable public service and positioning ourselves to benefit from it. At least that's the way I see it. I hope I'm not just rationalizing."

Bill was always the voice of reassurance.

"You're not. We're not. We're not breaking any rules or commandments here."

A hint of amusement could be seen urging its way into Lincoln's reserve.

"Actually, it's pretty ingenious. It's both naughty and nice."

Jamila seemed satisfied that there was an undercurrent of consensus in favor.

"All I can do is reiterate my own opinion. There's nothing to be embarrassed or hesitant about here. This *is* democracy in action. Maybe it's democracy that's been mutated somewhat. But we live in mutated times."

"Congress is certainly full of mutants."

"Well, Bill. You're certainly right about that."

Martin cracks a grin.

"Why … I'll fit right in."

No one said anything. Martin looked at each of them.

"Hey, isn't anyone going to stick up for me?"

They all burst out laughing.

• • •

Four days later, they had their weekly late-Sunday-morning powwow and potluck brunch. It was a longstanding tradition, originally set up during Martin's very first campaign. The idea was to bring the week to a close with a summation of what each individual was working on and had accomplished, with an eye to shaping the direction for the following week. This early in the campaign, it tended to be heavy on eating and light on serious discussion of business.

Everyone was there except Imogene and Bob, who were in Columbus at a training function related to their jobs.

Jamila put her 20-piece box of Popeye's extra-crispy, spicy-Cajun fried chicken on the table. Soon everyone was on their second piece, complimenting her on her excellent, if nutritionally questionable contribution to the feast. She looked around. Greasy smiles and greasy fingers. Conditions were optimal for a brisk if somewhat slippery exchange of ideas.

She pulled the pin on yet another grenade.

"Listen, folks. I want to be absolutely clear about something. We can't have any connection between the petitions and this campaign. Martin Truth's fingerprints can't be on this."

This immediately launched a lively exchange between her and Phyllis. They both tended to be no-frills, no-holds-barred, no-nonsense debaters. It was an articulate brawl.

"Sweet Jesus! What now, Jamila? Why?"

"Because first off, it will look like a political ploy—"

"Gee, what a surprise! It *is* a political ploy. That's why we're doing it."

"And it'll create annoying if unfounded questions about their authenticity and objectivity. We can't have either or the whole strategy falls apart. At all costs, we have to make sure the petitions avoid the appearance of bias or a partisan agenda."

"Aren't we polling the public to show our sensitivity to them? To establish our commitment to properly represent them?"

"True. But we're also polling the public to ultimately make a fool of Gardner. To be able to say to people, this *here* is what you want. That *there* is what you get. Gardner's not on your side. He votes against all these things you want done. Don't vote for the bastard!"

Phyllis thought about it.

"Okay. You're right. If it comes from us, everyone will say we're just smearing Gardner. On the other hand, if independent polls establish voting public priorities, it won't look like the numbers were manufactured or skewed by us. It's less likely that anyone will claim it's a partisan hatchet job."

"In fact, it makes it impossible for them to even suggest that. This goes right down the line. *We* don't confront Gardner with the pledges. A citizen's group with no candidate affiliation, just a bunch of people who are concerned with the direction of the country, they're the ones who tell him that they're fed up with the games. The unspoken, the implied message is that they would like to vote for him, but by the same token they want him to go to Washington and represent the needs of his constituency."

"But that's such bullshit."

"Not really. Because when we take the petitions around, we never ask people who they voted for, who they might vote for, what their party affiliation is. Not a word. From all outward appearances and if conducted properly, this *is* an impartial grass roots initiative and we don't care what their affiliation is. Truth is, if Gardner signs the petitions — no offense to you, Martin — he most certainly *will* win this election by a sizable margin. And we'll make an honest man out of him."

"Then this could backfire."

"We've already talked about this. Of course it could backfire. But it won't."

"I wish I had your cocksure, devil-may-care attitude. Maybe I could sleep nights. This makes me very nervous."

"Trust me. He won't sign them. He can't sign them. They're in direct conflict with every single promise he's made to his campaign donors. He won't take them seriously. He'll laugh. He'll put on that big phony teeth-whitened smile of his, then make some stupid wise crack. Everybody in the room will laugh, because they're *soooo* in on the joke."

Phyllis wasn't completely convinced. It was obvious she was still processing what Jamila was saying. She glanced over at Martin who just shrugged. Lincoln nodded. Bill gave a thumbs up.

"Okay. You're probably right. But this still makes me very skittish. And to be honest with you, I'm not sure if it's because I think we're pulling a fast one, or because I'm afraid we'll get caught. Maybe a little of both."

Lincoln came to the rescue. Again he was as decisive as he was exacting.

"Listen. I can put this together. It can be campus-based, a research project. I'll put 30 or 40 of my brightest students right on it. We'll call it the *Current*

Voter Preferences Survey. The petitions will have that on the header, then below that the sub-title reflecting the specific matter being addressed: *Voter Petition Regarding Social Security and Medicare: Ohio's 3rd U.S. Congressional District.* We can have some sort of logo in the corner, an official seal with an organizational name. How about Committee on Public Policy Preferences? CPPP. That sound alright?"

Jamila was impressed. And encouraged that he was not only getting what she was saying, but embracing the nuances of the whole approach. Everything had to be in place or the strategy fell apart.

"Nice, Lincoln! I love it. Good names for both the committee and the petition itself."

Even if a bit naïve at times, Bill was always as supportive as he was cheerful.

"I could put them at my shop. There are some other petitions there. I'll mix these in and we'll get some signatures that way. Actually a lot of signatures. You wouldn't believe how many commies love my coffee."

Even Phyllis cracked a smile.

Then after sharing a few more asides and spontaneous jokes, all eyes eventually settled on her. It was understood that she had final say, a protocol that was born out of respect for her judgment, her unflagging dedication to the Green Party, and her many years in the trenches.

She was writing a note to herself. Her cross-every-t-dot-every-i mind had kicked in.

"Though I can't say I feel great about the subterfuge, I understand the necessity. It's about the greater good. I'll file a DBA in the morning. The Committee on Public Policy Preferences. My dog gets to be CEO of another small business."

Jamila felt enormous relief. It was settled. A decision had been made. The entire strategy was now in place. It was now just a matter of tidying up a few details.

Phyllis now wondered aloud who would be the public face of the Committee on Public Policy Preferences.

"It can't be any of us."

Lincoln was shaking his head.

"I disagree. I could do this, no problem. Absolutely no one other than my wife and my two goldfish know I work with this campaign. Not that I'm ashamed, just discreet. The campus thought police would make life difficult for me if they thought I was in any way committing significant amounts of time to electioneering. So I'm a clean slate. In fact, with my faculty job, I'm perfectly positioned. Something like the Committee on Public Policy Preferences, as a non-partisan entity doing work that is good for citizenship, the public good and all, that's great PR for both the university and my department. Phyllis, if you want to put my name on the DBA, I'm fine with that. I can't wait to present about 8,000,000 signatures to Gardner and watch his glib, self-satisfied expression turn to silly putty."

"8,000,000 might be a little suspect since there are only a quarter million registered voters in this district."

"That wouldn't stop the Republicans."

Phyllis actually looked pretty happy. As happy as she ever looked, which was that she just got the news she had three months to live instead of two.

"Then it's agreed. There is a firewall between the official functions of this organization and the *Current Voter Preferences Survey* project, though in fact there is overlap in terms of two of the participating members. Lincoln will prepare the petitions and Bill will spill coffee on them. To keep this on the straight and true, none of our funds should be used for anything related to the petitions or the pledges. I know we're talking nickels and dimes here. But I think it's best if there's no money trail. Make sense, Lincoln?"

"We're only talking about using a copying machine and a printer. It's mostly manpower. I don't see any other expenditures. I'll absorb it into my department budget at U. of D."

Martin closed the meeting with his usual benediction.

"I just want to say ... I really appreciate this. You're all great!"

• • •

Next meeting, Bob Phelps and Imogene Kurtz were back from Columbus.

They had a very interesting new announcement.

Both of them had discreetly shown the original version of the Social Security/Medicare petition around at work and discussed it with some of their colleagues. These were fellow social workers who were on the grim front lines and saw first hand both the impact of the faltering economy and the destructive consequences of government inaction.

So far the response by both the President and Congress to the ongoing economic crisis had been tepid and ineffective. To make matters worse, more often than not, what legislative action there had been, turned out counter-productive and further exacerbated the already intolerable living conditions and unconscionable suffering of the poor. Now as the blight of unemployment spread upwards to the middle class, once secure families were now regularly seen applying for welfare assistance, food stamps, and other forms of government aid programs. In the midst of this disgraceful and cruel punishment of the citizens who had played no part in the destruction of the economy, the legislatures at both a local and national level had seen fit to cut back on unemployment benefits and these vital assistance programs, severing the much-needed lifelines of the escalating numbers of Americans who were vulnerable and increasingly desperate.

There were a lot of very pissed-off, very distraught people showing up these days at the Ohio Department of Job and Family Services.

Bob and Imogene had explained to their colleagues there were similar petitions floating around which addressed the minimum wage, ending the war in Afghanistan, and increasing taxes on the wealthy. The reaction to the petitions was overwhelming and unanimous. Every single one of their associates offered immediately to sign them all as soon as they were available.

Then it quickly went a step further. A very big and significant step.

Much discussion was devoted for several days about the "legality" of soliciting signatures from their casework clients. This could prove to be a very huge source of potential supporters. On the five key issues, Bob and Imogene said that conservatively 95% of those receiving governmental assistance through their agency would be strongly in favor.

It made sense. These folks were beneficiaries, or hoping to be beneficiaries, of the very programs that were mercilessly under attack in Congress. Conservatives both in the House and the Senate were always talking about how broke the country was. Three of the pledges addressed that shortfall. Raising taxes on the rich would bring in more revenue. Ending the pointless war in godforsaken Afghanistan would save a bundle of money — over $10 million a day — which could then be put to better use here at home. Raising the minimum wage also meant more payroll taxes flowing into the Federal government. As a result, there would be no excuse for cutting any of the social programs, especially Social Security and Medicare, which the majority of Americans, not just the poor, considered sacrosanct.

And of course, absolutely every piece of legislation in support of the initiatives which were targeted by the petitions and corresponding pledges, had been opposed by Matt Gardner. He had a perfect batting record. The guy never flinched when it came to screwing the poor, even elderly retirees, despite his lofty campaign speeches. This hopefully meant that the voters who would be signing the petitions would be easy prey at election time. If they hadn't seen the light already, it should be possible to get them to abandon their knee-jerk support for their incumbent congressman and take a chance on someone else. And there Martin would be, more than happy to welcome them into the Martin Truth for Congress circle of friends and supporters.

But therein lay the potential conflict of interest for Bob, Imogene, and their sixty plus colleagues. No sort of political activity in any way shape or form, certainly none promoting a particular candidate or political party, was permitted on the job. In addition to getting fired, a state employee found in breach of this strict regulation could be heavily fined.

After much handwringing and gnashing of teeth, it was decided that the petitions were fine. This was the genius of formulating them purely as a means to increase voter awareness. There was no mention of anything political whatsoever in the text. It was a voter preference survey on policy, pure and simple. Since Lincoln was heading up the effort and he was on the faculty of University of Dayton, it would be viewed as an academic exercise. No one could prove otherwise. Certainly not this early in the game. Perhaps later, as the strategy played out and it became obvious who would benefit, there might be suspicions. But then it would be too late. That's how it worked on paper anyway.

The involvement of the caseworkers at the Ohio Department of Job and Family Services was not a trivial contribution to the petition campaign. Just in terms of the office that Imogene and Bob worked, this meant reaching out to over 5,000 people. Both of them also knew caseworkers at three other satellite branches of the department. If they could get the staffs of these offices involved,

Bob estimated that this brought the total to almost 14,000 people who would probably be open to signing the petitions.

Everyone was pleased. Jamila again counseled caution.

"Which underscores the need to keep these petitions as far away from this campaign as possible. Now we have Bob and Imogene's asses on the line."

Phyllis: "This makes me nervous."

Lincoln: "I promise you absolute discretion. No, I take that back. There'll be no need for discretion. Because I'll make sure that there's no way under any circumstance anyone can connect the CPPP to any of us. Certainly not to the Green Party or Martin."

Martin: "Phyllis, don't be such a worry wart. Lincoln's got it covered. We can do this."

Phyllis tried to look relieved. She was a terrible actress. It was her defining characteristic to worry. Which made her perfect for heading up the campaign. Nothing got by her.

"Just making sure. I do have faith in you guys. But as my favorite philosopher once said, 'If anything can go wrong, it will.' Words to live by."

Everyone stifled their overwhelming urge to laugh. Martin finally mumbled a rejoinder.

"Only if you have a lifetime prescription for Prozac."

Jamila looked at Phyllis with big inquisitive eyes.

"So who is your favorite philosopher?"

Phyllis didn't blink.

"Me."

• • •

Jamila had to admit. Martin's people were sharp. There was a lot of brainpower, passion and a generous amount of creativity. Unfortunately, the creativity had tended to be dormant. They needed to be prompted and prodded to get their imaginations to power up. Old habits die hard. It's impossible to think outside the box if you don't even know you're in one.

In some ways, this explained why no one in America seemed able to escape the paralysis of the current state of politics. Too many ideas were deeply entrenched which had long ago outlived their usefulness. Decay had set in. People not only couldn't let go of many deep-seated habits but were still enamored of much of the mythology that defined simpler, more innocent times. They wanted things to return to the good old days. But the good old days never existed. Things were screwed up then too, but in different ways.

To compound the stultifying national inertia, there was the deluge of disinformation that seemed to swamp every discussion. People were drowning in bullshit. It was intentionally so. The right wing had concocted and initiated this strategy almost forty years ago. Though they would resent the comparison, it was built on the methodology of systematic indoctrination which Joseph Goebbels had so effectively implemented as Reich Minister of Propaganda in Nazi Germany. The basic principle was as simple as it was sound. Repeat a lie so often that it became accepted as truth.

There were the immediate pernicious effects which came into play. Things people took as certain knowledge that were just plain wrong.

Sometimes these convenient untruths were broad statements.

Any government program which broadly applies to American society is socialism.

A free market economy is self-correcting and benefits everyone.

Free trade creates jobs.

America is number one and the rest of the world is jealous.

Liberals are commie-loving traitors.

Sometimes they were very issue-specific.

Life begins at conception, therefore abortion is murder.

Liberals want to take away everyone's gun.

Higher taxes on the rich causes unemployment.

Labor unions are making America uncompetitive and must be abolished.

Immigrants are stealing jobs from deserving American citizens or are here just to live off of the public dole.

Wall Street and big banks are overregulated.

The indirect effect of disinformation was arguably more devastating. The lies were so bold and outrageous, they destroyed any possibility of constructive discussion. Issues were framed in terms which had no relation to reality, so the resulting conversations were nonsensical and abysmally counterproductive. Time and energy which could and should have been devoted to dealing with relevant pressing needs were squandered in frivolous and frustrating yelling matches, the likes of which dominated and clogged all media streams.

It was madness.

Let's say the only thing a person could see or read about for an extended period of time was whether fire-breathing dragons should be regulated by the federal government or locally by the states. As the heat of debate is steadily cranked up and the pros and cons are bandied about, the ridiculous underlying premise becomes further reinforced, and woe be anyone who has the audacity and courage to point out that there is no such thing as fire-breathing dragons.

The public would be polled:

> *"Is the proposed regulation of fire-breathing dragons good for America? Do you feel safer?"*

Politicians and pundits would grandstand:

> *"Again we see the tax-and-spend liberals in another example of overreach, as they impose their socialist world view not only on fire-breathing dragons but on the rest of us who have to foot the bill."*

A huge divide would open up as opinion became more polarized and attacks more vicious. The media would dazzle their viewers with graphics!

> *"This map shows where things stand. The red states are the ones who believe they themselves have their fire-breathing dragon situation under control, the blue believe that the crisis requires greater oversight from Washington DC."*

In the meantime, the myriad of real problems would be ignored. No time to discuss the unsustainably high unemployment rate, the loss of manufacturing jobs in America, the illegal foreclosures on homeowners, the continuing abuse of money in politics, the increase of unnecessary surveillance on American citizens and their loss of constitutionally guaranteed rights, the bleeding of the U.S. Treasury by big investment banks, the pursuit of unnecessary wars and building more military bases throughout the world, the declining safety of food in the country, the bankrupting escalation of health care costs and the tens of millions of people who still could not afford private health insurance, the strangling of the economy by the ballooning national debt, the absurd and anti-constitutional surrender of control of the nation's money supply to private banks, the debilitating dependence of America on foreign suppliers for its addiction to oil and the lack of a comprehensive national energy policy, on and on and on.

But at least we would inch closer to getting those pesky fire-breathing dragons under control!

Martin's campaign committee in some ways was a microcosm of this type of dysfunction. Not that they were consciously so, or even had immutably surrendered to the myopia which overwhelmed much of the rest of the citizenry. But they certainly tended to "play by the rules" and unquestioningly accept some of the givens that had been given them.

There was really only one of these givens that was rigidly fixed in stone. That was campaign finance. Big money in politics had drastically circumscribed the playing field. The membership dues made it a rich man's game. The Green Party in general and their little Ohio chapter in particular, without question could not compete. Their total campaign budget for the two years of a congressional term was what Gardner's spent in a week. It even paled to that of Libertarian

Peter Potts, who had inherited daddy's money and consequently had an impressive war chest funded almost exclusively from his own bank account. The Democratic candidate for the district's congressional seat, the giddy charlatan Chris Castiglia, received support directly from Democratic National Headquarters in DC, in addition to what he himself raised, and at this early date had already piled up more than two hundred times what Martin's campaign had at its disposal for this latest run for office.

This meant TV ads were a non-starter. *Way* too expensive. A handful of ads even broadcast in the wee hours of the morning would clean out their entire bank account. This was a major problem. As Jamila had thoroughly disabused Martin about, television had changed everything. Nowadays it *was* everything.

Fortunately, it wasn't the whole story.

Jamila offered a fresh perspective on what might easily be viewed as a hopeless situation.

No, they couldn't play *that* game. They couldn't even get on the playing field. Which meant it was now a matter of opening up and finding other options. If you couldn't get on the field, then work the stands. If you couldn't get in the stands, work the parking lot. Truly think *outside* the box. Get outside all of it. Surrender the battle of the air waves as unwinnable. Now look for the battles that could be won.

Yes, it was a truism that people sat slumped in front of their TVs for too many numberless hours. Without a doubt, they would see Gardner's and Castiglia's feel-good ads sandwiched between their favorite sitcoms, sporting events, reality shows, news programs, and soap operas.

But they had to leave their bean bag chairs and La-Z-Boy recliners sometime. They had to eat, whether that meant going to the drive-thru window at McDonald's or KFC's, or actually buying something resembling real food at the supermarket. Some of them even still had jobs. Many went to church. They attended sporting events, little league baseball and football games at the local high school.

"So let's grab them when and where we can. On real turf. Not the manufactured reality of the boob tube. And not when they're submersed in the hypnotic stupor of a TV screen. Grab their attention when their attention is grabbable."

"The restroom of a gas station? Now there's a captive audience."

"Martin, this is *not* a joke."

"Come on, Jamila. A little levity is healthy."

"I agree. Let me know when you come up with something."

"You're a tough audience."

"Not as tough as the folks you're trying to get to vote for you."

She was right, of course. Martin was just trying to find a way to laugh, so he wouldn't end up crying. Sometimes his campaign felt like an impossible battle with unbeatable odds against an invincible enemy. Those were in his more upbeat moments.

But they were making progress. Hopefully somebody would notice.

"Listen Martin. I have something to show you. Now don't freak out. It's a new campaign poster Phyllis and I have been working on."

She unrolled it and laid it on the conference table.

"Oh my god! Where did you get that?"

It was a large 36" x 24" mock-up. Across the top it read:

Martin Truth has always been there when someone needed him . . .

Below that was a eye-catching reproduction of a front-page article that had appeared almost twelve years ago in the Cincinnati Enquirer.

DAYTON HIGH SCHOOL STUDENT SAVES FOURTEEN IN HEROIC RESCUE

The article described the accident and near catastrophe which unfolded when the vehicle full of elderly retirement home residents had crashed into a utility pole in front of the Circle K where Martin was working his senior year. There was a black-and-white photo of him pulling one of the passengers out of the burning vehicle.

"I'm so embarrassed."

"You shouldn't be, Martin. This is amazing! Why didn't you say something? Phyllis dug this news clipping out of the back of a file cabinet."

"I guess ... I mean ... it *was* a long time ago."

"Not that long ago. I bet people will remember this."

"But ... it's just—"

"Martin, this says something about you. Something you should be proud of. Please, *please* don't say we can't use this. It's so perfect. It's you. It's who you are. It's the congressman you want to be."

He stood there for the longest time. Staring at the poster. Revisiting a time he had buried in memory. Looking at 17-year-old Martin Truth as he might look at a stranger, or someone he had ages ago only casually known and had forgotten.

Finally, he broke out in a sheepish grin. There was a shyness there Jamila had never seen. Martin for a brief moment was that 17-year-old boy again. He turned around, not wanting her to see that he was blushing.

"You guys do what you think is best, Jamila. You're right. I shouldn't be embarrassed. It's just that … I …"

Jamila stepped over next to Martin. She smiled when she saw his red cheeks.

"It's just that you're sweet beyond words, Martin Truth. I really mean that."

• • •

The last week of June arrived with a lot of heat. Temperatures were over 100 degrees. But Phyllis and Martin had even more cause to sweat.

Money was the immediate problem. They were broke.

This was a truly horrible time for this. They were only days away from when they had to spend considerable amounts of hard cold cash for t-shirts, baseball caps, promotional fliers, bumper stickers, and other giveaways, intended to build some name recognition for Martin. But Summer was the worst time to solicit contributions. People were either thinking about their vacations, on their way somewhere, or staying home but pre-occupied with enjoying the good weather months. July was almost as bad as December in terms of getting money in the door. It looked like they'd be struggling just to make it through the month. Phyllis frankly had no idea how they would pay the rent and electricity on the building.

Not good at all.

The office was modest but necessary. Years ago, they had tried to run things out of someone's apartment. Then someone's house. Then Phyllis's house. It was just too much. Too much traffic. Too much noise. Too much chaos. Too much of everything.

Things ran much more smoothly now. They had been at this location for over two years, a bona fide place of business, just off the main drag through Kettering, an upscale and liberal leaning suburb of Dayton.

It was store-front property, though the entire display window was covered in hanging bamboo blinds. There was a single main entry door opening into a large front area, filled with filing cabinets, two large and three small tables, two desks, three computer work stations, a snack area with a hot-plate, coffee maker, and a full-size refrigerator. In the rear half of the building, segregated by a wall with a door which generally remained open, was a conference area with an old wood table and folding chairs. This is where they spent hours brainstorming, planning, and engaging in usually cordial, sometimes heated, occasionally hysterical meetings. Off this conference room were two small offices. The slightly larger belonged to Phyllis as executive director of the Green Party chapter. The smaller was occupied by Helen Bueller, officially Phyllis's administrative assistant, but functionally the gofer as well as the 'go to' for everything going on there. She had been with the organization even before Phyllis arrived ten years ago.

Because it was in Kettering, the rent on the building was high. But it was a good location. While much of metropolitan Dayton and certainly the more agricultural outlying regions within the 3rd Congressional District boundaries, leaned quite conservative in their politics, this sector of the suburbs was populated by Democrats and progressives of various stripes. With the better schools, the cleaner air and streets, modern government buildings, lovely parks, and the characteristically upscale milieu of most upper middle-class neighborhoods, this is where the new money and professional class parked themselves. Here the locals were better educated and had the economic freedom to be community minded. People had more expendable income and were more inclined to flaunt it than to hoard it.

Not that money poured in to the tills of the Green Party or Martin's dedicated campaign fund. But enough usually dribbled in with predictable consistency to keep things going. Especially when they periodically got out and let the folks know that there was a candidate who would stand up for a cleaner environment, peace, love, and a better world. Phyllis called these the bleeding heart donors. People who wanted to *feel* that they were doing the right thing, wanted to *feel good* about themselves, wanted to *feel* they were doing their part. These were civic-minded people who could be counted on to throw a few dollars at the Green Party and specifically at Martin's campaign, even though they believed that he had no chance of winning.

Unfortunately, under the present circumstances, there wouldn't be time for any kind of focused solicitation. It took weeks to organize an effective fundraising assault. Their next big drive was scheduled for September.

What could they do? They barely had enough of a balance to cover the next monthly service charge on their checking account.

Bill, Lincoln and even Helen offered to put up some of their own money. Helen had some savings, Bill and Lincoln thought they could swing second mortgages on their homes.

Martin was stretched the limit. There had been a little money in a joint savings account with Alison. When she left, it left with her. She claimed it was all her money, that he hadn't contributed a dime. He wasn't in a position to argue. He never kept track of things like that.

Phyllis told them all to hold off a little while. She would think of something.

Then a strange thing happened.

A check for $1500 arrived in the mail. The return address on the envelope said it was from Soros Fund Management. Soros? As in George Soros?

Two days later, two more checks arrived. One was from Democracy Alliance and was for $5000. The other from American Bridge 21st Century. $9000!

Everybody naturally knew who George Soros was. But nobody had heard of the other two organizations.

Except Jamila.

"It's all Soros money, actually."

"You know about this?"

"I have some friends in low places."

"Is this for real? Can I deposit these checks?"

"I don't see why not. Soros personally didn't exceed the legal limit with his contribution. The other two are Section 527 PACs he underwrites to promote responsible and fair elections. You know, to try to save representative democracy before it gets cannibalized by big corporations. I sent out a few letters about Martin and what you guys are doing here. No one likes this Gardner asshole. I'm sorry I didn't say anything. I didn't want to get hopes up in case nothing happened. I hope you don't mind."

Phyllis took a moment to collect herself. Mind? Over $15,000!

Jamila sensed her discomfort.

"Look. I'm just a pushy niggah girl. I'm not much of a team player. But I get the job done."

Phyllis flinched like someone had just shot her with a BB gun when she heard Jamila use the 'n' word. She looked away, then discreetly reached in her purse and took out some Kleenex. She turned around, blew her nose, and quickly wiped her eyes. She wasn't a public crier.

"Thanks, Jamila."

CHAPTER FIVE

On July 5th, Defense Secretary Chuck Hagel figuratively dropped a bomb on the country.

It could have been an actual bunker buster for the impact it had.

He described a comprehensive strategic plan for making America an invulnerable fortress, able to foil or repel any attack in any form. What he was proposing was new generations of both defensive and offensive weaponry: reconnaissance and surveillance systems, both cyber and real-world intrusion detection, trans-internet cloud-based command and control, the total militarization of space, a unified global military dominion entirely coordinated and linked by artificial-heuristic intelligence and self-activated, self-monitoring cybernetic supercomputers. The idea was to take human error out of the equation by taking humans out of the loop. The system would be rigorously programmed to confront every possible challenge and consider every possible option, loftily remaining above passion, petty squabbling, ideological agendas, politics, temptation, impulse, distraction, subjectivity, or practical joking. It was the ultimate technological warrior allegedly with the singular mission of preventing war.

It became known as the Hagel Plan, though it was officially titled *New Millennium Defense System Architecture for Protecting the Homeland and Preserving the Peace*. What it actually had to do with protection and peace had everyone guessing. Even a cursory look at the laundry list of its sub-projects suggested that the vast preponderance of them were about blowing things up and a tiny inconsequential handful about actually defending the homeland. It was 95% Hitler and 5% Gandhi.

The *New Millennium Defense System*, as it was known for short, would be developed and implemented over the next decade at an estimated $4,800,000,000,000 — that's 4.8 trillion dollars for the zero challenged. To put this in perspective, 4.8 trillion dollars laid out end to end would stretch to the sun and back *twice*.

Because the announcement proposed unprecedented spending, it provoked a firestorm of controversy, commentary, opinionating, bloviating, harumphs and harangues, and grabbed huge chunks of media bandwidth for several days running.

It also provoked one of the best speeches of Martin's career, unfortunately at the time heard by far too few people. Interestingly, much later in his career this very speech gained enormous notoriety and greater appreciation. This came as the result of an attempt by a future political opponent to discredit him, to label him as an enemy-loving, peace-at-any-cost hippie freak. This unsavory and unsavvy opponent mockingly dubbed it Martin Truth's "Hug A Baby Go To Jail" speech. The attack on Martin backfired miserably, and if anything, dramatically increased Martin's stature in the political world. Even when Martin initially delivered the address, it was warmly received.

The weekend following Hagel's announcement, there was a low key, modestly-attended workshop being held at University of Dayton on parenting. It went on for three days and much of the event was devoted to the psychological and social aspects of raising children in a time of unparalleled distractions and challenges. One afternoon session was reserved for broader talks and discussions on exactly what kind of world were kids growing up in.

Several community leaders, one bona fide futurist from MIT, and both major-party congressional candidates were invited to speak. Gardner politely declined. The Democratic challenger agreed. Lincoln put in a good word for Martin and also got him on the speaker's list.

As fate would have it, Martin spoke last. It was almost as if he were an afterthought, one of those speakers who act as sonic wallpaper for an audience which has been exhausted by many hours of intense listening and can handle no more. He would provide a good opportunity for a bathroom break, grabbing a smoke, checking phone messages, or maybe a quick breath of fresh air, before the concluding Q&A panel session got underway.

Regardless, Martin took the opportunity very seriously. He was deeply disturbed by what Hagel's plan contained. Actually, *outraged* was more like it. So outraged that it would have been easy to just launch into a tirade about how skewed America's values had become, how the lessons of history had been forgotten or intentionally ignored, how the American Dream had been co-opted and now good Americans like themselves were being held hostage by a small group of mad megalomaniacs driven by delusions of empire and world conquest.

But this was a workshop on parenting. The room was full of people who were probably already extremely concerned about the direction of the country. Maybe they couldn't in so many words say exactly what troubled them, but they were there for encouragement. They were there because they wanted to do what they could, to make America and the world in general a better place for their kids and subsequent generations.

He bottled his rage and spoke to the seventy-some people in the calm, warm tone of a friend who stopped by for a neighborly chat. His voice was thick with concern and respect for every single person in the audience, as well as the gravity of the subject matter.

> *"I recently saw a movie which I would describe as emotional and provocative. It wasn't a very good movie but it had an interesting premise.*

The story was about a young mother who was so plagued by guilt that it ended up destroying her marriage and almost her entire life. Her newly born baby had died and she was convinced that she herself had killed it. Not intentionally, of course. She believed she had hugged the baby so closely, held it so intensely in her arms, had pressed the infant so fiercely and lovingly to her body, she had smothered it. She thought that her love was so overwhelming, it had gotten the better of her judgment and resulted in the helpless little child's death.

When I look at the recent announcement by our own Secretary of Defense, where he talks about how vulnerable America is and how determined he is to protect America, I can't help but think of that pathetic woman.

Let's put aside arguments about politics and economics. I've certainly done my part in contributing to these brawls. Let's not talk about whether this is just another boondoggle — definitely a very expensive one at that! — just another high-tech program sold by a defense industry with a ravenous, apparently insatiable appetite for profits, to a bunch of gullible imperialists who never saw a weapons system they didn't like. Let's put aside all discussions and arguments about the virtues of this system over that system, and over motives and agendas. Let's not even begin to entertain theories about secret cabals and tempting allusions to conspiracies and shadow governments.

Let's just assume that all of the key players are altruistic, patriotic, unbiased, selfless and motivated by only the purist possible priorities.

Alright. What's the parallel I'm drawing here? Am I saying that our leaders are smothering the nation with too much love? Actually, that. That may be. That <u>is</u> probably true. But I think more importantly, they are smothering us, the citizens. Citizens who are the lifeblood, the essence of America and American democracy. <u>We</u> are being smothered. <u>We</u> are being shut out. You and I are no longer allowed to be part of the process of governing. We are being 'protected', or I should say, 'overprotected'. Just as a child is protected when a parent believes that he or she isn't ready for something, we are being denied our rightful role, our duty and responsibility in our unique and magnificent system of self-government.

Certainly it makes sense for parents to exercise their best judgment at critical times and offer necessary guidance and protection for their children. Especially when they're young and vulnerable.

But are we children? As citizens, as fully-enfranchised voters who in the voting booth exercise our constitutional rights and responsibilities, as duty-bound participants in a political system which demands that we have a say in shaping the America we want, the future we want for our children, are we to be treated as toddlers being potty-trained?

This country was founded on faith and trust. Faith in a new form of government. Faith in democratic self-determination. Faith in government of the people, by the people, for the people. Faith in new sorts of institutions, and in organizing those institutions around the idea that we would all be engaged, that we would all do the right thing for ourselves collectively. America was founded on the simple, fundamental notion that we would work together, rely on, be responsible to, have faith in, and most of all trust one another.

But that trust is gone. Wariness and suspicion are now endemic in America and the institutions we have established.

Let's look at national security.

We've just been told by our Secretary of Defense that, despite the fact our nation is nearly broke, despite the fact that for every five dollars we spend, one has to be borrowed from the Chinese, the Japanese, and the Europeans — who by the way have their own problems — that we now need to spend another 4.8 trillion dollars. We all know how these things go. That will be 7.8 trillion dollars or 10.8 trillion dollars before we even figure out where the first trillion is going to come from.

So as citizens, we ask: What's this all about? We get back: 'It's very complicated. It's too complicated for you to know about.' And we say: Complicated? What's that supposed to mean. And they say, as they always say: 'It's a dangerous world. It's too dangerous for you to deal with. Don't worry. We'll take care of it.'

Excuse me! This is our country. We're big people. Adults. We're not little children. Since when is America run by an emperor and a few close confidants? Didn't we get rid of monarchy almost 240 years ago with a document called the Declaration of Independence?

The point it this: America is supposed to be a democracy, governed by the many and all, not the few and far between.

We're already spending — and this is the real cost, not figures massaged by some spin doctor — we're already spending just under a trillion dollars every year, that's every year, on defense. Now we have to spend another four to ten trillion? For what?

We all know what comes next.

They'll find some bearded weenie with a copy of the Koran in his backpack, a bomb in his ear or strapped inside his jock strap, and that's all we'll hear about for the next two weeks on Fox TV.

Mr. Hagel will have cloned himself so that he can be on five different news shows at once, reminding us of what a terrifying world this is and it's a very horrifying situation we find ourselves in. That there are countless terrorists still out there, just like the jock strap bomber, who hate us and are determined to destroy America.

Then they'll put their big protective arms around us, tell us everything's going to be all right, pat us on the back like they're burping us, and give us that big daddy's here or mommy's here protective hug.

What I have to say to everyone here today is this.

I don't know about you. But me personally? I can't breathe. I don't care why. Either I can breathe or I can't. If I can't breathe, even if I am being smothered for the best of reasons — love, for my own good, because it's too complicated, because it's a scary world out there — the result is the same. I'm going to die. Just like that baby in the movie I referred to earlier. I will be hugged to death.

Let's talk about America, what our nation stands for, what kind of America we want to see our children grow up in.

Everyone wants it to be safe. But the truth is, even though it is a dangerous world — it always was and always will be — America has been relatively safe for most of its 200 plus years. And it is relatively safe now. The chances of being killed by a foreign terrorist even now post-911, is less than that of being hit by an asteroid or being buried in a mud slide.

So enough of the bogeyman talk. Let's have an adult conversation. Let's talk about what the real threats are to the America we want for our children and our children's children.

As I look out at this audience, I see faces full of kindness, concern, love, and true caring about the world we are living in and the world we will be handing off to future generations.

We hold in our hearts and minds a vision of those young faces who are counting on us to create that world.

We know in our hearts and minds what kind of world that is.

We also know that children must be nurtured and protected.

At the same time, we all know that when the time is right, just as important as holding on is letting go. It's knowing when your child has become an adult. Which is not always as easy as it sounds.

The simple truth is that sometimes it's the child himself or herself who has to say: 'Mom. Dad. I'm grown up. I can handle it. Really.'

Let's tell our President and Secretary of Defense, both honorable, well-meaning public servants, enough with the secrecy. It's time to let us in on the big plans. It's time we had a say in shaping the America we want for us and for our kids. This is our country too. We're grown up. We can handle it. Really."

• • •

Coming out of the mouth of a less attractive, less phenomenally brilliant person than Jamila, some of the stuff she said would have gotten most people killed. Or at least slapped silly.

"Anti-intellectualism has become so virulent in this country, America embraces stupidity as a religion. And that ain't some dumb niggah talkin'!"

"Can I use that in my speech to the Rotary Club Wives Association this weekend?"

"You might skip the 'niggah' reference. But I wish you would. Somebody's got to break the bad news."

"What prompts this outburst?"

"Nothing in general. Everything in particular. Look at this headline. *Pastor Claims God Told Him To Strangle Neighbor's Dog*. Here's a good one. *Woman Protesting Credit Card Charge Chains Herself To Liberty Bell*. Or how about this? *Doctors Warn About Using Caulking Compound For Penis Enlargement*. Has everyone gone bonkers?"

"And that's the cute stuff."

"Exactly. The fluff. Sensational and senseless. But proof that stupidity is an epidemic. There are many sinister, extremely powerful people in this world doing some very ugly things. Getting away with it because no one seems capable of seeing it for what it is."

"Or they're not paying attention."

"Or they're too stupid to pay attention."

"Politicos definitely get a free ride these days. At least the ones in bed with the right people."

"It's a fuck fest for the fortunate and a clusterfuck for the rest of us."

"I absolutely will use *that* at the Rotary Club Wives shindig. Most people don't know these society women all talk like truck drivers and ride Harleys on the weekend."

"Politicians. Corporate CEOs. Bankers. Wall Street tycoons. Judges. Priests and ministers. Even celebrities. Power and money only leads to corruption. A corruption of their values, a corruption of their souls. They become other than human and end up completely incapable of feeling other people's pain. They can rationalize all they want but the fact is they're worthless mutants."

"I take people at face value. Different strokes. Different philosophies. The rich people in this country come up and live in such a different world. It shapes the way they see everything, the way they see other human beings. I don't think anyone sets out to be cruel to others. Look at Gardner. He served his country. He got his law degree. He got married. Raised a family. Walks the straight and true. Sort of. *He* thinks he does."

"But he came from privilege. His parents and grandparents all made big money in banking and real estate. When he spews all that shit about being one of us, about caring for the regular Joe, I want to puke. The only regular Joe he might have come in contact with is the guy who valet parks his car at the country club."

"Whoa! Jamila. You've got a little anger built up in there. I still believe he has to think he's doing the right thing. Otherwise, how could he sleep at night? Being rich doesn't exclude a person's having beliefs and conviction, however misguided you and I might think they are."

"You're too generous, Martin. You give Gardner way too much credit. I'm not claiming to be judge and jury here. All I'm saying is that I look at it more on a personal level."

"Meaning?"

"If someone looks like an asshole, talks like an asshole, and acts like an asshole, he's probably an asshole."

• • •

Besides the high school and college students who did busywork at the office, ostensibly related to their classroom studies in political science or civics, the Dayton chapter of the Green Party had between 30 and 40 part-time volunteers to do the grunt work of campaigning — handing out leaflets, doing house calls, manning the phones, attending rallies to increase body-count, putting up posters, sometimes just standing at busy intersections waving big signs. There were a handful of core members to this volunteer army, maybe eight or ten who showed great commitment and staying power. But it was mostly a revolving door. People would sign on, then disappear after a few weeks, discovering that campaigning is both difficult and tedious work, short on fun and gratification, long on exhaustion and boredom.

Despite the high level of turnover and fleeting presence, there were some general things which could be said to characterize these adult volunteers with Martin's campaign.

Most were much older than him, pushing or well into their 50s, some even retired. They were typically white, educated, solid, successful, coming from professional backgrounds. They were teachers, public employees, small-business entrepreneurs, counselors, social workers, community planners, managers and administrators or executive assistants to them, graphic designers, architects and health care providers. Many had worked for corporations, but they hadn't become consumed by corporate culture and still had a robust sense of responsibility to their communities, local schools, and other institutions and organizations which contributed to the general welfare. They were people with a social conscience and a frustration with the direction the country had been taking over the past couple decades. Maybe giving time to the Green Party was an attempt to promote some of their personal values and priorities: protecting the environment and implementing sound energy policies, providing a strong safety net for the less fortunate, assuring transparency in government, getting money out of politics, creating educational and vocational opportunities, furthering peace, justice, a kinder gentler America. Just overhearing them talk among themselves, it was obvious they all recycled, many grew their own vegetables, they mostly ate organic food, lamented America's reluctance to sign the Kyoto Treaty, wanted the senseless wars ended and our troops immediately brought home, thought the Republicans were out to destroy the country. Many thought the Democrats had gotten away from their core values and were just as bad. Some whispered that they had voted for Ralph Nader either in 2000 or 2004, and a few admitted to voting for him both times.

The common bond was simply this: They were fed up with business as usual. They had had it with both the Republicans and the Democrats. The system was broken. Someone had to do something to fix it.

Dayton, Ohio was not an obvious choice as a place to start a political revolution. It wasn't even a likely place for the Green Party to set up shop. Ohio itself, at one time a blue-collar state with strong unions and a large Democratic majority, had like many formerly liberal bastions become considerably more conservative. It was now a swing state in most national elections. Every two years, it was a toss-up whether it would go Red or Blue. Currently it had a Republican governor. 13 of the 18 United States congressman were Republicans. But even more tellingly, it had gone for Bush both in 2000 and 2004. It's support for Barack Obama in 2008 and 2012 was often portrayed as an anomaly.

Dayton itself had a long history of conservatism. It was a thoroughly military town, home of Wright-Patterson Air Force Base, its largest single employer. Because the base was a research-intense facility, there was a host of military contractors in and around Dayton as well. These business centers and labs were funded by millions of dollars in defense contracts, federal dollars underwriting the vigorous ongoing effort to keep America in the lead, in terms of both defensive and offensive weaponry and battle systems.

It was certainly not on its face fertile ground for demilitarizing the planet, implementing a green revolution, and promoting world peace.

At the same time, Dayton was a very family-oriented city, one that placed a lot of emphasis on community, education, healthy living, quality of life and social responsibility. Certain themes which ran in a separate parallel dimension to the prevailing narratives of the local military and defense establishment, included a number of causes which would be considered progressive by the standards of any community: People were concerned about the environment and proactively recycled. Seventy-five hazardous waste Superfund sites had been identified and targeted for clean-up. The twenty-nine worst industrial polluters in the area were under pressure from an increasingly vigilant core of concerned citizens. There was growing awareness about deficiencies in the typical American diet. Out of that sprang an organization called Vegan Dayton which promoted strict vegetarianism, and concern for animal rights. Area activists were pushing for stricter regulation of gas drilling procedures, especially those involved in the highly contentious business of fracking near aquifers. There was a small but zealous group of anti-war activists. They were always banging the drum, urging the city to build on the historical signing of the Dayton Peace Accord there in November 1995, the treaty which ended the Bosnian War. They actively campaigned for declaring Dayton a *City of Peace*, recognized world wide.

But in the big picture, these symptoms of progressivism were more the exception than the rule. They were tiny white feathers scattered few and far between in the vast swirling vortex of a cyclone that had swept up thousands of tons of debris over miles of destruction along its path. The positive sentiments and promises of a better world, of an America at harmony with itself, were but faint whispers in the yelling match and ugly cacophonous din which modern life self-destructively now embraced.

It was very easy for the progressive-minded to adopt a victim mentality and fall into an insular us-against-the-world frame of mind. Sometimes Martin and his supporters felt completely walled off from the vast majority of "buzz-cut central", consigned to a tiny insignificant corner of a marginal universe, sequestered and operating in a vacuum.

The "divide and conquer" strategy of the right wing zealots had been very effective in cordoning off and demonizing anyone who didn't agree with their ultra-conservative agenda and world view, one that was now being advocated and promoted at every opportunity, from every pulpit, podium and public platform.

The message was clear: You're either with us or you're against us.

That was the beauty of the petitions and the pledges. This unique and powerful strategy transcended much of what divided people, and neutralized the ugly forces which put individuals in convenient little ideological boxes with labels that isolated them from one another, preventing them from seeing and sharing what they had in common.

The petitions offered a much-needed voice to the voting public and the pledges were an ironclad means of guaranteeing that at least on certain critical issues, their elected representatives indeed *would* represent them — do the job they were sent to Washington to do.

It could even be argued that the petitions and pledges were *unifying* and *empowering*, that they built on trust in the democratic system, put faith in the best instincts of the participants, and exemplified the overall good will of the citizenry.

Martin Truth For Congress could only hope and dream that this good will would translate into support for his bid for Congress.

They could only hope that people would not arbitrarily pigeonhole Martin as a member of the lunatic fringe, an irrelevant third-party delusional, or a "spoiler" as Ralph Nader had been baptised, and see him just for what he was: an honest man whose only intention was to do the right thing for the country.

Were there rewards anymore for doing the right thing?

That was the million dollar question.

• • •

Sometimes Martin really hated the Q & A part of the program immediately following his prepared remarks. He had good reason.

Tonight was a truly off-the-wall gathering. It was being held at a VFW Hall in Middletown, a suburb only six miles from where he grew up. It was an open meeting, so in addition to the usual attendees, mostly member veterans who lived in the area, there were a number of regular citizens. There was also a very unusual contingent from distant easternmost counties of Ohio. This was an all-citizens paramilitary group called the Ohio Valley Militiamen. They were in town trying to stir up interest in putting together a regional citizens militia for Montgomery, Miami, Champaign, Clark and Greene Counties.

The meeting was being hosted by the AMVETS Ladies Auxiliary and the purpose of the get-together was to honor women in uniform, particularly those currently serving in overseas theaters like Afghanistan, Kuwait, Saudi Arabia, and South Korea, where tensions were high and there was a significant level of threat.

Martin had just given his standard stump speech, emphasizing the need for more democracy and citizen involvement in directing the country. It got a lukewarm reception. The same way that a dog can sense fear, their guts must have told them that Martin had never been in the military.

He now opened the floor for comments and questions.

"The gentleman in the uniform. What can I do for you, sir?"

"Retired Lt. Colonel Morton Pinkerton here. Served in 'Nam fresh out of high school and left the military right after Operation Desert Storm."

"What's your question, Lt. Colonel Pinkerton?"

"I just wanna set the record straight. We've got a serious problem in this country. There's a lot of ugliness out there. Crazy fanatics. Religious nuts who know nothing but killing in the name of their false prophet. These Muslamic jee-*hay*-dees want to take this country down by blowing it up. I ain't gonna vote for anyone who isn't gonna stand strong and put these sick animals in their place. As far as I am concerned, the only place for them is in the ground, with about six feet of dirt piled on top."

"Have you personally seen any of these terrorists lately, here in the Dayton area?"

"Well, ain't that the kicker now? These slimy bastards are stealthier than a ground mole, so you see them every day and you don't even know you're looking at them."

"Alright. Something to keep in mind. Thanks for sharing those helpful insights with us. Next. Over there, the man in the camouflage jacket and cowboy hat."

"I suppose you and your tree-hugging friends want to create more handouts for the leeches that are turning this country into one big soup line. If you want my vote, I say we take all these welfare queens and Freddie freeloaders off of unemployment and social security and put the money to good use. If they don't like it, ship 'em off to Cuba or North Korea. Or just line 'em up in front of a firing squad. Give me a goddamn gun and I'll take care of the suckers!"

Martin didn't even have to respond. A number of people booed and yelled.

"Sit down and shut up, you idiot!"

"Go back to the 9th Century where you belong!"

"Stuff it, retardo! Suck on a beer and listen to Rush Limbaugh."

"Why don't you go and pepper spray your sick grandmother while your at it!"

"Yes. The lady there in back."

"So you are with the Green Party. That means you're into all that environment stuff?"

"Right, ma'am. It has nothing to do with being Irish."

"So you think the world is getting hotter and now you want to spend billions of dollars on ... on stuff about that. The government is very broke right now. I have to live within my budget. So how can you say we should spend all this money we don't have?"

"Well, it's not just about money. It's literally about survival, and not being reduced to being hunters and gatherers again. But if you want to just talk about money, doing something about climate change now will down the road actually save trillions of dollars."

"Mr. Trust, we—"

"It's Truth, ma'am. Martin Truth."

"Well, whatever. Mr. Truth, then. We don't know for sure what's going on with the planet. I'll have you know that I have to defrost my freezer now twice a week. It used to be maybe twice a month at the most."

"I see. Well, that's sure a pain in the butt. And frankly, it is possible that climate change might be responsible for that. If you want to talk about it, after I take a few more questions, I'll meet you in the back of the room and explain the science behind it."

He took four more questions. All were actually legitimate questions by coherent people. Then they packed up and left.

On the ride home, Jamila suddenly burst out laughing.

"That was really rare. Oh my god, Martin. Global warming causing refrigerators to ice up. Absolutely priceless."

"I only said it was possible."

"You know, this is a good sign. She was obviously a plant. Someone sent her."

"You think? She didn't even know my name."

"Granted, they didn't bother to send the sharpest pin in the cushion. But you've gotten someone's attention. Definitely a hired heckler. Probably the same with the ex-military moron and the guy who railed about welfare queens."

"Don't you want to know how climate change can wreak havoc in the kitchen?"

"Save it for the zanies, Martin."

"Thank god. I'm only capable of so much bullshit. Then I always hit a wall."

"Maybe now. But if we get you in Congress, you'll be studying alongside the best."

"That's what I'm afraid of."

• • •

When Jamila stepped into Phyllis' cramped little office, she was pouring from a pot into one of her floral-patterned cups.

"Tea?"

"Thanks. But I've had so much coffee I'm about to float out to sea."

"Truly amazing considering the nearest ocean is over 1000 miles away."

Jamila took a seat.

"Jamila, I know you're busy but I need to get something off my chest. Maybe I'm looking for some reassurance. So I wanted to talk. Just you and I."

"Great. What's on your mind?"

"Something about this pledge strategy of yours is bothering me. But I can't put my finger on what it is. I just feel uncomfortable and I don't know why."

"It's not in the textbooks, that's for sure."

"Not even in the appendix."

Jamila came off as a street fighter most of the time. But it was moments like this when she was probably at her best. Calm. Attentive. Reflective.

"Phyllis, I see it this way. Textbook democracy is great for textbooks. But it doesn't exist anymore in the real world. Maybe it never did."

"I know what you're thinking. But I'm not entirely a by-the-manual kind of person. I've been at this a long time and I see how the game is played. It's just that … it just seems very negative."

"Negative? What's negative about it? All we're doing is collecting signatures on petitions. We're just out there feeling the pulse. It's a tremendous service we're performing. Giving voters a chance to express their feelings. We're giving them a voice."

"Right. But in October, we're going to drop this on Gardner like a bomb."

"That's the plan."

"But it'll be negative campaigning at its worst. It's like swift boating the guy."

"Phyllis, I respect you and what you're doing here. But I have to be blunt when you're dead wrong about something. Swift boating is making up derogatory stuff, creating horrible and completely fictional rumors, then paying some actors to mouth the lies on camera to create vicious and arguably slanderous campaign messages. All we're doing is identifying what the voting public wants here in this district and then showing them that the clown they have been voting for is in direct opposition to them. We're not making anything up. This is Gardner's own voting record."

"But it … it certainly focuses on the negative. I've always believed that campaigns should present positive messages, offer hope … and …"

"And?"

"And … it just makes me uncomfortable. What can I say?"

"Here's what I say: Fluffy feelgood campaigning doesn't seem to work very well anymore, does it? Look at it this way, Phyllis. Murder is murder. You could call it an 'unfortunate abrogation of the life options of an individual by the introduction of space-time discontinuity.' But it's murder. Plain and simple. Gardner is a fucking traitor to his constituents. We're not even using that word because we're so damn civil. But the voters should know that he isn't representing them. He's representing big corporate donors and special interest groups. He's not listening to the people. He's listening to lobbyists and investment banks. He's a complete toady to the military-industrial complex. We're not smearing him. He's smearing himself by being such a hypocrite to the power of ten."

Phyllis took a slow sip of her tea. It was her favorite. Jasmine.

"Maybe you should cut back on your coffee a bit."

Jamila laughed.

"You're probably right."

Chapter Six

Martin tried to be discreet.

Actually, for the longest time he just lived in denial. He had more or less convinced himself that his original rush of emotions — the school boy crush that started the moment she arrived, then gripped him for several weeks — needed to be countermanded by the stuff of reality. Jamila was too young, too beautiful, too professionally and academically committed to the thankless but demanding tasks of the campaign to even notice him. Plus it was an obvious and gross breach of professional ethics to be hitting on an intern. And certainly, at this stage in the campaign, neither one of them needed the distraction of a courtship, or even a playful dalliance.

Constantly reminding himself of these factors worked for a while.

But slowly, ever so slowly, the carefully crafted if fragile state of self-deception was edged aside by urges that cannot be extinguished by things as feeble as reason and common sense.

Lately, he found himself testing the waters. It wasn't conscious or intentional, rather just him in typical male fashion responding spontaneously to purely incidental and entirely innocent interactions. They could be anything.

"Want a donut?"

Yes! She really digs me.

"Is Phyllis coming in soon?"

Aha! She's hoping we can be alone.

"Do you know where that new Johnny Depp movie is playing around here?"

Alright! She wants to get me in the dark.

As intelligent as Martin was, his intelligence was hosted by a male brain. Nourished by the same blood stream as the rest of his body, thus subject to the same testosterone bath, it tended to generate the same erroneous male fantasies which had plagued *homo erectis* since two human prototypes of the opposite sex first reached for the same banana — and predictably produce the same erroneous reactions.

As a result, he began more and more to react to what he perceived were subtle overtures and what he sometimes decided were outright flirtations on her part.

His concerns for professionalism and propriety were gradually muscled aside by a more *anything goes* attitude. Soon he was making himself available for whatever might happen.

When after a long evening of work on the campaign, four or five of them would head out for a late night snack or beer, Martin always sat next to Jamila.

Or in the car he was driving, he would somehow maneuver her into the passenger seat up front with him, a position of honor he had previously always reserved for Phyllis.

Finally, in a make-it-or-break-it attempt to close the distance between them, he asked her out on a date. Not that he characterized it.as a date.

"I mean, we could, you know, head over to Cincinnati. Maybe check out a night club or a nice restaurant. You've been ... we've all been working really hard. We deserve a break."

"Sure. I'll talk to the others and see if they're up for it."

"Well ... no ... actually I just thought maybe just this once, it could be you and I. Even though we work together all of the time, I don't really know much about you. Your family. Your boyfriend. Do you have a boyfriend?"

"Hmm! I see where this is going, Martin. You want me to come over to the other side."

"Now Jamila, I don't see it that way. Not at all. I think I'm pretty color blind. So what if you're black and I'm white. In fact, I'm kind of surprised—"

He had never heard her laugh so hysterically.

"That's not what I meant. Black and white isn't the issue."

"Well then, what is?"

"Martin ... I'm a lesbian."

He was dumbfounded. A lesbian? This was absolutely, without any doubt, undeniably, inestimably, and cosmically the last thing he would have ever guessed. Was he that out to lunch? Had he missed something?

After a long silence, he mumbled something, not even sure himself what he was trying to say.

"Wa ... so ... jes ..." He took a deep breath. "Let me start again. Are you serious?"

"Did George Foreman name all his kids George for nothing? Of course I'm serious. Serious as a heart attack! Here's a fact, little known outside of Africa. 'Jamila' is Swahili for lesbian. Or more accurately 'lover of labia'."

"Really?"

Now he knew what Rihanna would look like with a belly laugh.

Jamila managed to compose herself. She reached over and pinched his cheek. Pinched his cheek? He felt like he was five.

"Don't worry about it. And don't look like you put poison in the peach pie. It's alright. Really! Now can we get some work done?"

• • •

The Democratic candidate for the 3rd District congressional seat was a nice guy.

That's about all that anyone could say about him. That's about all that anyone really knew for certain.

His campaign had managed against all odds, and against the best intentions and expert advice of the DNC (Democratic National Committee), to create a wash. A gigantic blank slate. He was like the chalk line around where the victim's body had been found at a crime scene.

His name was Chris Castiglia.

Of course, everyone knew he was a Democrat, for what that was worth. Beyond his party affiliation, what he actually stood for was a big void.

His campaign theme song was "Blowin' In The Wind". It fit better than he possibly could have imagined. His schizophrenic public statements outlining his conflicting positions on just about every important issue canceled one another out. Castiglia put the flip in 'flip-flop' and as a result, his bid for Congress was definitely looking to be a big flop.

One time he said he supported leaving Social Security alone. The next week, he claimed he in principle supported the recommendations of the Simpson-Bowles Plan on fiscal discipline. Which, of course, *decimated* Social Security. He spoke at a union rally about the need for a strong labor movement. Then he was cited in the media as being among the most adamant and vocal supporters of Ohio Governor John Kasich's blatant attempt to demolish public service workers unions in the state. He claimed that income disparities meant we needed to have a more progressive tax system, putting higher taxes in place on the exorbitant earnings of the ultra-wealthy. Then on his Facebook page he heralded the Ryan Budget plan as the remedy for all of the federal budget woes. Of course, the Ryan plan actually *lowered* the taxes on the upper 1%. Speaking of which, he peppered a few speeches with praise of Occupy Wall Street as the noble and constitutionally protected expression of free speech, then later vilified the protestors as a bunch of "unruly, drug-addled troublemakers who might benefit from attempting a day of honest work before they go complaining about the system."

With all of the dancing around and switching sides, he could have been accused of being conniving and manipulative. It was more likely he was just confused. The complexity and enormity of the many problems facing America just seemed to overwhelm him.

Castiglia had been in politics for six years now. This was his second run for U.S. Congress. He had served in the Ohio State House of Representatives for three terms. Before that he had been a commercial real estate developer, responsible for many of the ugliest strip malls in southwestern Ohio.

His big claim to fame in the state legislature was sponsoring several pieces of legislation asserting and protecting the rights of dyslexics. Castiglia felt that the public at large as well as local lawmakers had been insensitive to the plight of this "invisible minority" for far too long. It was never explained how and why he had latched onto this particular cause. But he was as fiercely loyal to dyslexics as they were to him. At campaign rallies could often be seen posters that said things along the lines of, *Chris Stacligia, we've back your got!*

Martin's people rarely spoke of him. They rarely thought of him. Whatever support he got at the polls was probably knee-jerk voting by die-hard Democrats who voted strictly party line. But this was an oversight that needed correcting.

However you explained it, the last election he did pull 32.2% of the vote. That was some 82,000 votes that Martin didn't get. Martin Truth For Congress needed every one of those people this election.

Bill stated the obvious problem.

"It's hard to attack a candidate who comes down on both sides of every issue. Talk about a moving target!"

Lincoln wasn't daunted.

"Not really. He's got serious credibility issues."

Imogene and Bob agreed with Lincoln's take on it.

"I get the feeling that even hard-core Democrats this time around are fed up. That they're running away in droves. Castiglia is becoming the town leper."

"My clients of color don't vote anymore. They gave up. They figure, what's the point?"

Bill appeared to be joking but there was always something to what he was saying.

"Maybe we should contribute to his campaign. The more this guy is out there, the faster his numbers go down. At the present rate, he could end up the first candidate in history with negative voting stats."

Even though she got a smile out Bill's facetious comment, Phyllis keyed in on the critical matter at hand.

"Whatever happens, we can't let those voters get away. We need to get their attention, then get them into the voting booth. So how are you going to charm them, Martin? What are your thoughts?"

"I assume that's where the pledges come in. It's the perfect way to capture the disheartened and disenfranchised Democrats. Without even going negative, they lay it out very clearly that I'm on their side, at least on the five critical issues. Gardner's on the wrong side. Castiglia's all over the map. I'm the one who signed the pledges. Clear choice. I'm their man!"

Which brought up a very touchy subject.

With the petition drive now under way and October soon approaching, they had to make a critical decision with respect to the bewildering and bewildered Democratic candidate.

Should Castiglia be presented with the pledges?

Jamila was adamant.

"There's the right thing. Then there's the smart thing. In this case, the right thing is truly the cosmically dumb thing. Even if this Castiglia guy is as confused as you say, he might just sign the pledges and then we're screwed."

Time for a new round of the ongoing welterweight boxing match between Phyllis and Jamila. Jamila had just delivered the first jab. Phyllis countered and off they went.

"Every candidate should be able to get on board."

"If Castiglia wanted something like this to kick Gardner's ass, then he should have come up with it himself."

"So this is just a dirty campaign trick."

"No. It is what it is. I know one thing. We're not doing all this to put a moron like Castiglia in office. We are doing it to offer a legitimate choice in this election, to *empower* the voters of this district to vote for someone who will represent their best interests, who will represent *them* and not a bunch of rich bastards. We're doing it to get *Martin* elected!"

"Then the approach is not fair. It's not impartial."

"Impartiality is intrinsic to the petitioning process. Impartiality is irrelevant in terms of the pledges. When this blows up, there's going to be plenty of publicity. They know where to find us. Or I should say, where to find the Committee on Public Policy Preferences. If anybody really wants to sign on the dotted line, let them show up with a pen in their hand. We definitely shouldn't go to them. Not Castiglia. Not Potts. Only to Gardner."

"Why?"

"Because it'll split the vote. Only not in our favor. There were 82,000 people dumb enough to vote for Castiglia last time. If they see he is on board with the pledges, it's a sure thing they'll go with him again. Simply because he's the other guy. He's the other major contender. People don't think in terms of third or fourth party candidates unless they are forced to."

"So that's it. We turn our backs on ..." Phyllis made quotation marks with her index fingers. "... the 'right thing', for purely *political* reasons. *Self-serving* reasons. This turns my stomach."

Jamila softened her tone but hardened her line.

"What should turn our stomachs is losing this election and having the magnificent and exemplary talents of our dear Martin here go to waste. Please! Let's put this in perspective. As much as we all might wish it would happen, using this pledge strategy in this one election in our tiny corner of Ohio, is not going to fix an entire system that's badly broken. It's not going to get rid of the horrifying corruption of our political process. We're not going to magically put a stop to the way money and corporations and abuse of power have gutted our democracy. We're just doing what we *can* and *should* do. And that's to get one piece of shit out of office and replace him with one of the good guys. *That's* what these pledges are about."

Martin was as incorruptible as they come. He had a solid foundation of personal values and the strength of character to stand by what he believed in. At the same time, he understood the battle being waged here.

"Jamila's right. We can't fight this without weapons. The pledge is our weapon of choice. People can believe what they want about them. We're not deceiving anyone. There is certainly nothing noble about throwing away the election by delivering the pledges to Castiglia, in doing so handing a victory to either a confirmed liar or a complete idiot. There's nothing requiring it. There are no rules. The whole pledge strategy is outside the box."

Bill tried to lighten things up again.

"Castiglia wouldn't understand them anyway. He'd think he was buying a time-share in Boca Raton. Or renewing his subscription to Us Magazine."

Phyllis: "I can't win."

Jamila: "But Martin can."

Phyllis: "Is that all that counts?"

Jamila: "Yes."

Bill: "I'll second that."

Lincoln was able to put Phyllis's conscience somewhat at ease.

"No matter how you dice it, the very act of presenting the petitions to our voters is a very positive thing. It's a step forward in a process that's been going backwards for some time now. People will be given a voice which, if we do our jobs properly, will be heard. The petitioning in some sense is one thing, the pledges another. The petitions put the candidates on notice. Asking them to sign pledges is a whole other thing, more like declaring war. It *is* blatant bullying, a strong-arm tactic. Make no mistake about it. It *is* a political ploy. And it's a necessarily brutal strategy in a battle not of our choosing. *They* created the battlefield. *They* destroyed any honor and civility. We are just protecting ourselves and trying to restore some sanity and democracy to a system that's been hobbled by big money and corporate power."

Phyllis was always attentive. Particularly so to Lincoln. But as was the case right now, she sometimes got defensive.

"What's your point?"

"My point is this. We're doing a great thing with the petitions. The public will have spoken. Nothing we subsequently do can take away from this. Who we decide to hammer with the pledge strategy is whole other matter. It's not a pretty picture. But we do what we have to do. This *is* about getting Martin elected. I personally am in favor of avoiding Castiglia. Never even giving him the opportunity to sign the pledges. I doubt if he'll track us down. He's simply too disoriented and disorganized for that. But on our part, we should do absolutely nothing to bring the pledges to his attention. Jamila is dead on. It would muddy the waters. No, I take that back. It would completely muck everything up. If he signed the pledges, people being the lemmings that they are, would flock to him. Bye bye Martin Truth."

If Martin had been asked to articulate his own detailed views, 99% of the time they would align perfectly with what Lincoln had to say. He was grateful, particularly in this instance, for being spared the appearance of favoring something that might be viewed as purely self-serving. Or worse, his giving yet another thumbs up in support of Jamila, who he also agreed with 99% of the time. This was not a good time, if ever there were a good time, to have "factions" emerge. Even more important, though Phyllis often was the brakes to their accelerator — the person keeping the campaign from speeding uncontrollably off a cliff — it would have been rude and counterproductive if she were ever to feel she was being ganged up on. This was one of the main reasons Martin often said very little at these meetings, never desiring as the beneficiary of all of their hard work to appear divisive, or to play favorites.

It never came to a vote. Or an official approval by Phyllis. Everyone tacitly acknowledged the validity and necessity of Lincoln's rationale. He was both brilliant and solid. There was rarely any arguing with him after he presented his characteristically well-reasoned and balanced take on even the most contentious matters.

The pledges would hopefully do their job.

And Gardner would be out of his.

• • •

If there was one thing that Phyllis was good at, it was badgering. It was applying relentless pressure to get her way.

She had assets which she worked ruthlessly to her advantage. One was her age. As a mature woman of 52, still attractive and formidable in a post-menopausal way, she came off with class and a wizened air of distinction and competence. Whoever was on the receiving end of her harassment never felt insulted. Another priceless asset was her keen ability to know precisely when to back off, to never push over the line that would invite animus and assure rejection. Combining a mature charm, patience, certitude, and a convincing show of regard for the person she was bludgeoning with her entreaties, her nearly 100% win record was hardly a surprise.

This time she was facing a formidable opponent.

As always, she refused to give up.

Her target was Gregory Ganz, the chairman of the panel which oversaw the forthcoming televised debates for Gardner's congressional seat. Plugs on WHIO-TV were already announcing the showdown between Republican incumbent Gardner and his Democratic challenger Chris Castiglia.

Every ten or so messages, Ganz would finally take her call.

The conversation typically went like this.

"Why don't you give up? It's not going to happen."

"Martin Truth deserves to appear. He actually has something to say."

"But nobody ever heard of your guy."

"Gee, I wonder why."

"These debates are not about giving every fly-by-night person who comes down the pike the chance to spout nonsense on the most watched TV station in Dayton."

"Apparently you've never listened to either Congressman Gardner or Chris Castiglia, then."

"Excuse me! Mr. Gardner has been our congressman for almost ten years."

"It's no wonder! Because you never allow anyone to debate him who can call him out on his horrible voting record and his ridiculous ideas. Like that missile defense system on the East Coast to defend against North Korea, for example. Now that was a brilliant idea!"

"I'll have you know that Matt is a personal friend of mine. And I don't appreciate—"

"Oh really. Personal friend, eh? Well then call him up and ask him. Does he believe in real democracy or is this debate going to be another two hour song and dance number for his campaign?"

"I'm sure he could give you some lessons in democracy. He is our congressman. But I'll tell you what, Mrs. Wagner—"

"That's *Ms*. Wagner, sir."

"Whatever. Just for you, just so you'll stop bombarding me with phone messages, I'll have my people call Gardner's people and see what he says. Okay?"

Of course, he never did.

What finally worked was both unorthodox and in its underhanded way pretty funny.

Prompted by some joking around and a dare by some regulars just sitting around shooting the shit at his café, Bill called Gardner's campaign office. Posing as just an average citizen, he accused Gardner of being a coward, afraid to go head-to-head with someone who might have some debating chops.

"Tell Mr. Gardner that unless he's a complete chicken, he should have Martin Truth appear. Otherwise it's going to look like a sumo wrestler and a midget up there. Castiglia couldn't put together a good argument for wearing a warm coat in a winter storm."

"I'll pass your suggestion along. Thanks for calling."

While she was passing the suggestion along, they were passing the phone around the café. They took turns, coming up with more outrageous language, to suggest that Gardner was a total cop-out and trying to fix the election by staging a phony debate.

"Debate? What debate? Gardner's going to get carpal tunnel syndrome from patting himself on the back so much while that other guy just smiles and looks clueless."

Bill told Lincoln about the prank calls. After he finally stopped laughing, he got inspired. He talked it up in a summer session poli-sci class he was teaching, prompting a number of students who had a subversive streak start to make similar calls. They tended to be less subtle.

"You're pissing off a lot of young voters by not letting the Green Party candidate be in the debate. What kind of totalitarian campaign are you running there?"

"Tell Matt Gardner he's a fucking fascist! He doesn't believe in government by the people. He believes in government by Matt Gardner."

Soon the calls Gardner's campaign office was getting were too numerous to be considered a fluke. Someone brought it to his attention. The only concern for Gardner and his campaign manager was whether this upstart from the Green Party would cause serious trouble either way, whether Martin could embarrass the incumbent if he was not included in the debate, or do so if he ended up on the stage with him that night.

Gardner's people checked out Martin Truth. They weren't impressed with the videos of Martin's speeches posted online. To them he looked like the typical third-party policy wonk, long on self-righteousness but short on charisma and plain old sex appeal. Martin Truth just didn't have the right stuff. They unequivocally declared him no threat.

Gregory Ganz then got a most unexpected call. It was Gardner himself, who personally told his good buddy that he welcomed the opportunity to have Martin

Truth be included in the coming debate. And not only Martin, but the Libertarian candidate Potts as well.

"The more the merrier! What the hell, Greg. Let's show the public what they're missing."

Gardner's entire staff got a great laugh out of it. They assumed that having three idiots on stage with Gardner would just make him look that much better.

"This'll be a rout!"

"Maybe when it's done, you should thank the special education teachers in the area for making it possible for these three lemon brains to make it this far in politics."

Ha ha ha!

"Ain't it the truth! Isn't America great? Truly the land of opportunity, where any nitwit can get on the ballot and even make it on TV without teaching his dog to lip sync to Lady Gaga."

Ha ha ha!

Yes, they were sure it would be all fun and games for their guy Congressman Matt Gardner.

It didn't quite turn out the way they expected.

• • •

Phyllis, Jamila and Helen had been working non-stop for three days. Now Martin and Lincoln were there to see the results, exactly one week before the televised debate.

Lincoln was looking intently at a laptop, quickly scrolling from one thing to the next.

"This is phenomenal. Great job, everyone."

Tonight Phyllis seemed willing to surrender her role as quarterback.

"I'm exhausted. Jamila or Helen, you talk about it."

Helen was terminally shy. Jamila was terminally outspoken.

"What we've put together for you, Martin, is four hours of the essential Matt Gardner. Essential, as in the essence of the man's public face. We have videos, transcripts of speeches, audios of his speeches, interviews on camera and in print, the published literature and online policy positions that define Gardner. In sum total, these are where he comes down on the issues. The idea is to completely prepare you for what Gardner's going to claim he stands for."

"Perfect. Let me guess. In addition you have a detailed summary of his voting record, which sends a rather different message."

"Exactly. You obviously missed your calling as a mind reader. Now what we think you should do is spend the next three days studying this stuff. Know it better than Gardner himself. It would be great if he were to slip up on something and you were able to coach him on exactly what he's said. But he seems like a pretty sharp cookie, so you probably won't get that chance."

"Okay. Got it. Three days. No sleep. No fun. No turns on the mechanical bull. No foosball. Nose to the grindstone."

"This *will* be fun, Martin. This is your chance to flap the unflappable Mr. Stonewall. His voting record is such a glaring contradiction to what the guy has the audacity to promise to his clueless, apparently very inattentive supporters, you should be able to dice him up into tiny pieces by the end of the debate."

"Better for digestion. So. Three days studying this crap. Then you've got me booked for shock treatments at Kettering Psychiatric Hospital?"

"Worse than that. The four of us are going to be your sparring partners. As in role play. We'll spew the nonsensical mucous Gardner will be spewing that night. You can practice with your comebacks. If you're cool with it, we'll help you fine tune your responses. Give them the meat-cleaver edge to get the job done right."

"Jamila. Jamila. The things that come out of those pretty lips. And yes, not only am I open to suggestions, I insist on them. One thing I don't want to end up doing is two hours after the debate thinking, 'Damn! I wish I had said it this way.' This meat-cleaver needs to be able to slice, dice and chop. *Haieee!*"

After executing his best ninja karate chop, Martin stopped clowning and his eyes softened. They slightly glistened with a not infrequent warmth.

"Listen. Helen. Phyllis. All of you. I *so* appreciate this. Phyllis, I know how hard you worked just to get me into this debate. There's no way I'm going to let you down. This might be my only title shot."

Phyllis actually blushed. Jamila grinned from one dangling earring to the other.

"Go get him, Rocky!"

"I'll start tonight. Thank god it's the weekend. I promise. I'll have this stuff down so pat, you might think *I'm* Matt Gardner when I'm done."

Jamila did her best to look poker-faced.

"As Jesus Christ so beautifully said in one of the deleted passages of the New Testament: 'Know thine enemy well, whence he doth not cast his lot with thine on the true path of enlightenment, then you can beat the shit out of the asshole.'"

Martin tried not to laugh.

"Hmm. I missed that one."

"Would I make up something like that?"

"Yes."

"Well … I *am* paraphrasing slightly."

Lincoln was typing away on the laptop.

"Hey. She's right! I found it on deletedpassagesofthebible.com, right here."

Jamila looked as surprised as the rest of them.

"You did?"

"There's some disagreement as to the precise translation. You were quoting the King James version."

"I was?"

"The World English version and the latest Young's Literal edition has the ending as, 'then his wife be forever barren and his skull fill with the boiling entrails of his enemies.'"

"Are you serious?"

Lincoln looked directly at her and grinned.

"Gotcha!"

• • •

The televised debate turned out no more and no less farcical than political debates typically are in these times of talking points, sound bites, and bumper sticker cogitation.

But it had its moments.

Unfortunately, the occasional emergence of a genuinely dynamic exchange of ideas was sabotaged by having four candidates on stage. Three was an uncomfortable crowd. Four was a ragtag mob.

Chris Castiglia, the Democratic challenger, of course was there. And as per Gardner's request they allowed Martin to appear, as well as Peter Potts, the self-proclaimed Libertarian. Potts had been for several months mounting his own crusade to be included. Crazy as the guy appeared, he was sometimes quite effective at promoting himself and had been exhorting the debate committee almost as zealously as Phyllis. His annoying and persistent supplications were like water torture to the committee chairman, Gregory Ganz, and tonight's moderator, the editor-in-chief of the Dayton Daily News, Jana Collier. She began to feel like Potts was stalking her. They were both relieved that Gardner had made the decision for them.

Sadly, whatever persuasive and modestly coherent argumentation Potts was sporadically capable of off stage was entirely missing this evening on stage. If any television viewers had a modicum of confidence in his adequacies for public office before the debate, his garbled and repetitious ramblings throughout the evening made short order of this prior support. Even worse, Potts's remarks, rebuttals and interjections without fail brought all discussions to an abrupt halt. Every time he opened his mouth the room filled with mind-numbing incoherence, which instantly induced amnesia in anyone within earshot. Nobody had a clue as to what they had been talking about.

Democrat Castiglia did himself no particular harm, nor any particular good. He came off as the innocuous, irrelevant candidate that he in fact was. He was affable to the point of appearing frivolous, preferring at all costs to safeguard the entire event from what he perceived as untoward displays of animosity. As the self-appointed peacemaker, he was always trying to smooth things out, to keep it PC and friendly, ignoring the fact that what drove people to watch these confrontations was their appetite for blood sport. After all, these viewers had given up their usual sitcoms, psycho-drama, CSI blood baths and reality shows, to see some serious political cage fighting, not a dainty display of amicability, climaxed with a group hug at the end.

Thus it was by default that the highlights of the entire debate, those which managed to survive the buoyant buffoonery of Castiglia and the disjointed derangement of Potts, were a number of heated exchanges between the conspicuously cocky incumbent Matt Gardner, and the unknown upstart Martin Truth.

Not coincidentally, the most intense and spirited of these clashes centered around the five issues Martin's people had identified as essential grist for the pledge strategy.

Early in the debate, when Jana Collier, the moderator, brought up Social Security, the result was both articulate airing of several salient points, and indelicate trading of some serious blows. Neither Martin or Gardner was pulling his punches.

MARTIN: "There's been a lot of muddying the waters on Social Security. Republicans like the esteemed Mr. Gardner talk about needing to reduce the national debt. But Social Security doesn't contribute one dollar to the national debt. Social Security is a self-sustaining trust and its monies are by law intentionally sequestered from the ongoing spending of the government for its other functions. It is a completely separate fund and has no place in the debate about reducing the national debt."

GARDNER: "I hate to have to keep calling this gentleman 'Truth', since I hear so little of it come out of his mouth. Mr. Truth here seems very confused. This fund and that fund. He's like a kid who can't figure out which cookie jar he hid his marijuana in. All I can say is what I've said all along. And that simply is, we owe it to our elderly, our retired citizens who've worked hard all their lives and now just want to relax and enjoy their golden years, we owe these good people the security of a decent pension check every month. Enough to live on and surround themselves with the comforts that we've come to expect in this great nation of ours."

MARTIN: "Then why have you consistently voted to gut Social Security, resulting in reduced payments to its recipients. You've also voted in favor of increasing the eligibility age to 68—"

GARDNER: "Excuse me! I will not have you distorting my—"

MARTIN: "On March 29, 2012, you voted for the first version of the Ryan budget proposal. Then on May 10, 2012, you voted for the second version of the Ryan budget proposal. Both of these horrible pieces of legislation included huge cuts in Social Security to pay for more tax breaks for the already filthy rich in this country."

GARDNER: "You need to get your facts straight, young—"

MARTIN: "I've got my facts straight. With all due respect, maybe you need to get your story straight. You're either for keeping Social Security the way it is, which is a self-funded, self-sustaining program, the most successful and popular in our history — a program which by the way is solvent until 2038 — or you're for stealing the money people have contributed over the course of their lives so that you and your country club friends can buy another Rolls Royce or send the money to a numbered bank account in the Grand Cayman Islands. Which is it, Mr. Gardner?"

GARDNER: "I'll have you know, my mother gets a Social Security check every month. Do you think I would do anything to hurt my own mother?"

MARTIN: "I guess we need to ask her. Does anyone have a cell phone we can use?"

JANA COLLIER: "Okay okay, gentlemen. You both need to confine your remarks specifically to the question I've asked. And you're both a little, actually you're way over your allotted time and we haven't heard from Mr. Castiglia and Mr. Potts. Mr. Castiglia?"

CASTIGLIA: "This sort of sticks-and-stones approach to politics is exactly why we have so much gridlock in government now. We can disagree. We can even agree to disagree without making personal attacks, eh? Social Security has been around for a very long time, and will continue to be around for a long time. Let's just work together, to keep it together."

POTTS: "There is no doubt in my mind where the problem stems from. All of this mess started when that damn Nixon took America off the gold standard. When money isn't backed by the most revered precious metal in human history — which by the way many believe receives its value and ennobling power directly from the intrinsic interaction of the sun with objects in the galactic sphere — you have to expect things to spin out of control."

MARTIN: "Actually, in direct response to Mr. Potts's pining for the gold standard, I wonder why America doesn't go on the uranium standard, since we have so much of it sitting around. What do you say to that, Mr. Gardner. You're the expert on matters of defense. Why does our country have over 800 tons of pure bomb-grade uranium stockpiled? The Soviet Union broke up. We're not under any threat of attack that I know of by France, India, or any of the other nuclear powers. Why are we on such a war footing armed to the teeth with nuclear bombs, when the rest of the world seems more preoccupied with stealing our jobs than stealing our flag?"

GARDNER: "I suppose it's easy for armchair generals like you to sit around smoking a peace pipe and believe that since you can't see through the cloud of smoke, it means it's a safe world out there and everyone loves us. Maybe you missed it because you were playing sitar in a park somewhere, but we were ruthlessly attacked on September 11, 2001. When the Islamic jihadists flew those planes into the World Trade Center, they weren't stopping by to check out the back-to-school sale in the stationery shop. They were declaring war on the greatest country in the world. They were declaring war on our freedoms. They were declaring war on our democratic system of government, the most noble experiment in self-determination in the history of the world. They were declaring war on the American Way!"

MARTIN: "So we should have tried to shoot them down with an intercontinental ballistic missile armed with a 2 megaton hydrogen bomb?"

GARDNER: "See! Right there. That's the kind of sarcastic remark we've come to expect from people like you. I'm quite sure you've never been in the military. Other than playing with little plastic soldiers when you were a boy, you haven't the slightest clue about the kinds of systems we have in place, about the enormous military capacity of this nation, of what's required to defend our land, our people, our way of life."

MARTIN: "I'm merely asking. What has nuclear weaponry got to do with defending the nation against shoe bombers, underwear bombers, crazies hijacking commercial airliners, letters full of anthrax, cyber-sabotage of the internet, any of the stuff which poses real threats to this country and its people? Are we safer with 800 tons of nuclear bombs? Or are we just making ourselves a bigger target for the world's resentment and enmity?"

GARDNER: "The voters of this district have sent me to the venerated halls of the U.S. Congress ten years in a row now. Do you know why? Do you have a clue? I'll tell you why. It's because they know that Matt Gardner doesn't negotiate with terrorists. Matt Gardner stands strong in the face of barbaric threats to the loyal citizens of this great nation. Matt Gardner will <u>not</u> rest until every single one of these maniacal fanatics who would impose their evil demented religious beliefs on us, until every last jihadist and suicide bomber is locked up or dead. That's why they send me to Congress. I love peace as much as any man. But Matt Gardner doesn't sacrifice his wife and children or any of the good people of this great nation under God, to some naïve belief that if we just play tambourines and give peace a chance, all the bad people will go away."

MARTIN: "Well, even if all of our spines are now tingling from your magnificent declarations on behalf of America the beautiful, it must be obvious to everyone in this room and watching this debate on television, that you are not going to answer my question. I can't blame you. If I were you, I too would choose to blow my patriotic horn rather than admit that the programs you sponsor and support in Congress are a huge waste of taxpayer money, though they fill the coffers of your defense contractor campaign supporters. How did that idea for putting a missile defense shield on the East Coast to defend America from North Korea work out? You know, the one facing the wrong way?"

GARDNER: "Amateurs like you make me laugh. The enemies of America don't have to do very much when know-nothings like you are doing their work for them. The missile defense system you are referring to wasn't facing the wrong way. It was facing up. That's where missiles come from. Or maybe you thought they burrowed through the ground like moles. Sure, anyone can find waste in programs that are as complex and comprehensive as the ones we're trying to build to protect the homeland. What's your solution? Look for a mushroom cloud and say, 'Now that would've been a good spot for a missile defense system!' You're in way over your head, young man."

CASTIGLIA: "Now I'm not going to point fingers, but while we're bickering about silly details, there are hateful people out right now putting the finishing touches on some bizarre plan to attack America. These terrorists know no boundaries, they don't play by the rules of the Geneva Convention, they will stop at nothing in their attempt to destroy us. I don't want to get into what I think motivates them. It doesn't matter what I think. I do know we need to be vigilant, we need to marshal all of the resources at our disposal. If need be, we must confront them on their own soil before they can ever get anywhere near our borders. But most of all, we need to be united as a people, and put trust in those who are charged with safeguarding America.

GARDNER: "That would be me."

Everyone seemed to think that was very funny. It relieved some of the escalating tension. Peter Potts then waved his hand, looking like a school boy who needed to go number one.

JANA COLLIER: "Mr. Potts, did you have something you wanted to say?"

POTTS: "Going back to your original comment, Mr. Truth. Having a uranium standard for our currency would never work. You put that much uranium in the vaults in Fort Knox, you're gonna end up with a meltdown. Like Chernobyl."

The embarrassed silence which followed his airhead comment was broken by the moderator, who moved on to the war in Afghanistan.

JANA COLLIER: "The American public is becoming increasingly anxious, maybe impatient would be the better term, about our ongoing military presence in Afghanistan. It is now on record as being the longest military conflict in our history. Where do you see this going? Do you see an end in sight? Mr. Gardner?"

GARDNER: "It's a very difficult mission. Our boys are doing a phenomenal job. Phenomenal! But it's messy. Very messy. Even so, America has never been a country to walk away from a tough challenge. There are never any easy answers when dealing with madmen. Or terrorists. When those 3000 innocent people died in the World Trade Center attack, when the plane smashed into the very bastion of our military defenses, the Pentagon, and that other aircraft crashed in Pennsylvania, it was clear that those responsible had to be brought to justice. That is what we're doing there. Bringing these international criminals to justice. Of course, I want the war to end. But that's not something you can just put on a Day Planner. It's not like soccer practice or the World Series. But we will prevail! Whatever it takes, however long it takes, America will prevail!"

Applause broke out in the audience, punctuated by some yells and cheering.

JANA COLLIER: "Mr. Castiglia?"

CASTIGLIA: "Nobody wants war. We didn't choose this war. America is a peace-loving nation with good people. We've become a target of a small but deadly group of rogues, religious fanatics, who will stop at nothing to impose their twisted ideologies and narrow religious beliefs on us. The good news is that we both have the moral high ground and God on our side. Just as the distinguished Mr. Gardner said, we will prevail. God bless America!"

MARTIN: "We're all with you on that, Mr. Castiglia. Those are great sentiments. But I'm not exactly sure how that addresses the quagmire which Afghanistan has become. More troubling are your remarks, Mr. Gardner. It seems that someone with your military experience and your position on the Armed Services committee in Congress would better equip you to give a truthful and lucid answer to the question. It's very troubling that you seem woefully ignorant of both the political and historical record. Mr. Castiglia is right. We didn't choose this war, meaning the people of this country. But someone did. And the alleged someone invaded Afghanistan on the pretext of capturing Osama bin Laden. But the Taliban government had offered prior to our attacking them, to turn bin Laden over to a neutral country for us to apprehend. We had other opportunities in the course of this horrible mess to capture him. Somehow we screwed that up. Then just last year, a handful of crack Navy Seals did the job. They did the job that whole divisions couldn't do, even after killing an untold number of civilians and sacrificing over 2,100 young soldiers. So what have our troops accomplished? At one point we had 110,000 of them over there, running around doing what? I hate to bring up that other disaster, our war in Iraq. But conservative estimates put the cost of the two wars, the one to hunt down one man, the other to find and destroy non-existent weapons of mass destruction, at 1.27 trillion dollars. In case anyone out there didn't get that, let me repeat. Iraq and Afghanistan are costing at minimum 1.27 trillion dollars! Putting aside the money, we have 2,100 young men cut down before their lives ever truly got going, thousands more maimed, crippled, and psychologically damaged by this pointless war. The Veterans Administration says that on any given night, there are 107,000 of these former soldiers walking the streets and homeless, victims of Post-Traumatic Stress Syndrome. And you want to offer patriotic slogans. The American people want our boys home. And they don't want any more being shipped back in body bags. In fact, a recent New York Times/CBS News poll indicates that 76% of Americans want—"

JANA COLLIER: "Mr. Truth, you're way over your allotted time."

GARDNER: "Can I say something to Mr. Wave-The-White-Flag here? You've never been in the military, so you find it easy to sit around sipping your latte and yelling 'surrender' when the going gets tough."

MARTIN: "Why don't you answer the question, Congressman? What are we doing there? Why are we still fighting in Afghanistan? You voted for the war and every appropriations bill to keep the war going. What exactly—"

Gardner now started yelling.

GARDNER: "Maybe you haven't been paying attention because you were too busy hugging a tree. But there have been no attacks, that's zero attacks on the United States of America since 911. That's what we're doing there. Fighting terrorism!"

MARTIN: "That begs the question."

GARDNER: "What are you talking about? Begs what question? This isn't some high school debate here."

MARTIN: "I've been using Dial soap all my life and haven't been hit by any asteroids. Does that mean that Dial soap keeps me from getting hit by asteroids? [Laughter bubbled up from the audience and Martin paused till it died down.] Just humor all of us, Congressman, and give a simple, straightforward answer to the question. What are we doing in Afghanistan? Other than wasting a lot of taxpayer money and killing off America's brave young soldiers."

GARDNER: "No one said war was pretty. It has always required sacrifice. I just want everyone to understand that I, as your congressman, have and will continue to do everything in my power to preserve the honor of this country, so that those we lose in battle will not have died in vain."

MARTIN: "Well, nobody dies in vain if—"

JANA COLLIER: "Gentlemen! Enough! We really need to move on here."

And so it went. Through health care …

GARDNER: "This health care that the President shoved down our throats, deceptively named the Patient Protection and Affordable Care Act sure didn't solve any problems. If anything, it made things worse."

MARTIN: "See. We do agree on something. But the rest of the story is that serious reform was blocked at every turn by you and the rest of the Republicans who have your bread buttered on both sides by the health care industry."

CASTIGLIA: "This is a very difficult issue. Both sides of the aisle did their best. The President did what no one else has been able to accomplish for over five decades. I think he deserves some credit here."

Increasing the federal minimum wage …

GARDNER: "I'm for everybody earning as much as they can. But the simple fact is that this is a down economy. Employers have to tighten their belts just like the rest of us. If you force them to pay more for each employee, they'll just go with fewer employees. You might think with your bleeding-heart mentality that you're helping the average worker. But the fact is you're going to put a lot of them out on the street."

MARTIN: "It's common knowledge that employers, at least the major corporations, are sitting on over two trillion dollars. That's money that's doing nothing for the economy. They're <u>not</u> *tightening their belts, they're floating in a huge ocean of cash that they're afraid to invest. Common sense tells you that the best investment is paying a livable wage to your employees. Guess what happens then. They can actually afford to buy your products! They spend money and the economy starts rolling again."*

GARDNER: "This minimum wage debate is just another example of big government interfering in areas where they don't belong and just end up mucking things up. Wages, like the price of products, are fairly determined by the laws of supply and demand. If someone doesn't like what a prospective employer is paying, he or she can go someplace else and get a job more to his or her liking."

MARTIN: "Well, that's a nice fairy tale but the facts tell a different story. Tens of thousands of jobs have been shipped overseas, then in 2008 the investment banks crashed the economy causing 2.6 million jobs to go up in smoke. The result has been that unemployment — that is, real unemployment, not the massaged numbers we get from the current administration — is well over 15%. So this someplace else you would have our job seeker go doesn't exist. Thousands of the people now desperate for jobs were laid off by the very corporations who underwrite your campaign. It's quite obvious whose team you're playing for, and it's not the guy who works on the loading dock at Walmart and just wants to be able to pay his rent."

CASTIGLIA: "I think we need to enforce the existing federal minimum wage. It's been pointed out to me that waiters and waitresses sometimes only make $4.00 per hour, sometimes less."

POTTS: "If we returned to the gold standard, all money would actually be worth something. Right now, it's just like paper. In fact, it is paper."

A discussion of Medicare heated up, then veered right back to Social Security ...

GARDNER: "Let me make this crystal clear. I have always been and always will be committed to Medicare. It's been in place for over forty five years and is among the most cherished government programs in our history. I speak regularly to groups of senior citizens and understand their needs. I have people in my own family who are retired and depend on Medicare. And let's not forget, not only does Medicare serve the needs of over 40 million elderly Americans, it also provides support and necessary services for some 8 million others who have disabilities."

MARTIN: "Then I have to ask again, why in 2012 did you vote for both versions of the Ryan budget bill? Both versions of this onerous piece of legislation contained language which hack away at Medicare turning it into a voucher program, which would truly stick it to current recipients. It increases the personal out-of-pocket medical bills each person will have to pay by over $6,000 a year. As if retired citizens have an additional $6,000 laying around every year to spend on doctors and treatment. Then the Ryan budget proposal went on to fundamentally change Social Security, significantly reducing benefits, raising the age of eligibility, and so on. I might mention that 58% of all Americans oppose this awful piece of legislation, and more specifically 74% of senior citizens oppose it. You're definitely on the wrong side of this issue, Congressman."

GARDNER: "It's a question of solvency. If our whole economic system goes bankrupt because guys like you think the government can just print money or pull it out of thin air, there won't be anything for anybody."

MARTIN: "Funny thing is, Social Security is solvent. As things stand right now, it remains solid until 2038. That's 26 years from now. And if we could raise the cap just a bit, meaning again to ask the wealthy to pay into the fund a bit more, it would be entirely solvent indefinitely. As it is now, income above $106,800 is not subject to social security contributions. So, let's take one of your campaign donors as an example. Mr. Shelby Kuhlmann."

GARDNER: "I don't think we need to name names or—"

MARTIN: "Mr. Kuhlmann is CEO of Capital Nine Investments and has a salary of $1,250,000 per year. That's just his base salary. He makes much more with sweetheart stock options and other perks. But let's just go with $1,250,000. So while probably everyone in this audience, myself, the camera crew, and even our lovely hostess, Jana Collier, pays into social security on every dollar we earn, Mr. Kuhlmann only pays on $106,800 and on the rest — the $1,143,200 — he doesn't pay a single penny. Does that sound right? [Martin looked around at everyone in the room and shrugged his shoulders.] Folks? Is that fair? Seems a little off to me."

GARDNER: "Who are you to decide what's fair or not? Do you even have a job?"

MARTIN: "What does Mr. Kuhlmann do with that $1,143,200 that he can't chip in a few extra dollars so that people who've worked hard all their lives can enjoy a decent retirement? It might come as a surprise to both Mr. Kuhlmann and you, Congressman Gardner, that retirees are not exactly living the life of high-rollers. In fact, many of them just barely get by and some of them don't. According to <u>your</u> tax returns, sir, you spend more in one week than the average Social Security recipient spends in one year. I think you might be a little out of touch with what it takes for the typical senior citizen to survive. As a result, you've consistently voted to cut the current Social Security pittance down to an even smaller pittance. It's very sad. Very sad."

GARDNER: "Could I maybe get a word in here?"

JANA COLLIER: "Yes. I have to warn you, Mr. Truth. You consistently go well beyond your allotted time. I know you see me waving, trying to get your attention. Let's try to tighten it up a bit and avoid the long speeches. Okay, Mr. Gardner, go ahead."

GARDNER: "Trying to make this personal is vicious and a cheap insult. The man you referred to, Shelby Kuhlmann, is an upstanding citizen, contributes to many charities, and I can say from my own personal experience, is not someone who would do anything to hurt other people, especially our elderly citizens. Your harangue is just an attempt to point the finger and pin certain nettlesome problems on people like Mr. Kuhlmann and myself, who happen to make a little more money. As I said before, my own mother is on social security. Sweet lady. She just turned 76. I know how much that monthly check means to her. So, Mr. Truth, I'm not out of touch. I'm well aware of the challenges people face in their golden years."

Martin didn't even have to say anything to that one. Castiglia did it for him.

CASTIGLIA: "With the money you make, your mother is living on social security?"

Jana Collier let the groans from the audience close that discussion.
They moved on.
Increasing taxes on the rich unleashed a full-on battle royal …

GARDNER: "So you want to punish success, is that it? Maybe when someone sets the world record for the 100 yard dash, we should cut off his legs. Is that what you have in mind, Truth?"

MARTIN: "No. But I don't think just because someone is rich they should be able to drive their Maserati in the 100 yard dash. [Again the audience showed their appreciation with scattered chuckles and even a few catcalls, 'Make 'em pay their fair share.'] Warren Buffett has pointed out that under the current tax code, he pays a lower rate than his secretary."

GARDNER: "Well if Mr. Buffett wants to try to remedy the enormous hole we've dug ourselves in with our out-of-control spending, let him. There's no law preventing him from paying extra. All I know is that the more dollars you take from the job creators, the less money they have to create jobs. This is simple logic, Truth. I think even you can understand it."

MARTIN: "Logic, as you call it, that flies in the face of the facts. When the income tax rates on the upper 1% were over 90% during the Eisenhower administration, unemployment hovered consistently around 5%. Now the highest tax bracket pays only 35% and the official unemployment numbers have been consistently over 7%. Actually, the rich in this country, the ones that keep your campaign awash in money, pay much less than 35%, since the bulk of their income is taxed as capital gains at a mere 15%. Your most recent tax return shows that with all the special tax breaks you get, <u>you</u> only paid 13.7% of your seven figure income in taxes. Warren Buffett is a very rich man and an American who thinks that the more you make, the greater your debt of gratitude should be to this great country. A bill was introduced into Congress built around what was called the Buffett Rule, which would have at least begun to address the enormous discrepencies that now exist in our tax code. As we've come to expect, you voted against it."

GARDNER: "Well, Mr. Buffett is welcome to send as much of his money to Uncle Sam as his heart desires. No one is stopping him. The point still remains, there are some people who've worked hard and properly benefited from their industry. You want them to give away their hard-earned money to welfare moms, lazy deadbeat dads, and undocumented immigrants. It's always the same with you socialist types. Take take take. And frankly, to my ears you all sing the same song. The Battle Hymn of Class Warfare. The rich versus the poor. You're just envious. You're jealous of <u>my</u> success and have *to insult the good patriotic Americans who support me. You attack me personally, or I should say you slander me, just because many good, God-fearing voters want a strong, knowledgeable, dedicated, experienced person as their representative in Congress. You've got one solution for all the problems of the world: take take take. I suppose next you'll be asking me for a hand-out, so you can promote your anti-American socialist message and turn this country into Cuba."*

MARTIN: "Nope. Not at all, Congressman. I'm not in the least interested in your money. We already get our fair share of legitimate contributions from concerned voters. The difference with my campaign is we don't accept bribes."

GARDNER: "How dare you—"

MARTIN: "All people need to see is the list of your biggest campaign donors and they'll see why you vote the way you do. And why you are so dead set against the wealthy of this country paying their fair share. You don't want to upset all your country club friends, who can count on you to keep their taxes at an obscenely low rate, while you and the rest of the Republican storm troopers put the American Dream on the chopping block, hacking away at Social Security, Medicare, benefits for the unemployed, funding for public education and college tuition, even lunch programs for children of the poor, heating oil assistance for low income families. I could go on. But your record speaks for itself."

GARDNER: "Truth! What a joke! If there was ever someone with a more deceptive surname. You can lie all you want, but the voters know the real truth. In November, guys like you won't have the opportunity to malign people like myself, or even my worthy opponent Mr. Castiglia. You'll have to go back to doing whatever you anarchists do between elections."

Finally, they each made their closing remarks …

CASTIGLIA: "We are one people. We are one nation. We are all children of a higher power, regardless of what you choose to call it. My personal and political philosophy is one and the same. Respect others and work together for a better world. That's exactly what I will do if I'm elected to office. Washington has become its own little world of insiders. It has become divided into cliques and little nuclei of power and influence. That's not my game and I don't intend to play it. I will go to Washington DC representing you, the good citizens of this district."

POTTS: "I call myself the One-Man Political Posse for good reason. What's a posse? I'll tell ya! It's guys that get the job done. They see evil, they track it down, and bring it in tied up and ready for trial. Ready for justice. I go it alone because I don't want to compromise my principles. There's work to be done. I don't have time for a bunch of excuses. This country's in big trouble. There's evil all around. It's coming after America. You got terrorists coming from the outside. And I hate to say it, but you got a lot of people inside this country too, who whether they mean to or not, are destroying the greatest nation in history. What can you expect from me as your congressman? Well, I'll track 'em down and bring 'em in. Nobody owns me. I'm at your service. The good people of Ohio. The good citizens of the United States of America. God bless our great nation. Let's stand proud and stand tall ... together."

GARDNER: "America is the greatest country on Earth. The greatest country in all of history. We got there by excelling at everything we set out to do, by never accepting 'good enough', by being resourceful and feisty, maybe at times a little rough around the edges, but never afraid to step forward and defend the things we believe in — those ideas and values which define our democracy, our way of life, the American Way. When I look in on my kids late at night, tucked away and lost inside their dreams, I see the future. And I see my responsibility to make this country all it can be, the kind of place I want my children, and their children, and their children's children, to live in. I see it as a place where everyone can thrive, where everyone has an opportunity should they choose to take advantage of it, to enjoy all of the riches and rewards that only a nation like ours can offer. Our best days are not behind us, as some of the nay-sayers, the cynics, the glass-half-empty types would have us believe. [He gave a subtle but unmistakable glance right at Martin.] Our best days are today and tomorrow and the day after that. That's what I see my job is. To go to Washington DC, as I have for almost ten years now, and do my part to make that happen. Yes, to represent you as today's citizens of this district, but also to represent the future generations of our great nation. Thank you! And God bless America!"

MARTIN: "I agree with Mr. Gardner. Our best days are now and tomorrow. But unfortunately, that's just for a tiny few. There's a party going on in this country but most of us aren't invited. The wealthy are getting wealthier but for the rest of us, you know the story. We're losing our jobs or have jobs that don't pay enough to live on, our houses are being foreclosed on, we can't afford to send our kids to college, on and on. My message and the goal of my campaign is simple. I want to see this country back on its feet. I want to see all of us enjoy the benefits of living in the richest country in the world. And I don't think we need Mr. Gardner to decide what kind of America this should be. The American people are smart. They know what they want. But they don't get it, do they? 75% want the wars ended and our young soldiers back home safe and sound. The wars keep going. They want to earn a decent wage. We make about the same in equivalent dollars as we did back in 1956. 1956! 70% of Americans want the filthy rich to start paying their fair share in taxes. But all we hear about is more tax cuts for the wealthy. We want Congress to leave Social Security and Medicare alone. But our elected representatives —

from both major parties I might add — want to hack them to pieces. Cuts and more cuts. You and I don't even get a say in the matter. And that's the problem, isn't it? We elect them to do a job — to represent <u>*us*</u> *— and they vote to please their wealthy patrons and corporate donors."*

JANA COLLIER: "Mr. Martin. Again you are exceeding your allotted time."

MARTIN: "The Supreme Court, in one of the most heinous decisions in our history, Citizens United, decided that money is free speech. Since then, all of our smiling elected officials have been swimming in campaign contributions. Our democracy is being bought. Your vote doesn't count anymore. Congress now decides the critical matters that affect you and I, based on who picks up their $600 lunch tab, who fills their campaign coffers. My campaign is about restoring democracy to this country. About having your voice, the good people of America, heard again. About letting we the people decide for themselves what kind of America—"

JANA COLLIER: "Excuse me! Mr. Martin!"

MARTIN: "I can't order God around. I can't tell him to bless America. But I know one thing for sure. He <u>*will*</u> *bless our great nation if we again elect responsible leadership. Thank you."*

JANA COLLIER: "Are you done? Whew! I thought we were going to have to get a grappling hook. Anyway, I want to thank the participants. Distinguished Congressman Matt Gardner, the Republican incumbent. Mr. Chris Castiglia, his Democratic opponent. Mr. Peter Potts, the Libertarian candidate. And finally, Martin Truth, from the Green Party. I want to thank our audience here in the studio, and all of you out there in the television viewing audience. Our next debate will be Wednesday, September 26th. The final clash of the Titans will occur October 17th. Thanks and good night!"

There's always the big discussion after a TV debate about who won and who lost, who landed the big punches, whether anyone scored a knockout, who will see the big push in the polls now that the gloves are back in the locker and the cut men are patching up the fighters, readying them for the next bout.

Martin by any measure came out way ahead this evening. The big problem remained as always, nobody knew who he was. They might remember his name — in large part due to Gardner's several lame jokes about it — but that still might not translate to any kind of results at the polls. The election was still nearly three months away. A long time to remember. A long time to forget.

A little boost might have come from the post-debate coverage given by the local channels. All the pundits agreed that a feisty new personality had emerged on the local political scene, as they discussed what turned out to be a patently one-sided performance. Sadly, the issues and the contrasting positions took a back seat to how pissed off Gardner looked, how wussy Castiglia came off, and how certifiably insane Peter Potts apparently is. Plus the commentary on and the scoring of the debate only lasted a couple days. Then the focus of reporting moved on to other high drama stories and sensationalized dispatches of local and national news.

It soon became evident that Martin would not be invited to the next two televised debates. No explanation was given. But it didn't take a genius to figure out what happened. Gardner made the call. He wasn't going to again be humiliated by some third-party punk who had no chance of winning.

That still couldn't take away from what had just occurred tonight. Triumph was in the air. Martin's whole staff was there. Their guy had done extremely well. Phyllis was beside herself with joy. Bill looked like a kid who had just gotten a new bicycle. Lincoln kept a comfortable distance but undeniably looked pleased. Bob and Imogene talked excitedly with Helen, who uncharacteristically was also a bit of a chatterbox.

Jamila caught up with Martin as he milled about shaking hands with members of the audience, fielding their congratulations, comments, and questions.

"Hey, Martin. Something happened up there at the end. You know, when the whole thing was over. You shook hands with Gardner and said something. The guy looked like he wanted to kill you. What was that all about?"

"I just said, 'You're going down, sucker!' He seemed to take offense. Can you believe it?"

"Oh my God! That's awesome! I'm surprised he didn't deck you. So the question is this: Do you believe it? You think you can take him down?"

"I have no idea ... but it sure felt good saying it!"

• • •

The debate did have one immediate and powerful impact on the election. It made the job of the petitioners much easier.

A surprisingly high percentage of the 3rd District voters gave up their usual mid-week fare of sitcoms, sports and reality shows for two hours, and watched the four candidates have at it. As a result, their attention was very much drawn to the issues which the petitions addressed — Social Security, Medicare, raising taxes on the rich, increasing the federal minimum wage, and the hot button issue of them all, ending the war in Afghanistan.

This largely resulted from the choice of topics by the committee in charge of the debate, which were indeed the things voters were concerned about. But it was significantly reinforced by Martin himself, the way he kept hammering away at the message: *This* is what you the voting public wants, but *that* is what you get. The 'that' in question was not just Congress as a whole enacting unpopular legislation, but more troublingly their very own Congressman Gardner, opposing what the majority of his constituents wanted.

Now when student volunteers went around house-to-house presenting the Committee on Public Policy Preferences petitions, people were already fired up about the issues, or at least tuned into them. That was what they were reporting to Lincoln for at least three weeks following the debate. Voters, of course, at first showed some reluctance to look at anything resembling a petition. But as soon as they saw it was about Social Security or the Afghanistan war, the minimum wage or getting the rich to ante up more in taxes, they perked right up. They practically grabbed the pen from the volunteer.

Maybe most voters didn't make the explicit connection to Martin's highly charged comments during the debate. They certainly weren't picturing Martin Truth when they signed on to the commitment: *"I will only vote for a candidate who ..."*

But they definitely were taking the petitions seriously. They were taking seriously the idea that they should have a voice in running their country. They were taking seriously the idea of being taken seriously.

• • •

Martin's campaign people didn't want to let dissipate what political capital might have been accrued with Martin's strong showing in the televised debate. This was easier said than done. The nation had been long suffering from a massive epidemic of ADD. Yesterday's news might as well have been someone's journal entries during the Peloponnesian War, as stories as ancient as one or two days ago were quickly swamped and erased from memory by new scandals, disasters, crimes and gossip.

They worked hard and worked fast to mount a new publicity offensive.

A new ad campaign was coming together. It was everything that could be expected and more.

"It's not good enough."

Jamila. Never satisfied.

Phyllis, usually the bad cop in these situations, looked confused. She was feeling confident they were making serious progress.

"What do you mean, not good enough? This is a thousand times better than what we've had. People are seeing Martin in a whole new light. People love the new logo."

"Too bad we're not selling t-shirts."

Even the unflappable, eternally optimistic Bill appeared to be getting impatient.

"Everyone I talk to thinks highly of Martin. Whenever he or his campaign comes up I only hear positive stuff. *Very* positive stuff."

"And how often is that?"

"Well ... okay. I see what you're saying. But—"

"We have a problem here. A fundamental problem. I guess it's intrinsic to being green. Somehow we've got to get this campaign on the front page, that's all. And then keep it there. I'm not sure there's any way to do that. Anything realistic, anyway, that's not illegal. Sorry if I seem like a curmudgeon. I'm just frustrated. We need to do more and I don't know what it is."

Martin for once was having trouble agreeing with her.

"I don't think you should underestimate what we've accomplished, Jamila. You were right. I was boring. Maybe I still am. But the posters, the website, the new graphics set a new tone. Everyone's done a great job. I think people will be paying more attention. This has breathed new life into my campaign. It's fresh. It's exciting. It's new."

"But so what? It's like laundry detergent. Every box says, *New!* or *Improved!* or *Now With Moon Dust!* Somehow we've got to take this to a whole new level."

"What are you thinking? Do you have some ideas? I mean, I'm open to anything."

"I'm still thinking. There's something missing. Critical mass. Do you get critical mass? It's like the one additional snowflake that triggers the avalanche."

"What's missing? Is there some vulnerability of Gardner's we're failing to target? A vote or a position he's taken that would get people riled up? Is there some issue we've overlooked?"

"I'm talking about the big picture, Martin."

"But it's about individual issues. It's all in the details. It's all the little pieces that go into creating the big picture. Am I completely off on this?"

"Yes and no. All of that's important and we've got most of that stuff covered. Everyone's done a great job. I'm not talking about individual issues. Or what's right or wrong or what's good for the country. What I'm talking about is kicking some ass. I'm talking about fire power. And that's something that's sorely lacking in this campaign. It doesn't matter how righteous your causes are. Nothing's going to happen. Nothing's going to change. Not without a big bang. The shot that's heard around the world. Something of biblical proportions."

"So what do we do? Fire power? Maybe I should ride around town in am M1A1 Abrams tank. Now *they* blow things up *real good!*"

Martin wondered if he should be joking around like this. Jamila looked slightly possessed tonight.

"Look. It's not so different than a war. But I'm not talking about violence literally, as in guerilla warfare or overthrowing the government. Even if we're talking about picking them off like a sniper. Even if we intend to take them out one at a time until the ranks of the corrupt motherfuckers are decimated and they're all wandering around a fucking desert wondering how they fell off the camel. But we don't use bullets. We use ballots."

"That's good! We should do something with that."

"What?"

"A new campaign motto: Join the revolution! We don't use bullets. We use ballots."

"You're losing it."

"I just meant ... I was giving you a compliment. I thought it was pretty cool."

"Well, I appreciate the nice sentiment. But I could come up with fifty of those a day. It still wouldn't get the job done."

"What job is that, Jamila? Usually I'm right in sync with you. But I'm not following you."

"Make you the big story. Have everybody talking. Make it so Martin Truth pushes Lindsay Lohan's puffy drug-addled puss right off the screen and *you* be the lead story. Tonight. Tomorrow night. Every night!"

"Maybe I need to check into rehab."

“Would you do that for me?”
“You know I would.”
It turned out that Jamila would get her wish.
Martin would indeed end up as the lead story.
But it wasn’t the result of their best laid plans.
He didn’t even have to check into rehab.

Chapter Seven

During a public outdoor appearance at Garden Station Park in downtown Dayton, someone tried to shoot Martin. The would-be assassin fired two rounds but was a lousy marksman.

The first missed him by several feet and tore a branch off a nearby tree.

The second was even further off the mark, but unfortunately found a target.

Jamila was more than a little busy these days and now rarely accompanied Martin on his campaign stumping. Today she happened along with the tempting promise of some decent barbecue. She was standing off to the side of the makeshift stage, next to a P.A. speaker stand, munching on a chicken wing. The second shot by Martin's would-be assassin grazed her left arm, inflicting a long flesh wound between her elbow and shoulder. It required fifteen stitches. She was very lucky. The bullet passed just a few inches from her heart.

The assailant was immediately apprehended by two policemen who were standing only a few yards away from the man as he fired his weapon, a Colt M1911 handgun.

Though the specifics of his agenda were a bit vague, it was obviously politically motivated. When interrogated by the police in custody, he replied through clenched teeth, with spittle lubricating the path of his venomous tirade, "I'm doing my patriotic duty. Just ridding this sorry fuckin' world of one more fascist, socialist, pinko, cocksucking piece of shit! When I get out of here I'm gonna finish the job. I'm gonna kill every last one of these evil motherfuckers! Just you wait."

Not exactly the best way to kick off a good defense when it went to trial.

His place on the extreme lunatic fringe of the right was further corroborated by his history. He belonged to a Michigan militia, an extreme paramilitary group who had for the past several years been on an intense search-and-destroy mission in preparation for the much-anticipated arrival of the anti-Christ.

His name was Walter Kurtz, though within the ranks of the militia itself he was known as General Gam. He was one of three high-ranking group leaders still at large, after its headquarters in Clayton, Michigan had recently been raided. The attack on Martin was at the tail end of a shooting spree which had been unfolding for two weeks along a trail from Clayton southward into Ohio. Police immediately identified him as the man who had shot up a bar in Toledo, emptied his entire clip into the façade of a post office in Findlay, blown out the cab windows of a FedEx truck near Wapakoneta, then randomly shot at passing cars from an overpass on the I-75 freeway thirty miles north of Dayton.

Obviously, Martin never got to finish his short address. At the time of the attack, no one seemed to be paying much attention anyway. People were stuffing their faces, kids were running around screaming, and easily within earshot on another stage, a rock band was doing a sound check. It was hardly the ideal conditions to try to charm someone into voting for you.

Of course, once the gunman got off a couple rounds, everybody perked up. They were all eyes and ears, even as they scrambled for cover. Nothing like a little gun violence to grab people's attention.

After Jamila was patched up and sent on her way from the emergency room at Miami Valley Hospital, Martin gave her a lift back to her apartment.

"Funny thing, I was just thinking the other day I could macho up my image a bit by dressing like a Navy Seal and bringing a gun to these campaign appearances. Maybe an Uzi or some other nice shiny assault weapon."

"To shoot yourself in the foot before you put it in your mouth?"

"I can always count on you for a vote of confidence."

"Martin, you were doing great today! It was unanimous."

"Unanimous?"

"Everyone listening to your speech was very impressed."

"How can you be so sure?"

"Because I was the only one listening."

• • •

They were at campaign headquarters.

Jamila was smiling ear-to-ear.

"You can't buy publicity like this! This is awesome!"

She had been scanning all of the national news sites — Yahoo News, MSNBC.com, CNN.com, Google News, Fox online, Huffington Post, ABC News, USAToday.com — when Martin walked into the office and couldn't help but hear her animated exclamations.

"What's up? Did Tom Cruise get back together with Katie Holmes?"

"You're a star, dude! Martin Truth is all over the internet. You're the lead bleed today."

"Okay. Just 'fess up. Did you hire this guy just to give my campaign a shot in the arm?"

"You are unbelievable! Have you been reading my email? The good news is that now that this loser is in custody, I won't have to pay him the other half. You know, the standard hit deal. 50% up front. 50% upon completion of said assignment."

"And just what was the assignment?"

"It sure the fuck wasn't to shoot *me*!"

"How's the arm?"

"The arm sucks but I'm diggin' the painkillers. But something very good has come out of this."

"What's that? If gangrene sets in, you'll be getting a 20% discount on a prosthetic arm?"

"Better than that. This has inspired an idea for a whole new promotional campaign."

"I don't think I want to hear this."

"Picture you standing at a podium, smiling, gesturing grandly. But superimposed over it are the crosshairs of a rifle. On the top of the poster it says: *Martin Truth For Congress*. Then at the bottom: *You don't have to put a gun to his head to get what you want.*"

"The scary thing is I think you might be serious."

"Okay okay. It probably needs some fine tuning. Maybe instead of crosshairs, someone should actually be standing right in front of you pointing a gun at your forehead. One of those big monster weapons they have in all of the action movies now!"

"Maybe you should cut back on the painkillers. Are you sure you're not working for Gardner?"

"You *have* been reading my email! So I suppose you know he's leaving his wife for me?"

All joking aside, Jamila was right about one thing. Martin was all over the news.

While often shorting substance for spectacle, a significant number of media outlets actually did a respectable job of reporting on his uphill battle, painting him not only as the victim of an attempted assassination, but as a come-from-behind third-party underdog, literally risking his life, to take on the big boys of politics. It was a made-for-modern-media story combining the sensationalism of gun violence and the high drama of soap opera, with the hard truths about contemporary political campaigns.

The best pieces included a short clip of Martin himself, videoed as he sat with Jamila in the emergency room right after the incident. It was an impromptu interview in a dramatic hospital setting with doctors bandaging up a gunshot victim. He milked it in grand style.

> *"We've been trying something new in my congressional campaign. It hasn't been seen in national politics in quite some time. It's called honesty. No double-speak. No obfuscation. We tell it like it is. And we guarantee to represent the constituents of this district, not a bunch of high-roller campaign donors or paid lobbyists. What can I say? We're doing what we can. Unfortunately, as one of my most dedicated campaign workers here will tell you [Jamila looked into the camera and gave her most charming if somewhat pained smile], sometimes you have to take a bullet for what you believe in."*

The response over the next week was staggering. Of course, both the media and television viewers are massively ADHD, so the wild whirlwind of attention would die off quickly as new Hollywood gossip, political scandals, natural disasters, airline hijackings, industrial explosions or nuclear meltdowns climbed aboard the runaway train of 24/7 news. Martin Truth would soon be archived.

But what a week it was while it lasted!

Martin had to cancel almost all of his scheduled appearances just to keep up with the constant requests for comments and updates. Even Al Jazeera did a feature story on him called, *American Politics, A Dangerous Business*.

There was no way to know accurately how any of this was playing out with the local voters. Polling was unreliable under the best of circumstances. Something like this might cause a huge spike of interest and what might appear to be real voter support, only to have it suddenly vanish, as people became distracted again by the ubiquitous campaign ads they were bombarded with on television and in the press by the other candidates. This was the truly Sisyphean challenge he faced by not having money. At least not having the kind of money that the two major-party candidates had. As election day approached, every media vehicle — especially commercial TV — was saturated by feel-good spots which, for all of the informational value they packed, could have just as easily been about some new feature-loaded automobile or miracle-producing hay fever medicine. Constantly seeing Gardner and Castiglia waving at adoring crowds, playing with their kids, walking their dogs, spending an afternoon in the park with their friends and families, and either going in or coming out of Sunday worship service, accompanied by soporific sloganeering and patriotic pit-a-pat, was a sure-fire way of bending minds and melting hearts. The Madison Avenue types who created these vapid but enormously appealing and subliminally persuasive 30-second sound-bite and sight-bite gems, didn't get paid the big bucks for nothing.

Even more significant and a huge negative was *not* seeing anything comparable on Martin, no minimum amount of videogenics which would keep his image fresh in everyone's mind, fix him in their consciousness as a real candidate, confer him legitimacy and name recognition.

But at least he had gotten his Andy Warhol 15-minutes of fame. And as Jamila pointed out, it was better than free. People might actually walk away from a good number of the news reports on the attempt to kill him, not only with some basic impression of Martin Truth the man, but hopefully a sense of his message, and the courage and integrity of his campaign.

America loves an underdog more that someone who just walks their dog.

America loves a martyr, even if the bullet missed.

When much of the hubbub had dwindled and life was almost back to normal, Martin, Jamila, Phyllis, all of them got one last big laugh. Bill had found something unusual and unexpected — to put it mildly — on the internet.

"You're not going to believe this! This is hysterical."

"Watcha got, Bill? Coffee beans that generate their own Nitrous Oxide?"

"You, Mr. Martin Truth, have your own fan club. A very special fan club."

They gathered around the big monitor in Phyllis's office. Bill typed in a URL.

"What are we looking at here?"

"Just wait, just wait. Trust me. It'll be worth it."

He hit enter and a new web page came up.

There it was. Martin's latest claim of notoriety.

Welcome to the Justin Bieber Fan Club
Fans of Martin Truth Page!

Jamila shrugged a comic shrug and smiled a daffy smile.

"There you go, dude! Like I was saying, you can't buy publicity like that! If you can just hang in there until these tweeners come of age ..."

• • •

Another day. Another dollar.

Even if the campaign was now in full swing and Martin was burning the candle at both ends and in the middle, he still had to show up for work.

"Good morning, Evelyn. You're looking exceptionally lovely today."

"Well thank you, Marty. It must be the cucumber aloe facial mask I've been using every night. Martin ... Mr. DeCorte would like to see you in his office."

Martin instantly got a sinking feeling. Perhaps it was his intrinsic discomfort with authority figures, a vestige of his adolescent years. More likely, it was his inherent distrust of "corporate" types, people whose fixation with making money always seemed at odds with his own humanistic, progressive world view. He assumed they were all Republicans, and anyone in the local corporatocracy probably buddies with Matt Gardner.

Conrad DeCorte was the founder, CEO, and majority shareholder in Future Perfect, Ltd. Martin had only talked to him once before. That was the day he interviewed for his job there. DeCorte was perhaps the least amiable person on the planet. Not arrogant or offensive, just intent and pathologically preoccupied. No one knew anything about his personal life. But if the guy had kids, they probably thought he was a deaf mute boarder in their upscale home.

He turned and headed over to DeCorte's door, only a few short strides away.

This was it. His throat tightened. Martin was positive he was getting the axe.

His first shock was when he stepped into the executive's office. It looked more like the hobby craft room of some homebound adolescent. There were hand-built scale models everywhere. On the shelves, on work tables, on the floor. Scale models of planes, boats, houses, forts, buildings, whole towns. In the center of what was probably supposed to be an executive desk, was a half-completed scale model of an oil drilling platform.

The second shock was the reception he got. DeCorte immediately stood up, came around the desk and went right over to Martin, who walked in assuming the worst. DeCorte wiped his hand on a rag, and extended it in a warm handshake.

"Martin Truth, come right in. It's a pleasure. Let me clear a spot so we can take a load off and talk a bit."

He moved some boxes from a Naugahyde couch sitting against one wall of the cluttered office, and they sat down.

"Martin, you've been with us for over six years now. You've never asked for a raise, never missed a day of work, and been perhaps the most dependable, solid employee we've ever had."

Wow! He noticed?

"We've, of course, known about your interest in politics. While we don't in principle agree with everything you stand for, there's an awful lot of common ground. An awful lot. Our use of only natural gas powered vehicles is not a PR stunt. My partners and I have a longstanding concern about the environment and share the belief that the way things are typically done is really mucking up the world's ecology."

Frankly, Martin *had* always pegged the eco-friendly trucks as just a PR stunt. But from what DeCorte was saying, it went much deeper. Maybe this should have been more apparent to Martin. It was certainly a huge capital expenditure to go with these vehicles, and they had done this from day one of the company.

"We don't want to lose you. At the same time, we know what this election means to you. And it looks like we almost lost you anyway on the wrong end of a handgun. To be blunt about it, it sure wouldn't hurt this town or this fucked-up country of ours, to have someone of your intelligence and integrity in office."

Martin wanted to pinch himself to make sure he wasn't dreaming. He liked what he was hearing, but at the same time, felt it was too soon to let down his guard.

"Here's what we've come up with. How long before this election thing is over? Six weeks? Two months? Anyway, we're definitely heading into the stretch, and if you're going to give asshole Gardner a run for it …"

Asshole Gardner? This guy is definitely not a Republican.

"… you've got to give your campaign *all* your time and energy. So here's what I'm proposing. I shouldn't just say 'I'm' because all three of us agree on this. You know, the three guys who own this dump. Effective tomorrow, you're on a paid leave-of-absence. We'll keep you at full pay right up until election day. If for any reason after the election you need to take some more time, we'll keep you on till the end of the year at half pay. And I don't mean to jinx your efforts to make it to Congress, but just in case you lose the election, your job will be here waiting for you. We'll hold it for you till, say, January. End of January."

Was it possible? Was this really happening? This was a gift from on high!

"I … I … I don't know what to say. I mean … thank you so much! This is unbelievable. What a—"

"Listen, Martin. It's okay if I call you Martin? I mean, we're not exactly bosom buddies. Anyway, we don't talk politics around here. It's too divisive. We have a company to run and I don't think it's a good mix. People get nuts when you get into any of that shit. But I can say personally and quite sincerely I've been disturbed for a long time, a *very* long time, about the direction of this country. If someone doesn't do something pretty soon, we're going to lose it all. America, I mean. We're already losing our democracy. Our economy is a shambles, people are at each others throats, everyone hiding from the bogeyman terrorists. Whoever's running the show has certainly got us where they want us.

A bunch of clueless, cowering idiots. So this is just our way of doing something about it. It's a small thing but it's what we can do."

"Mr. DeCorte, I can't thank you enough."

"Just do what you say you're going to do. Go get 'em, Martin Truth!"

• • •

Politics is certainly full of surprises. Sometimes things take a completely unexpected turn.

What started as a regular blog posting, earnestly made but made just in passing, ended up becoming a centerpiece for much of the rest of Martin's campaign.

At Jamila's urging, Martin had been writing a new personal editorial piece every week, which was then posted on martintruthforcongress.com/truthblogs. Sometimes they were casual and anecdotal, other times serious and a bit wonky. Jamila and Phyllis could view the site stats to see which ones were popular and got the most hits. They could also see how much time visitors to the site spent on various pages and individual postings, giving them some insight into what seemed to capture their interest, even excite them, and what on the other hand, turned out to be not very engaging.

Martin mixed it up pretty good. One week he would discuss a certain piece of legislation. The next he might tell the story of someone who lived in the area who had survived some catastrophe or was the victim of bureaucratic bungling. The human interest stories were by far the most read. Ranking at the top of the list was one where he talked about the trials of the prostitute he met at the sports bar. Without going into all of the details as to how he had met her, he offered her as an example of how the current system and the resulting wealth gap was leaving good decent people behind, driving them to desperate measures just to survive. There were over 100 comment replies, all of them sympathetic and supportive.

His latest piece was one of the more wonky ones. Martin didn't want his site to come off as a gossip column or a soap opera symposium, so he always balanced things out with this type of thought-provoking policy statement, outlining his official positions on critical matters facing the district and the nation, and offering his vision for the future. Doing so gave a clear and solid perspective on him as a candidate, and the kind of congressman he would be if elected to office. This particular posting turned out to be a watershed moment in the campaign.

Published a little less than three weeks after the televised debate, it was called *Retooling America For Peace*. In it, he lamented the state of the economy, the lack of good jobs, and was unambiguous in assigning the blame.

Retooling America For Peace – posted September 10, 2014

When we needed to fight World War II, in a matter of a few months we converted all of our factories — all of our nation's manufacturing capacity — to the war. We made guns, boats, and planes in order to defeat the enemy. Items for personal consumption and use were in short supply and rationed. The economy of America was a war economy.

When the war ended, with the Germans and Italians defeated in Europe, the Japanese defeated in the Pacific, we converted all of that industrial capacity back into making things for a better life. America was back on a peacetime economy. People made a good living and enjoyed all of the new comforts which American goods provided.

Our problem now is we are on a war economy again. We make lots of military stuff. But we don't make much else. Most of what we buy for our personal use is made in China, Vietnam, Malaysia, even Mexico. What do we make anymore?

Now think about it. We are on a war economy, and …

THERE IS NO WAR!

Sure, there's the "War on Terror". But the terrorists are a bunch of disorganized ragtag crazies, not divisions of well-trained, well-equipped troops with the huge industrial might of a Germany or a Japan behind them.

Ask yourself <u>this</u>:

Why is half of our entire federal budget
spent on the military?

Then ask yourself <u>this</u>:

What if we put that to better use by retooling
this country to make things again?
To put people back to work?

Back in 1989 when the Berlin Wall came down, followed by the collapse of the Soviet Union in 1991, we were told a new era had begun. The Cold War was over, they said. Now we can finally scale back our military. We'll save all that money we've been spending to fight the Evil Empire of the Russians. Our national leaders dubbed it the "peace dividend".

Well, the peace dividend never happened. In fact, we spend more on the military now then we did back then! If you add up <u>all</u> of the money that we actually spend on both offensive weapons and defending the homeland — which includes the bloated budget of the Department of Homeland Security, special allocations for the State Department and USAID, nuclear weapons expenditures by the Department of Energy, the top secret budgets of the NSA, CIA and numberless other new counter-espionage organizations — plus the ongoing wars in Afghanistan, Iraq (yes we're still spending trainloads of money there), Libya, Yemen, Syria, and countless other hotspots which don't even get into the news, it comes to over a trillion dollars. That's a TRILLION DOLLARS <u>every year</u>!

Do you know that the Pentagon has a slush fund of $83 billion dollars unobligated cash sitting around in case they need it? That's a lot of mad money, if you ask me.

Where is all this money going? For what? Is there a war? I don't see a war.

If you took half of that, meaning $500 billion, and simply hired people, that would put well over 14,000,000 Americans back to work at an annual salary of $35,000!

The unemployment problem in this country would be instantly solved!

Now I'm not suggesting that the government just create out of thin air and hand out 14 million jobs — though the idea actually has some appeal.

But I am saying it's time we stop wasting so much money fighting wars that aren't happening, fighting enemies that don't exist, and keeping this country on a war economy just to line the pockets of the military contractors. You know who they are. Raytheon, Lockheed Martin, Northrop Grumman, General Dynamics, Boeing, BAE Systems. For a complete list just look at the list of corporations who make enormous contributions to the campaign of my opponent, Congressman Matt Gardner. I say we take all this money for making bombs and invest it in America, modernize our factories, support research and development of peacetime products, and create a viable American economy that makes things again.

When we needed to fight World War II, we retooled America for war.

I say it's time to retool America for peace.

— Martin Truth, Candidate for U.S. Congress

Perhaps still smarting from the humiliation Martin inflicted on him at the televised debate, Congressman Gardner decided to reply to Martin's blog the following Sunday via an editorial in the Dayton Daily News. This was, of course, foolish on two counts. First it drew attention to both Martin and *Retooling America For Peace*, a policy statement which might have on its own only been viewed by a handful of people, many of whom wouldn't even have finished reading it. Second, it came off as whiny and vindictive, as if Gardner was taking a break from licking his wounds to try to bitch slap Martin, rather than add something constructive to a legitimate debate of the issues.

In any case, Gardner staked out his position in predictable fashion:

Defending America Can't Be Entrusted
To Armchair Idealists
(An Exclusive Daily News Editorial Essay)
by Congressman Matt Gardner

> Beware of the false prophets of peace! Beware of the pretend patriots and armchair generals! Beware of the little boys in sandals with peace signs painted on their foreheads who get their understanding of politics from Jon Stewart on the Comedy Channel!
>
> I recently read an essay on the internet which would have gotten a failing grade in any high school civics class, written by a third-party (third-rate) candidate for my congressional seat, Martin Truth. I am taking the time to talk about this, not because anyone takes Mr. Truth or his candidacy seriously, but because his ideas, while appearing noble and innocent, are in fact dangerous, if not treasonous.
>
> Right off, the guy insults America by saying we don't make anything here anymore, except military weapons. I guess he and his hippie friends never need to buy shampoo or tooth paste. Funny thing, when I take my family to the Dayton Mall, we come back with a carload of stuff made right here in the greatest country in the world.
>
> Then right on cue, with his friends gathered in a drum circle behind him, he goes on with time-worn and tedious "beat swords into ploughshares" cheerleading.
>
> Well, I have news for this naïve and misguided charlatan and everyone else who buys into this hug-thine-enemy nonsense and turn-the-other-cheek peace-and-love rhetoric. First, the world is a dangerous place. There are many ignorant, fanatic fools on this planet, people who reproduce like rabbits, truly don't know what a day's work is, but hate us because we have so much. These envious wannabes hate us because we do work hard and

> have built the greatest nation in the history of the world, a society with everything a person could possibly want.
>
> Second, we happen to have the largest and most productive economy in the world! So we can do both. We are America. We can have our cake and eat it too. We can build bombs and fighter aircraft and keep America strong. And we can manufacture all of the things we have come to accept as part of the great American Way of Life. Cars, boats, televisions, smart phones — why even shampoo and tooth paste.

Ignoring the increased casualties in Afghanistan from individual attacks on American soldiers and shelling of the military bases themselves, plus the recent spate of anti-American riots throughout the world which included both killing of American citizens and bombing of numerous U.S. embassies, Gardner went on to say:

> In case Martin Truth and those who think like him hadn't noticed between hits on their bongs, free love orgies, and dancing in the street, since 911 there hasn't been a single successful attack on the United States of America. That's what a strong America is about.
>
> Wishful thinking and 'visualizing world peace' will not keep America safe. Perhaps in Martin Truth's world, where people still fight with swords and till the soil with ploughshares, his storybook fantasies might work. But we don't use ploughshares anymore. We use big sturdy agricultural equipment manufactured by excellent industrial firms like International Harvester right here in Ohio. And swords went out with King Arthur. Now we have the most sophisticated weaponry known to mankind. America has satellites, smart bombs, cruise missiles, fighter jets, and unmanned drones like the amazing and advanced ones being developed and tested at our Air Force facilities right here in Dayton.
>
> I am committed to keeping America safe. To keeping America strong. To keeping America safe by keeping America strong, and not pretty-please pretending the enemies of our great democracy and our way of life will just go away.
>
> I am committed to spending the next two years as your congressman, to protecting the American Way of Life, keeping the American Dream safe from its vicious enemies, who threaten it both from without and from within.
>
> — Rep. Matthew Gardner, Ohio 3rd District, United States Congress

Powerful stuff. The kind of gut-level appeal that had gotten the man elected over and over.

But as a result of a tragic event which no one could have possibly predicted, his singling out with great pride the unmanned drones being developed and tested at Wright-Patterson AFB turned out to be a very unfortunate choice.

• • •

They were just beginning the flight testing of a new domestic surveillance drone. It wasn't a big craft but was very agile and carried twelve gallons of aviation fuel. It had been in the air only ten minutes.

Now panic filled the control room.

Drone Pilot: "Shit. We've lost it."

Flight Safety Commander: "What's going on here?"

Software Systems Engineer: "We've lost control of the craft, sir."

Project Manager: "Have we got a comm link?"

Communications Engineer: "We've got a clean pingback. It's not the link."

Flight Safety Commander: "Are we getting nav data?"

Software Systems Engineer: "Not a byte. Nothing's getting in or out."

Project Manager: "It looks like the onboard processor locked up. We got no data. No control. But we're tracking it on radar."

Flight Safety Commander: "I say we shoot the fucker down."

Project Manager: "That's pretty risky. Besides, can we scramble that fast?"

Software Systems Engineer: "What happened to the backup processor? It should have automatically kicked over. It has a basic command set embedded in the firmware. At least we could have landed the bird."

Communications Engineer: "No way to know. It's not telling us anything."

Flight Safety Commander: "Where is this flying turd right now?"

Drone Pilot: “Radar has it heading due north. It’s out in farm country right now. But it’s got enough fuel to keep going for another eleven hours.”

Project Manager: “It’s barns and cows all the way to the Michigan border.”

Two minutes later, it became apparent the drone was not going to Michigan. As if it had a mind of its own, it banked into a slow turn and reversed its direction by almost exactly 180°.

Just after re-entering the edge of Dayton’s northernmost suburbs, the pilotless aircraft began acting very strangely. It dipped, then climbed, banked left, then right, then left again. Abruptly it accelerated, then slowed to near stall speed. Suddenly it picked up speed again and was now in the airspace of Dayton International Airport. Air Traffic Control had been alerted and all flights were temporarily suspended. It continued flying erratically as it headed toward the northern suburb of Vandalia.

Vandalia was a rather non-descript, middle-class community of a little over 12,000 people. It boasted three elementary schools, two middle schools, and one high school.

Murlin Heights Elementary School sat in the midst of grassy lawns just north of beautiful Dayton Memorial Park. West of the school’s courtyard was a recreation area with swings, two slides, a teeter-totter, monkey bars, plus a large paved zone for kickball, tag, and general frolicking.

Lunch recess had just finished when the drone crashed into the school grounds. All of the children were back in the school building on their way to their homeroom classes.

Except one.

Jessica Meyers had left her backpack at the foot of the monkey bars and had rushed back outside to retrieve it.

She never heard it or saw it coming. The drone had less than a minute before gone nose up into a steep climb, stalled, started to tumble back to earth, then inexplicably cut its engine, and dove nose first. By the time it hit the ground, it was doing over 250 mph.

The drone exploded when it impacted the ground only ten feet from little Jessica. She was immediately enveloped in the fireball that resulted from gallons of aviation fuel being set ablaze. The entire surface of her body was burned and she died only hours after being rushed to the hospital.

The death of eight-year-old Jessica Meyers instantly became the main story across the entire nation. Every television channel, internet news site, radio talk show, print and digital news source was filled 24/7 with interviews, commentary, video clips, and sound bites which captured the grief all of America was feeling.

The President went on TV and made a short but powerful address to the nation. He looked close to tears as he talked about his own children and how when he heard about Jessica, he felt like he had lost one of his own daughters.

But then he closed his address with a gross misrepresentation and a puerile pandering to patriotism.

> *"While it in no way mitigates the enormous grief we are now feeling as a people, nor justifies the loss of an innocent life, let us understand that this is the price we too often pay in the ongoing War on Terror — a deplorable, heartbreaking price in this case — in order to defeat savage fanatics who have no hesitation taking precious innocent lives, like those of Jessica. We must all of us devote ourselves to vanquishing this enemy, redoubling our every effort to fight the bloodthirsty extremists in the world who are determined to destroy the American Way of Life. We owe it to ourselves. We owe it to little Jessica Meyers."*

Not that he expected anyone to notice, Martin immediately issued a statement.

"On The Tragic Death of Jessica Meyers"
This transmission is from the Campaign Headquarters
of Martin Truth for Congress – Ohio 3rd Congressional
District, and is for immediate publication.

> Our sorrow, our lamentations, our prayers go out to the family of Jessica Meyers, whose short life ended in a horrifying tragedy which defies all comprehension and denies any justification.
>
> It is painful beyond words to consider the loss of this innocent, young girl. Jessica Meyers died in an incident so random, yet so predictable, given what dangerous times we live in.
>
> That's all we can manage to say right now. That's all any of us in our shared grief can say right now.

Three days later, however, Martin did have more to say — a lot more.

Posted on martintruthforcongress.com, issued as a press release, videotaped and posted on You Tube, forwarded to every media outlet, news corporation, press site, public blog, letters to the editor, public opinion forum, and even printed the old fashioned way on hundreds of fliers, it was an incendiary editorial essay expressing his total outrage over the tragedy and the spin that had been put on it:

Little Jessica Meyers Did Not Have To Die
by Martin Truth, Candidate for U.S. Congress,
State of Ohio – 3rd Congressional District

> I need to take issue with what the President said the other night on national TV.

This is not to politicize this painful tragedy. The President has already done this. I only write this because my conscience demands that the truth be brought to light.

The President claimed that Jessica was a victim of the War on Terror. This is a boldface lie. She was a victim of the war on us. Yes, *us*. You and I.

It was glossed over by the major media reports of the incident. But the pilotless drone being tested at Wright-Patterson AFB was not a drone for use on the battlefield, or in any of the theaters of operation where we have established a military presence — Afghanistan, Iraq, Yemen, Libya, Syria, anywhere in the Middle East, or our bases in Europe, Australia, South Korea, Japan, Taiwan. This drone was a domestic reconnaissance plane. Let me repeat that: a *domestic* reconnaissance aircraft, to be flown over America.

In straight talk, a domestic reconnaissance aircraft is for spying on Americans. Let me be clear: This drone is being developed for spying on *you* and *I*.

The militarization of this country is out of control. The military in conjunction with and as directed by the Commander-In-Chief of our armed services — meaning the President of the United States — is running amok! *That's* what little Jessica Meyers is a casualty of.

Ask yourself this: With reconnaissance drones like the one that killed this poor little girl, designed not for battlefields or for fighting terrorists in the War on Terror (as the President disingenuously claimed), but for spying on U.S. citizens right here on U.S. soil, who are *they* protecting *us* from?

And who will protect us from *them*?

When our government decides it must listen to our phone calls, read our email, and keep track of our every movement with Big Brother domestic surveillance drones, all of which is currently being done in the name of 'fighting terrorism', this is not an America I recognize anymore.

I am sad and insulted that the President would use the horrible and tragic events surrounding the death of little Jessica Meyers to promote a lie to the American people. We deserve better.

Jessica Meyers did not have to die. The development, testing and deployment of military equipment for the sole purpose of spying on American citizens is both against the time-honored

> traditions and values of our country, and in direct conflict with the clear intent and language of our Constitution. Such a drone is *illegal* and should have never been built, much less flown on that fateful day.
>
> Jessica Meyers did *not* have to die.
>
> Jessica Meyers should *not* have died.
>
> That drone was *not* for the War on Terror.
>
> That drone was for a war on American citizens.
>
> Little Jessica Meyers was killed by military madness.
>
> We deserve better. We want an America we can recognize.
>
> Let's truly honor the memory of Jessica, and all of the soldiers who have died in the struggle to defend our country. Let's work together to restore democracy and rule of law to our great nation.
>
> Let's start now before we all end up like little Jessica Meyers.
>
> Let's reclaim in her name the free and democratic America little Jessica Meyers should have grown up in.
>
> May her precious and innocent soul rest in peace.

When Martin read it to the campaign staff, there was unanimous agreement on two things: First, this editorial essay could turn out to be political suicide. And second, it *had* to go out. Campaigning and winning elections be damned. It said what had to be said.

"Martin, this is both brilliant and courageous."

"The gloves are off. Gardner's either going to shit his pants or have you assassinated."

"Probably both."

"I hear Guantanamo is lovely this time of year."

Everyone dug in and for the next 24 hours they sent it everywhere it could be sent.

Then they waited.

They didn't have to wait long.

Among those media outlets which were part of their blitz were OpEdNews, Truthout, Buzzflash, The Nation, Truthdig, Counterpunch, and a host of other progressive publications. These not only published it but made it a featured article. As a result, news aggregators picked up on it. Huffington Post gave it a prominent spot on its main page. So did Aljazeera English Edition. Soon it was everywhere: CNN, Great Britain's The Guardian, BBC.com, even the Washington Post, New York Times, Wall Street Journal, and Financial Times.

Within only 48 hours, they had their answer. It was obvious they had done the right thing. With the predictable exception of the extreme right wing wackjobs like Rush Limbaugh and Bill O'Reilly, the response was overwhelmingly positive.

Suddenly, the phone at Martin Truth For Congress was again ringing off the hook. The two incoming land lines were proving inadequate by a factor of ten. Local news stations sent crews to their office for on-the-scene coverage of the man who had all America talking. Even NPR wanted Martin to participate in a national "audio roundtable", bringing in experts from think tanks, universities, and of course, the R&D sector of the Air Force who oversaw drone design and development.

Martin couldn't keep up with all of the requests for interviews and additional comment. Rather than spread himself too thin and risk muddying his message, he stuck closely to a brief but hard-hitting prepared statement:

> *"The facts speak for themselves. While the security of this nation is paramount, the authority to protect American citizens is being turned against them. We need to ask some vital questions about what is going on with our democracy — why our cherished freedoms are under assault. Ask the tough questions of your elected representatives. Demand some real answers, not politically correct mumbo-jumbo. Then reply by voting responsibly in the upcoming election. What have we learned from this heartbreaking incident? It's simple. We don't need more eavesdropping, wiretaps, cameras, operatives, drones. What we need is to stop wasting money of all of this onerous and illegal junk, and start putting people back to work. We need to stop constantly talking about war and start talking about how we can create a more peaceful world. Most of all, we need to prevent horrible tragedies like the death of little Jessica Meyers and restore an America where it's safe to be in a school playground."*

Even taking Martin out of the equation, it was blatantly obvious that Gardner's chest-thumping reference to drone development at Wright-Patterson had backfired in a big way. He saved what face he could with a carefully crafted public statement.

PRESS RELEASE: From the Office of Matt Gardner
U.S. Congressman – State of Ohio 3rd Congressional District

> While I am profoundly saddened by the death of eight-year-old Jessica Meyers, our shared grief also demands decisive action. As a sitting member of the House of Representatives Armed Services and Homeland Security committees, I will recommend that Congress initiate a full investigation into what happened in this fateful incident. We will determine if safety procedures

> were properly in place and faithfully executed. We will leave no stone unturned and accept no excuses. If the individuals conducting the test flight of the aircraft were responsible for its failure, they will be held accountable. Moreover, to prevent such a tragic event from ever occurring in the future, we will determine if sufficient and appropriate safeguards are properly configured and fully operative. As your congressman, it is my duty to do everything in my power to make this district a comfortable and safe community for you and your family.

Vis-à-vis the media coup that resulted from Martin's audacious and assertive condemnation of domestic drone development, Gardner's investigative initiative seemed paltry and apologetic. It was received with wary reserve.

At least for the present, Martin had struck a serious blow to Matt Gardner and put him on the defensive.

But the harsh reality was that this close to an election, advantage can be gained and lost in just a matter of hours. Overall, it was impossible to say where things really stood. The public had a frustratingly short attention span and sometimes seemed to suffer from total amnesia. Martin had without question benefited from a lot of publicity the last two months. It had been a mixed bag, some things a reflection of his competence and doggedness as a campaigner, others purely serendipitous.

He obviously had worked hard to do well in the televised debate. Whatever good came out of his victory was deserved. Subsequently, Martin had drawn tasteless and ill-conceived criticism from Gardner for his *Retooling America For Peace*, which in the end translated into more legitimately earned recognition.

But the attempt to assassinate him and the crash of a malfunctioning drone were unforeseen and unwelcome events which had ultimately also strengthened his hand. Martin felt guilty that the death of Jessica Meyers ended up playing to his advantage. It was a cruel and fateful twist in the already serpentine road of his campaign. At the same time, he *did* say what needed to be said. He exposed exactly what that drone was designed to do, how it equated to the wanton and illegal assault on the constitutional rights of Americans, and how in a tragic way the loss of a young girl's life was symbolic of the loss of much of what had made America a great country. Martin brought to light the frivolous and dangerous direction the militarization of the country was taking us. Regardless of how he did in the election, perhaps some good would come of it. Certainly he could hope. It was not hyperbole anymore to suggest lives were at stake. Or that democracy itself was on the line.

Even so, politics for too long to remember had become but another entertainment sport in the three-ring circus of main stream media. The pundit clowns and smarmy bubble heads were as remorseless as they were heavy-handed at reducing the most profound contest of ideas into churlish cat fights, at pandering to the public's ravenous appetite for scandal and innuendo, at demoting both the message and the messenger to the ranks of reality show narratives and laugh-track enhanced sitcoms, at turning every contest for public office into either petty soap opera or bloodlust cage fighting.

This was the reality within which the electoral process now took place.

As the month of September closed, the ringing of the phone lines at campaign headquarters returned to a more normal level, a desultory pace which offered not much encouragement.

Entering the crucial final weeks, the Martin Truth For Congress campaign was flying blind. Operating in a total vacuum. Polls, particularly at a local level, were notoriously inaccurate. Besides, Martin's campaign couldn't afford the time or money to do polling right now anyway. Any questions about his popularity, his perceived viability as a candidate, even his name recognition, would have to wait. They had a strategy mapped out. As far as they could tell, it was a sound strategy. Even that was a moot point. At this late stage, it was their only strategy. Their only shot.

This was it.

Hammer time.

Chapter Eight

It was the first week of October. Time to throw down the gauntlet with Gardner.

One month was perfect. It gave him enough time to make a considered response. He really couldn't make the excuse that it was too late in the game, claiming that this was some 11th-hour attempt to ambush him. At the same time, one month was not enough time for him to mount a very sophisticated counter campaign. Nor was it likely that the matter would dissipate on its own or be swallowed up in other election news developments. In fact, if things went well, the controversy they hoped to generate should be peaking right about the time voters were heading for the polls.

The petitions had been collected and the formal pledges prepared. Petitioning had gone better than expected, largely due to Lincoln's excellent organizational talents and his formidable skills at inspiring the students at University of Dayton to get involved. Inclusive of all four petitions, in excess of 90,500 signatures had been gathered. The petitions to bring home the troops from Afghanistan and for leaving Social Security and Medicare alone were the big winners, both in excess of 28,000. But the ones for increased taxation on the wealthy, and for increasing the minimum wage, each still came in at a respectable 17,000 plus. Slightly over 23,000 people signed two or more petitions. 10,656 signed all four!

Gardner was holding a big public rally on Friday evening. It was expected to draw about 600 people, the vast majority of which were his hard-core supporters. The occasion was for him to express his appreciation for the hard work they had all done on his behalf, give them a pep talk, fire them up and urge them to keep pushing right till the polls opened on election day. Gardner was a smart campaigner. Though he had won the last five elections and according to local news commentators had a very comfortable lead, he wasn't taking any chances. Or maybe he wanted to mount an even more impressive landslide than his last triumphant victory.

The press would certainly be there. If executed properly, this would be the ideal situation to confront him with the petitions and the four pledges.

Lincoln would have loved to do the confrontation himself. But there was some tiny but measurable risk that someone might connect him to Martin's campaign. This was far too important to take that chance.

Lincoln was faculty advisor to a grad student at U of D, a young man who he greatly respected and had been a key participant in the petition drive. His name was Gareth Tamblin, but everyone just called him Gary. Lincoln was sure he was perfect for the job.

Beyond his enormous intelligence, the guy was charming, funny, fearless and unflappable. He loved putting people on and thrived in situations where a lesser person would fold and run.

Gary was deeply committed to the cause as well. Lincoln had such a close relationship with him that under an oath of absolute secrecy he explained exactly what the pledge strategy was about and what they intended to accomplish. Gary was a raging progressive, a devoted environmentalist, and always eager to participate in anything which would challenge the existing order, which he loudly condemned as corrupt and loathsome. If the pledges would oust Gardner and make it possible for Martin to grab the congressional seat, Gary would do just about anything to get the job done.

The rally went pretty much as expected. Speakers droned on, spouting rah-rahs and vapid adulation. Gardner sat dead center on the stage, his chalky marshmallow-white smile never letting up, taking in all the praise like a giant ego sponge. Each speaker was introduced by a short, rotund master of ceremonies, Mike Finch. He had nerdy horn-rimmed glasses, a pumpkin-shaped head, sported a canvas top hat with *Gardner For Ohio* on the lamé hatband, and wore a short-sleeve white shirt with big perspiration stains spreading from his armpits, cinched under his two-and-a-half chins with a crooked red bow tie. His dull gray dress slacks were belted up just below his nipples, making quite a show of his plaid socks and black wingtips. He could've passed for the road manager of a Dixieland band.

Gary edged to the far end of the raised stage and waited for his opportunity. A plump middle-aged lady who looked frighteningly like a rooster was just finishing up her remarks. She had been gushing about what a great family man and personification of Christian values Matt Gardner was and how Ohio could do no better than send him back to DC for two more years. After her last shrill blast of adoration, she turned around and waddled over to the candidate to receive a big hug for a job well done. Gary jumped onto the stage and headed for the microphone.

Everyone on the dais was focused on rooster lady, but as she made her way to the side of the stage to exit, they suddenly heard Gary's voice confidently booming out over the P.A.

"Thanks, Mike. I'll just introduce myself. I'm Gareth Tamblin from the Committee on Public Policy Preferences. We just go by CPPP to make it easier."

Mike Finch, the MC, immediately appeared confused. This didn't seem right. He checked his speakers list to see if he had made a mistake. But Gary had such poise and total command of the podium, at least for the moment he dispelled any suspicions that he was not part of the program. He smiled with an almost giddy effervescence, gave a pleasant reassuring nod and two big thumbs up to both Mike and Congressman Gardner, then continued.

"Over the past three months, we have canvassed the entire Ohio 3rd Congressional District. We wanted to know how the voters felt about certain key issues, matters which have come up before the very legislative body that our fine congressman here has dedicated almost ten years of his life serving. Let me tell you, Congressman Gardner, distinguished guests, and all of you who have been so kind as to show up here tonight, we found so much *enthusiasm* among the voting public. As we went door to door, people weren't too busy. No! They didn't brush us off. Not at all! In fact, they welcomed the opportunity to speak out, to sign on the dotted line, so to speak, and to be heard. What a great country! What a great state this is! Ohio! Yes!"

The crowd yelled and cheered. They probably had no idea what they were cheering about. But Gary had such an infectious and exhilarating manner of speaking, it spread like fire through the audience, which up till now had been subjected to generous helpings of tedium.

For dramatic effect, Gary now turned around to Gardner. He took the microphone out of the mic holder and walked directly toward the congressman, smiling and continuing to speak as he gradually closed in on him. Gardner was beginning to grow suspicious and his stock-in-trade grin was looking a little strained. He sensed that something was off, perhaps getting an inkling that this might not be on the approved agenda for the evening's festivities.

Rather than be at a height disadvantage, he stood up to be eyeball-to-eyeball with whoever this young man was.

Gary was now toe-to-toe with Gardner, radiating excitement and dripping with sincerity.

"We at CPPP know you'll be proud to be part of our effort to restore true representative democracy to America. Now what we have here are two separate items. We have petitions and we have pledges. I couldn't carry the petitions with me because there were so many. But suffice it to say, we will be happy to show you each and every one of the 90,636 signatures. What I do have with me is these."

He held up the four pledges.

By now it was becoming evident to master of ceremonies Mike, that indeed, Gary was not supposed to be there. He appeared flustered and unsure of what to do.

Gary just charged ahead on the runaway train of good vibes he was engineering.

"Mr. Gardner, this is such a rare treat. I've never been so close to a person of national prominence, someone who is a vital part of making America run. Let's hear it for our congressman! Come on!" The crowd erupted in rowdy applause. "Congressman Gardner, sir, there are four pledges here for *your personal signature*."

Gary made a big show of pointing at the pledges for the audience, and miming someone signing them.

"I think you should know, Congressman Gardner, these pledges reflect the overwhelming majority of opinion here in our district. There is one on bringing home our troops from Afghanistan…" That instantly provoked a deafening roar of approval from the audience. "There's another for making the wealthy in this country pay their fair share in taxes…" An equally impressive outburst of cheering. "This one is for raising the federal minimum wage, which I'm sure would help a lot of folks here tonight…" A huge surge of yelling and clapping by the youthful crowd! "And lastly, this pledge is on Social Security and Medicare, two of the most successful government programs in our history. Most people are saying they don't want our wonderful Congress messing with them. That's it!" He waved the pledges in the air and the crowd cheered like the home team had just scored the winning touchdown.

Mike had finally gathered his wits enough figure out that since Gary was indeed an intruder, he needed to swing into action. He rushed toward the center of the stage, pulling by the arm a private security guard who had been standing nearby. Mike was determined. If this character with the microphone wouldn't leave peacefully, then necessary force would be applied.

As soon as Gary finished describing the pledges, he stuck the microphone in Gardner's face and stood there smiling. The confrontation had now become a smile-off, the difference being that Gary was thoroughly and sincerely enjoying every second of this, and Gardner was just buying time as he tried to size up the bold, impetuous young man standing so cocksure and mockingly, directly in front of him.

Before Gardner could reply, Mike and the rent-a-cop had closed in. Mike started to make threats, pushing the befuddled rent-a-cop toward Gary.

But then an amazing thing happened.

Gardner leaned away from the mic and said something to Mike, apparently suggesting he and the rent-a-cop back away, that the situation was under control, and he would handle it. With Mike still looking warily at Gary, they edged their way a few feet behind the seated row of distinguished guests, but remained ready to intervene in case they were needed.

Gardner then turned back to Gary and spoke clearly into the microphone.

"So young man. What did you say your name was?"

"Gareth Tamblin, sir."

"I can see you're passionate about this. I admire that. And whatever it is you've got in your hands probably represents a lot of hard work."

"Yes. You're absolutely correct, Congressman Gardner. Gathering 90,636 signatures on the petitions alone involved hundreds of volunteers and several thousand person-hours."

"Person-hours. Not man-hours. That's good. I like that."

"It's politically correct, sir."

"I'll tell you what, my boy. I promise to look these over and if they are in order and are as laudable as you claim they are, I will be happy to sign them."

Gardner waved to the audience. They responded with a booming yell of approval.

"You have 24 hours."

"Excuse me! What did you just say?"

"Congressman Gardner … sir. I said you have 24 hours."

A look of rage suddenly replaced Gardner's faux-amicability and plaster-of-Paris charm. He forcefully grabbed the microphone and held it away so it wouldn't pick up what he was about to say. But it still did.

"*You* are giving *me* an ultimatum? Just who in the hell do you—"

Gary theatrically pointed at his watch.

"24 hours. Starting right now. Have a nice day."

And he was gone.

• • •

The next day came and went.

Then another. And another.

Lincoln was beside himself with excitement and anticipation. He was so hyper, he had trouble dialing the phone.

"Congressman Matt Gardner For A Strong America."

"Is Mr. Gardner available?"

"Congressman Gardner is in a meeting. What does this concern?"

"This is the CPPP, a citizens organization. Three days ago we presented Mr. Gardner with some time-sensitive documents for his signature. We're still waiting to hear back from him."

"One moment please."

It was probably only thirty seconds but to Lincoln it seemed like an eternity.

Suddenly a voice came on the line. Lincoln almost fainted. It was Gardner himself.

"Is this about the pledges?"

"Yes, Congressman. We need an answer."

"You need an answer? Here's my answer. GO FUCK YOURSELF!"

Click.

• • •

An emergency meeting was convened for 7:00 pm that evening. Everyone would be there.

It was only 6:45 but Phyllis, Lincoln, Bill, Imogene, Bob and Helen were already in place. As usual Helen sat with her note pad and a digital mini-recorder in front of her in order to transcribe what was said. Bill had brought some of his best dark roast Sumatra coffee from the café and was pouring cups for his fellow caffeine addicts.

Martin walked in. A lively discussion was already in progress.

"He really said that."

"Yes. 'Go fuck yourself!' Quote and unquote."

"What a charmer."

"What an asshole!"

"No surprise there."

"Can we use that? I mean, he *did* say it."

"Let's put a photo of him on the web with 'Go fuck yourself!' above his head in one of those cartoon balloons!"

They were so boisterous it was more like free beer night at the bowling alley.

Lincoln restored some semblance of order.

"Okay okay. We shouldn't have too much fun with this. I think we can safely say I have on record that he's not going to sign the pledges. Now we have some serious work to do."

Right then Jamila arrived. She had earlier in the day already talked to Lincoln and was smiling ear-to-ear her trademark confident smile with a touch of sinister charm.

She was beautifully scary.

"Oh yeah, baby! I'm digging this!"

Martin's excitement also had him in a playful mood.

"Good evening to you too, Lady Parks. And how was your day?"

"Fucking fantastic! Time to hit the streets, my man. Let's pulverize that jerk!"

Despite experiencing five months of it, Phyllis still tended to recoil at Jamila's bluntness. But after a microsecond of hesitation, she got down to business.

"I know we've covered this before. But now it's on us and I just want to be absolutely clear. What's next?"

"We tell the world!"

"How?"

"Like I said before. All the stuff that works."

"I'm sure I don't have to remind anyone that we have some serious limitations. Meaning we don't have a million bucks to throw at TV ads."

"Understood. And yes, that will just slow us down a bit. But I think if we play our cards right, we can get a lot of free media coverage. Like I said before, there's all the usual stuff. Put your cyber-nerds to work. We've got Facebook, Twitter, Tumblr, Reddit, Digg, Pinterest, Delicious. You probably think we shouldn't quote Gardner. But in terms of the internet, trust me, *'Go fuck yourself!'* is pretty tame stuff. And it *is* an attention grabber! I say we build our social networks campaign around it. It could go viral, especially considering what a upright-johnny the guy supposedly is, with his bogus family values pitch and those horseshit ads of him going to church every Sunday. Trust me, it'll get around. People love seeing the high-and-mighty make hypocritical asses of themselves."

Phyllis still looked skeptical.

"By far the majority of the people we need to reach are not on the internet all that much. Most voters are not that computer savvy. Sure, everyone has email. But Facebook and Twitter? They definitely don't sit around surfing for videos on YouTube."

"That's just getting started. That's the easy stuff. There's a lot of ways to go. I need your help here on this. This is your playground. You guys live here. I don't know all the ins and outs. But I do know that in every community, there are little grapevines — news letters, bulletin boards, buyers-sellers-traders weeklies. There's always a way to get things on the news. It's all about properly framing it. Putting it in context. Either as a human interest story, which is a great way to go, or getting people to laugh. That's sure fire!"

"What does *that* mean? I'm not sure what we're talking about here."

Phyllis looked unusually tired today. She had not slept well since the confrontation with Gardner. On the surface, it came off better than anyone had expected. Apparently the crowd had shown a great deal of excitement about the pledges. And Gardner was caught off guard and totally lost his cool when Lincoln's plucky young grad student so insolently slapped him with the 24-hour ultimatum. At the same time, Phyllis was relying on second-hand reports, since she obviously couldn't be there. She still wasn't completely convinced it had come off as a clean victory. She wasn't confident they really had the upper hand. They'd certainly look foolish if they made a big deal out of his refusing to sign the pledges and nobody cared. It was *so* difficult getting people to pay attention these days. To anything!

She took a minute to gather her thoughts. Everyone there, including Jamila, had enormous respect for Phyllis. They recognized that she was the solid voice of reason in all these discussions. Perhaps she tended at times to be a little too cautious. But her method balanced the madness that sometimes ensued when enthusiasm got the better of common sense.

Phyllis looked up and glanced at each of them as she spoke.

"Actually, let me take that back. I completely get what you're talking about. I'm just apprehensive. This has to work or we end up with a lot of egg on our face. It's like telling a great joke poorly. No one laughs and everyone thinks you're an idiot for trying to tell it. This whole approach is untested. Which doesn't mean it won't work. But it does mean that we *have* to pull this off. There's no room for error. Am I making any sense here?"

Jamila nodded enthusiastically, obviously in total agreement.

"Absolutely! That goes for anything that's worth doing. Getting Martin Truth elected is something we definitely have to pull off. Otherwise, what are we all doing here?"

"No. I think there's more at stake here. We're way outside the box with this pledge strategy. If we don't pull it off, the vultures will come after us with more than their usual viciousness. They'll portray it as a dirty trick. They'll say the Green Party is a bunch of hoodlums, that we're underhanded. That we're desperate and we've sold out, abandoned all our 'high-minded idealism', that we're the kettle calling the frying pan black. That the people we find it so easy to criticize would never stoop so low. Of course, the major parties do worse stuff, but the facts never get in the way when it comes to manufacturing a scandal. If we get caught, it's curtains."

Lincoln shook his head and tried to smile. But he was obviously a little offended by what Phyllis seemed to be saying.

"You don't show much confidence in me. Have a little faith. CPPP is hermetically sealed. There's no way it's getting traced back to this campaign."

"I have all the faith in the world in you, Lincoln. I'm not saying it's *you.* But things happen. There's always a way. I never can figure out how a lot of stuff finds its way into the press. There's always some way — some fluke no one can possibly anticipate — that things can screw up."

Martin had been listening as he always did, attentively, thoughtfully.

"I don't have a crystal ball. I'm not a mind reader. Sometimes the mind of the voting public is like the Heisenberg Uncertainty Principle. The closer you look at it, the more it transforms into something indeterminate and unrecognizable. But here's where I think we stand. Even with all the exposure we've gotten recently, if the election were held today I'd get maybe 10% of the vote. And that's if Santa Claus drove all of the liberals to the polls in his sled."

That broke some of the tension. There were perceptible smiles.

"We've basically got nothing to lose. Well, okay. We could alienate the 10% who realize that Martin Truth is not a new board game, fun for the whole family from Hasbro. But I say we go for it. This pledge strategy is powerful. If we screw this up, it's not for a lack of effort. A lot of effort! We'll just chalk it up to experience. The Wright Brothers didn't get off the ground their first try. *But!* If we pull this off, even if we lose the election, it's going to create a whole new precedent. It's going to lay the groundwork. It'll be field-tested and get enough attention that maybe the next time some brave soul tries it, it just might work and send one of the corporate shills back to the minors. I know I'm mixing my metaphors again but you get my meaning. *Little Jessica Meyers Didn't Have To Die* was about as risky as it gets. But we decided to go for it. And why? Because it was the right thing to do. It was our responsibility to the citizens of our district here, and in a broader sense, to the citizens of America. We — and I include all of you for making a courageous decision and because you worked harder than I did to get it in the public eye — stepped into the ring ready to take our shots. Lady Luck was with us and it turned out to be the right thing to do for this campaign as well. Enough metaphors. I say the risk is worth it. Let's take it all the way."

Phyllis actually seemed somewhat relieved. A decision had been made. She didn't oppose it. She had just been feeling ambivalent and a little unsure of the consequences. Fear of failure can be a powerful deterrent even for someone with her store of unflagging fortitude. But to the degree everyone else in the room trusted her judgment, she trusted Martin's instincts.

"Okay. I'm sorry … sorry about my wavering. I just … alright! It's settled. I hope everyone understands where I'm coming from. I just want what's best for this campaign and for our little chapter of the Green Party. I'm just thinking long term. Now Jamila, even if you've said it before and we may think we understand it, let's go over again how you see this unfolding. How do we blow this up so big that no one can miss it?"

"Listen, Phyllis. I don't have all the answers. I need everyone here to build on the basics. Like I said, getting it rolling is pretty easy. We start with the obvious stuff. Facebook. Twitter. But we'll use the social sites just to draw attention to the street theater. That's how we pull in the media. That's the shit that delivers a big bang for the bucks."

"Street theater? Shakespeare in the park? Can I play Macbeth?"

"More like Cirque du Soleil, Bill. We dress up as clowns. Give out balloons that say *'Congressman Gardner. Sign the damn pledges!'* We'll stand at the busy intersections, hit the malls, parks, swimming pools, rec centers, ball games, everywhere there are people. We create scenes. We make noise. Weather's still good right now. People are out and about. We can have a demolition raffle. Give us a buck and we'll give you a sledgehammer for a big whack at a car. On the side of the car it says, *Congressman Matt Gardner won't sign pledge to tax his filthy rich friends*. Maybe we can get someone to donate an old Cadillac. That would be perfect."

"You can't hold big demonstrations anymore. They're cracking down on them. You can't even carry signs on public streets without the cops hassling you."

"But people wear clothes. There's no law against clothing, is there? You get fifty people all wearing a t-shirt that says *Matt Gardner refuses to protect Social Security and Medicare*, and have them bring some pastries to a retirement home. We'll get *that* on the news, I promise. There's always a way around petty laws. We just need to be creative."

Martin suddenly perked up. This was starting to sound exciting!

"Wheelchairs. Wheelchairs are a statement in themselves."

"What about wheelchairs?"

"Um … I don't know. Wait! I've got it. We line them up. They'll be holding a banner that says, '*Matt Gardner, why do you want to take my wheelchair away? Don't you own three cars?*' How many cars does he own? Anyway, you get the idea."

Jamila wasn't entirely sold on the wheelchair brigade but gave her guarded approval.

"Sure. Why not? Gardner is fucking with people. He's hurting people. That's why we're doing this. It's not right. We just need to let the voters know in no uncertain terms what the man is all about. He doesn't give a shit about anyone other than himself and his Daddy Warbucks friends. And the only reason he's running for office is to win. He sure doesn't need the money. He doesn't need a job. With guys like him, it's all about power and prestige."

Something just then occurred to Bob.

"Imogene? We've got access to the directories at work. How about if you and I put together a list of all of the nursing homes in the area? That and all city recreation facilities. Then we can figure out what sports clubs are doing what and when."

Jamila added that to her notes.

Lincoln had an interesting idea.

"Though veterans are understandably usually very patriotic, I'm reading that there's a growing sentiment among them now that the government is just using them, or using them for the wrong reasons. The VA hospitals are filling up with casualties from both the Iraq and Afghanistan wars. It's not just amputees and guys with their faces blown off. The incidence of PTSD is alarming."

"We should go to Dayton VA and talk to them. Ask them what they think about the wars. And what they think about their congressman's refusal to bring the troops home. Have them all wearing t-shirts that say, *'Congressman Gardner refuses to sign pledges ending the war in Afghanistan!'* or something along those lines. Do a press release and write an article."

"If they'll let a camera crew in, we could film it."

"They'll definitely let one of the local stations do a news story."

"Hey, I got it. Phyllis, you're pretty popular with the folks over at WHIO-TV, especially after talking them into letting Martin be in the debate. I'll bet they're dying to return the favor."

"Aren't we the comedian, Bill? Actually, one of my close friends is a producer at WDTN. He'd be open to doing something. He's told me that a number of times but said the condition would be that it couldn't be overtly political. They couldn't appear to be endorsing or giving preferential treatment to a candidate. Going in under Committee For Public Policy Preferences would work. Local non-partisan action group doing focus studies on vital contemporary issues. Visiting the VA hospital to get some perspective on the petition and candidate pledge to bring the troops home would make total sense. I'll tell him to expect a call from the Committee, pitch it as me just giving him a valuable lead on a story."

Jamila continued writing notes as she threw a question out to everyone there.

"Any more ideas? What other places do people congregate?"

"Since people live to shop, the biggest hot spots are Walmart and Costco. Any of the areas where you have a bunch of big box stores."

"Well, those places have zero tolerance for canvassing of any kind. Especially political. Their private police force will escort you off the property pronto."

"True. But they have parking lots. Sometimes they run one into the other, like the PetSmart, Toys 'R Us, Wingerman Furniture, and Bed Bath & Beyond. There's three or four other stores, I can't remember the names, which all share a huge parking lot."

"I heard about this environmental group in California. They got this enormous old gashog, maybe an Oldsmobile or Buick, and they painted it orange and blue, yellow and red. Crazy paint job and so loud you would see it from low earth orbit. Anyway, they put some message across both sides, 'Save the Planet' or something like that. Then they just drove it around. They drove the Walmart people nuts. They just kept driving and when the security guards would stop them, they'd just say they were looking for a good parking place. This went on for weeks before Walmart finally finagled a court order, a cease and desist. They probably paid off the judge."

"Yeah! There you go. We paint on the side, *'Gardner wants to keep you poor. He refuses to sign pledge raising minimum wage.'* That would work. If nothing else, the employees working at these low wage box stores would get the message."

Helen, as quiet as she was solid and efficient, the campaign's silent steady workhorse and Phyllis's administrative assistant, had never once in seven years spoken up at a meeting. Everyone looked surprised, if not shocked, when they heard her clear her throat and then timidly start to interject.

"I … there's … I have one thing I wanted to say."

"Sure, Helen. Everyone's welcome to say whatever they wish."

"Well … I'm no expert. But if I saw signs and t-shirts that said, 'Congressman Gardner refuses to do this' or 'Congressman Gardner refuses to do that', I'd think he was being attacked. But if the signs said, 'Congressman Gardner, please sign the pledge to protect social security.' Well, it's more polite … and it says the same thing. It's saying he refuses to sign the pledge."

It was like a giant light suddenly lit up the room. Jamila was first to respond.

"My god! You're so right. 'Refuses' is very aggressive. It *does* look like a personal attack."

Martin immediately concurred.

"Helen! Thank you! A citizens campaign would not attack him but appeal to him. If Jamila is right, he's still not going to sign the pledges. It'll accomplish the same thing."

Lincoln agreed but wanted to split the difference.

"Helen's correct. Especially for things like visiting retirement homes and the VA hospital. We can't come off like a mob. Maybe toward the end of the month, however, we could have a few student protests with the stronger wording. Right before the election, we can drive the point home, in case anyone missed it. Maybe something like, *'Only eight more days to sign our pledges. Do the right thing, Congressman Gardner!'* But, Helen, you make a really great point. You should speak up more often, eh?"

"I like to space my comments out a bit. I'll have something to say again around 2021."

Everyone but Phyllis had a good laugh.

Martin couldn't help but notice.

"I know what you're thinking. Please, Phyllis. Stop worrying. This won't come back on us. Lincoln's got it covered. The petitions, the pledges, now the stink he'll be creating about Gardner's refusal to sign them, it's just a citizen's uprising. It's voters who want certain things done and done right. There's no problem."

"Problems sneak up on you. I know…I know what you're thinking. I'm a worrywart. I just don't want this campaign, and especially the Green Party of this district, in any way implicated in rough house politics. It's what sets us apart."

Jamila thought this was settled. She had no patience for purist snobbery or paranoia.

"There's something else that sets you apart."

"What's that?"

"Your unbroken string of defeats."

"Touché."

• • •

Gardner really shined in the second and third televised debates. Of course, without Martin there to pose a serious challenge, and without Peter Potts there to belch elephantine phlegm balls of non sequiturs into the gazpacho of the exchange, it was a pretty dreary non-confrontation. Both events could have been billed "An Evening of Fluff and Smiles with Congressman Matt Gardner."

The only uncomfortable moment came during the last debate, held on October 17th and attended by a dwindling and more noticeably comatose number of people.

JANA COLLIER: "We're seeing a lot of attention being given to four pledges. These are the result of a citizens group called Committee on Public Policy Preferences. They are saying that they want their pledges signed by whoever represents this district in Congress this next term. These are apparently legally binding commitments reflecting the views of what they claim are huge voter majorities, on Social Security, Medicare, increased taxation of the wealthy, raising the federal minimum wage, and immediately ending the war in Afghanistan. What do you have to say to this? Have you or are you planning on signing these pledges?"

Castiglia pleasantly joked that he had heard something about them but didn't know the details. His ditzy admission blended in seamlessly with his cluelessness on just about every other topic discussed that evening.

Though Gardner looked a bit antsy as Jana was posing the question, he quickly recovered and dismissed them with his usual mix of snide mockery and jingoistic blather.

GARDNER: "Yes, Jana, I'm familiar with these so-called pledges. My people have looked at them and deemed them an amateurish stunt. Pledges? They're a joke. It's all a bit of childish buffoonery which has no precedent and no legal foundation. And this committee. Who are they? As far as we can tell, it's just a bunch of students at U of D with too much time on their hands. Let me say this: As your congressman, I stand shoulder to shoulder with the fine citizens of this district on all of these issues. I don't need to, nor do I plan to, sign these or any other scraps of paper someone comes up with to try to bully me around. I have better things to do. The very things I have been doing and will continue to do to make this district safe and comfortable for everyone who lives here. We owe it to ourselves and our children to build a strong America. And that starts right here in the great State of Ohio's 3rd Congressional District."

An interesting thing happened over the course of the next two weeks, starting two days after this final televised debate.

Helen brought the mail into Phyllis's office. A huge stack of mail. As she always did, she had opened and organized it.

"Phyllis, I think you're going to like this."

She set down over twenty-six personal checks, made out to Martin Truth For Congress. They were mostly modest contributions, $5 to $20. There was one for $35, another for $75.

Phyllis was understandably pleased and called everyone on the campaign committee to let them know about their little windfall. They all agreed it was a wonderful anomaly.

Turned out it wasn't an anomaly at all. In fact, it was just a preview of coming attractions.

The next day, the next and several nexts after that, more and more contributions arrived. Their postal carrier, instead of putting a rubber band around their mail as he typically did, had to dedicate an entire mail bag to them. It wasn't a huge bag, but nevertheless still held between 150 and 200 envelopes. With only the exceptional utility bill or junk mail flier, they were all checks supporting Martin's bid for Congress.

No one wanted to read too much into this encouraging turn of events. But something was happening out there. Something good was definitely happening.

• • •

At the risk of making a too obvious connection between the petition-pledge drive and Martin's campaign, each time Lincoln's CPPP guerilla army would swoop into an area with their *Congressman Gardner, please sign our pledges!* offensive, a few days later the same grounds or facility would be blanketed with simple but effective campaign leaflets.

For Martin Truth, promises are not just high-sounding
words to be forgotten after election day.

Martin Truth has signed four iron-clad pledges.

– To end the war in Afghanistan –
– To make the rich pay fair taxes –
– To raise the federal minimum wage –
– To protect Social Security and Medicare –

Martin Truth is a man you can count on.
Martin Truth is a man who will keep his word.

No more empty promises.

Martin Truth for Congress
3rd District of Ohio

Martin's leafleters — traveling in frenzied swarms of 15 to 20 — tacked them up, handed them out, tucked them under windshield wiper blades, taped them in bathroom stalls and above urinals, put them on benches and tables. With their singing-dancing-chanting and general exuberance, they caused as much fuss as they could get away with before being escorted away by bewildered and overwhelmed private security guards. Most of the leafleters were high school and college age kids. It was a big fun game to them and after each raid they left in high spirits and lighter by several hundred fliers.

Phyllis got numerous calls complaining. The infuriated callers would threaten legal action citing anti-littering codes, claim violations of anti-trespassing laws, and even deliver brutish warnings that next time skulls would be cracked.

She just laughed and usually mentioned the First Amendment somewhere in the exchange. She knew the callers had no legal ground to stand on. She certainly wasn't going to be bullied by some thick-skulled manager of a shopping mall or a bumptious parking lot attendant.

But she did wonder if they were pushing their luck.

At their nightly meeting, she recounted one of the phone calls she had gotten that day.

It came from the owner of an Econo-Lube-n-Tune on the west side.

"This one was screaming from the moment Helen picked up the phone. So I recorded it. Definitely a real swell fellow."

She reached back to the answering machine on the table behind her, scrolled to the appropriate message, and hit play.

They went back and forth as expected. Phyllis was calm and put on a show of being contrite while the caller raved on, sparing no expletives known to contemporary English. Toward the end, she jokingly asked the guy a question which sent him to the next level of insane ranting.

> *"I certainly have made a note here of your objection. I'll tell the kids to stay away from your place of business. But you know how kids are. So hard to control these days. Anyway, the important question is, will you be voting for Martin Truth in the coming election?"*

> *"Are you fucking crazy? I read your fucking socialist flier. Raise the fucking minimum wage? You've got to be fucking kidding. If my employees don't like what I pay them, I tell them, 'Don't let the door hit you on the way out, asshole!' And listen up, you dumb cunt! There ain't no free speech on my property. You want free speech? There was a little blond who was one of the brainwashed goon-squad brown-shirt commie-socialists you sent over here to spread your horseshit propaganda. She can spread something alright. Send that sweet little pussy and those innocent lips back here and she can practice some free speech by slick licking my dick! Let me say something else. They're just lucky I didn't bring my gun to work yesterday. Next time, I'll blow their fucking commie faggot heads clean off. In case you don't know, that's the Second Amendment, bitch!"*

"We went on to discuss some of the nuances of the wording of the Bill of Rights and the original ideas bandied about at the Constitutional Convention, but sadly I didn't get it on tape."

Lincoln: "No doubt about it. He's a bona fide constitutional scholar."

Martin: "Do you think he'd be up for doing some speechwriting?"

Phyllis just grimaced and shook her head.

"All in a days work. They're not all *that* bad. You know, the calls? I'm just wondering if we're making more enemies than friends out there."

Lincoln shrugged.

"This is election season. Everyone expects it. It's no big deal. That's all they get right now. By the way, earlier today I was thinking that maybe we should crank up the heat a little."

Jamila, who had been uncharacteristically quiet so far, perked up.

"Right on! We've got, what? Twenty-two days to make this happen. Yeah, I'd definitely say it's time to pull out the blowtorch."

Phyllis didn't say anything. But in the back of her eyes hovered the apprehension she was obviously feeling. Lincoln put it as diplomatically as he could.

"This campaign is right on track. We've spelled it out for anyone who notices. Anyone we can get to notice. Martin Truth is on their side. He signed the pledges. Blah blah. But the truly critical thing is letting people know that Gardner has not. This campaign can't highlight that without creating suspicions, without someone connecting the dots and saying, 'Oh, so you're the ones behind the pledges.' Only the CPPP can do that. So I want to turn up the heat, get the message out there loud and clear that Gardner has not and will not sign the pledges."

Phyllis wasn't sure she wanted to know but still had to ask.

"How do you propose doing that?"

"Direct action."

• • •

Six volunteers from the CPPP had set up across the street from the headquarters of *Matt Gardner, A Congressman Who Cares About You!* They were outfitted in t-shirts that left little to the imagination.

Matt Gardner, lapdog for
the rich and powerful.

They each carried a different sign …

Matt Gardner refuses to sign pledge
for fair taxes on the wealthy

Matt Gardner refuses to sign pledge
protecting Social Security

Matt Gardner refuses to sign pledge
protecting Medicare

Matt Gardner refuses to sign pledge
to bring troops home from Afghanistan

Matt Gardner refuses to sign pledge
raising the minimum wage

… and finally one that put plastic explosive icing on the cake …

Matt Gardner's perfect record in Congress:
More body bags for Afghanistan
More tax breaks for the rich
Destroy Social Security
Destroy Medicare
Keep us poor

There was a parking space reserved for Gardner directly in front of his storefront office. As he pulled up, he had a lot on his mind. Still he couldn't help but notice the small group across the street marching back and forth. Having a few kooks carrying signs within sight of his headquarters was rare but nothing new. There was always something. Protect the honey bees. Vaccine causes autism. Stop fluoridating the water. He usually just nodded and waved. If he was in a good mood, he gave them a thumbs up, then went about his business.

But one of the signs caught his eye. *Matt Gardner's perfect record in Congress: More body bags for Afghanistan...*

Gardner was a proud ex-military guy. Patriotism and service to his country were his bones and blood. He didn't mind the occasional John Lennon give-peace-a-chance sign. But this was personally insulting!

His ire increased as he read the rest of the sign. His temper went through the stratosphere when he looked at the other signs. Fucking pledges! So that's what this was all about. The little incident onstage three weeks ago with that fucking punk still irked him. Now they were right in his face, right in front of his campaign office.

He slammed his car door so hard, it almost blew out the windows, then broke into a full run, not even bothering to look for traffic. Two cars slammed on their brakes to avoid hitting him.

The girl carrying the *Matt Gardner's perfect record in Congress* sign was facing the other way and didn't see him coming. He grabbed her shoulders and roughly swung her around. She managed to maintain her balance and found his index finger jabbing her in the chest bone.

"How dare you lie about me? This is slander!"

The girl, of course, immediately recognized him. Never having seen this side of the man, face red and puffed with rage — a dramatic contrast to the delightful guy in the television ads — she took a moment to size up what kind of threat he posed. They were in a public place. He had an image to maintain. Even if he appeared rather agitated, she figured she was on reasonably safe ground.

She looked him squarely in the eyes and replied with extraordinary cool.

"The Congressional Record doesn't lie, sir. Perhaps your memory is slipping. Shall I give you a quick refresher course as to your voting record on these issues?"

"Why you bitch! You've got a lot of—"

What happened next happened so fast, it could have been the subject of speculation and volumes of interpretation, as in I-think and maybe-she and then-he and if-I-remember-correctly. But someone had pulled out their iPhone and caught the whole incident on video.

Gardner grabbed the girl's sign and started beating her with it.

Suddenly a police squad car pulled up and two officers jumped out.

Gardner pulled rank. The girl and five other protesters were arrested and hauled away. They put up no struggle but later were charged with incitement, assault, and resisting arrest.

Gardner would claim that he calmly had tried to talk to them but the girl assaulted him, then the others joined in.

> *"With my military training, I could've easily taken this whole lawless mob down, but I opted to show mercy on these six crazy, probably drugged-up anarchists. Fortunately, someone called the police and they intervened. As far as I'm concerned, they should lock these kinds of mental misfits up in an institution, to keep the streets safe for the good law-abiding citizens of Dayton."*

The video decisively rebutted all of this.

It was obvious that Gardner was the aggressor. In fact, the girl never lifted a finger. She did lift her hands and arms to try to deflect the blows Gardner was raining down on her. It was also clear that she was backing away from him with the assistance of the other protesters, who were trying to pull her away and out of harms way. There was absolutely nothing in any of their actions that could be construed as aggression.

The video of course was immediately posted on YouTube. By the next day, it showed up on TV stations both in Gardner's congressional district and much of Ohio.

Martin was interviewed for a couple of the local television dinner-hour news shows.

> *"Apparently, Mr. Gardner needs to cut back on his caffeine a bit. I watched the video several times and saw nothing these young citizens did which would provoke his attack on this young lady. Well, other than bring up the truth about his voting record. Maybe in Congressman Gardner's world of privilege and power, the truth is not something to be tolerated."*

• • •

A few days later, the hubbub had pretty much died down.

Gardner had his people apply some discreet threats. It was suggested that they could hardly keep spending the generous sums of money they were throwing at the television stations for campaign ads, if the same stations were going to run such "unflattering" and "biased" stories. Soon nothing more was aired about the incident in the street, certainly not the incriminating video footage. Public discussion of the incident ceased.

The protesters themselves were released without charge. The video had made it patently obvious there was nothing to charge them with. Demands by anonymous callers to the office of the Chief of Police proposing Gardner himself should be arrested for assault, were dismissed with a curt, *"We'll make a note of your recommendation."* Nothing, of course, was done.

Gardner's threats to pull his ads from the local TV stations didn't just muffle specific mention of the incident. It pretty much put the lid on anything which might be unsympathetic to the incumbent. The constant rotation of Gardner's official campaign ads continued and there were still news stories about him. But they were nauseatingly good-natured. One was a piece on his family. They followed his kids to school, showed his wife at home doing domestic tasks, then talked to them about what it was like having a congressman as head of the household. Another was about Gardner's love of dogs, featuring video footage of him playing with his four purebred Rottweilers on the expansive lawn of his estate.

In fact, there seemed to be an entire blackout of the discordant aspects of the congressional race. News of the other three candidates never came up, except when citing the latest poll numbers. Even this was done only sporadically now. In terms of politics, the big ticket news items were the race for the state's Senate seats, and the scandals which periodically popped up when a candidate in some other part of the country said something particularly stupid or offensive.

Lincoln, of course, kept sending his CPPP volunteers out and about in droves, armed with leaflets and signs. Though they were getting through to voters a handful at a time, in terms of TV and official print media, it seemed impossible to get any mention.

In spite of this dearth of reportage, the pledge campaign did continue to rustle some feathers. There were apparently undercurrents of public disenchantment over Gardner's refusal to sign. One cable news show featured some rather tame clips of people being interviewed in the street. Perhaps Martin's campaign was benefitting somewhat. It was hard to say.

Then things changed and Martin Truth For Congress got a huge shot of adrenalin.

This had nothing to do with what Martin was saying or the manner of delivering his message. He was still the intelligent, good-on-the-eyes pleasant-to-the-ears, mild-mannered and personable fellow he had always been.

The surge in interest was the direct result of a gross tactical blunder on the part of Gardner.

Apparently Gardner still smarted from the public humiliation by Gary at the rally, and increasingly in his face-to-face encounters with voters was taking heat about the pledges. Gardner decided to counterattack. He probably figured he would just deal with this whole annoying business in one grand gesture, brushing it off like some lint that had settled on his tailored suit jacket, then get on with winning the election.

He had his campaign staff whip up his *own* pledges. Immediately, brand new quickly-assembled but entirely polished, highly professional television campaign ads showed Gardner surrounded by a small but enthusiastic group of supporters, smiling and applauding as he signed them. It was staged to look like the President signing a bill into law. Gardner grinned his Pepsodent grin, then handed out the pens he had used to several excited citizens within arm's reach, and proudly held the pledges up to the camera. To close the ad, there was a shot of the American flag waving in the wind, with a thundering James Earl Jones-like voice-over declaring: *"Matt Gardner, not afraid to sign on the dotted line, a man committed to you, the people of Ohio."*

It completely backfired.

The press didn't take a first glance at Gardner's pledges themselves. Instead it picked up on the human interest aspects of the story. Suddenly the David vs. Goliath plotline was back in play. It was the poor underdog theme all over again. Martin Truth, a virtual nobody, had been shot at, had been written off as a joke, had comparatively no money in his coffers to mount a credible campaign, but now was apparently being taken as a serious threat by the incumbent. Martin Truth had signed the CPPP pledges and here was Gardner trying to play catch up. As part of the coverage, clips of the bruising he gave Gardner in the first debate were reprised. Martin was being called the Come From Behind Kid.

Most of it was typical fluff reporting. Martin nevertheless was all over the news and being again handed the opportunity to be heard.

He and his campaign crew made the best of it.

A press release went out immediately.

Crafted by Lincoln and Jamila, it scored a direct hit.

PRESS RELEASE: From the Campaign Headquarters of
Martin Truth for Congress – Ohio 3rd Congressional District

The incumbent candidate, Mr. Matt Gardner, recently made a big show of signing pledges on four key issues of great concern to the voters of this district. What prompted this piece of theater is anyone's guess but clarification is in order.

The pledges Mr. Gardner signed are of his own invention. They are not the pledges presented to him by the voters of this district, through the citizens group known as the Committee on Public Policy Preferences.

Moreover, there is no equivalency. The CPPP pledges have the binding power of legally enforceable contracts. His pledges are more campaign vapor. They're just more empty promises. Considering Mr. Gardner's voting record for the last ten years, we should expect him to ignore them the same way he has ignored the clear and certain will of the voters who in good faith have elected him in the past.

We here at the campaign headquarters of Martin Truth For Congress wish to go on record as stating unequivocally that Mr. Gardner's recent made-for-TV show of signing pledges is nothing more than a PR stunt and an insult to the good voters of this district.

As for the Democratic candidate, Mr. Chris Castiglia, since there is no public statement claiming otherwise, we can only assume that he likewise has not signed the CPPP pledges.

It should therefore be understood, that here in Ohio's 3rd Congressional District, Martin Truth is the only candidate who has signed the CPPP pledges. Martin Truth is the only candidate who has made an absolute and irrevocable commitment to properly represent the interests of the constituents of this district on fair tax policy, Social Security, Medicare, raising the federal minimum wage, and bringing our troops home from the pointless war in Afghanistan.

The specific text and certified copies of the pledges Martin Truth signed can be viewed at his website:

martintruthforcongress.com/pledges/

Martin Truth doesn't just talk. He will go to Washington and do the job he is elected to do. His commitment is irrevocable. He put it in writing.

For the next three days, Martin was repeatedly asked for comment. An interview he did with Amber Watson on the WRGT-TV local morning show was typical of his remarks, which reinforced in his own amicable but wry way, his campaign's press release.

AMBER: "Mr. Truth, thanks for being here this morning. What's your take on this pledge issue with Matt Gardner? First, he refused to sign them. Then just last week he came out with his own version of the pledges. You've probably seen his latest TV ads."

MARTIN: "Mr. Gardner's had nearly ten years to do the right thing. It seems peculiar that he's now getting around to signing a pledge to do what he should've been doing all along."

AMBER: "Those are harsh words."

MARTIN: "It's a harsh voting record."

AMBER: "Meaning?"

MARTIN: "Meaning the guy is batting a thousand. I will give him credit for consistency. He has voted against every fair tax increase on the rich, he voted for both versions of the Ryan budget and every other piece of legislation which would decimate both Social Security and Medicare. His voting against increasing the minimum wage is part of the public record, and he practically led a marching band on the floor of the Congress every time an authorization bill came up for the wars in Afghanistan and Iraq. People are fed up with seeing their sons and daughters coming home in body bags."

AMBER: "So you obviously don't think his own pledges have much merit. I understand that yesterday you said something to a reporter about a peace treaty. What was that all about?"

MARTIN: "I was merely making a comparison. I signed four pledges and they're legally binding. They're bona fide contracts with the citizens of this district. If I break the terms, I suffer very serious consequences. Very serious! What I said was that Mr. Gardner's approach was as if at the end of World War II, the Germans refused to sign an official armistice agreement. Instead they wrote something on a paper napkin which said, 'Hey, we're really sorry about that stuff we did, the bombs, the tanks, the whole Blitzkrieg thing, the 6,000,000 Jews. We promise to try harder from now on.' It's not something you're going take very seriously now, are you?"

AMBER: "So Gardner's pledges are like paper napkins?"

MARTIN: "I'll make a general statement and you can draw your own conclusions about Congressman Gardner's announcement. Most of what professional politicians promise during election season is best written on toilet paper."

AMBER: [Starts giggling] "I see. Not napkins. Toilet paper! Well, alright. Best of luck on your campaign. I know that we've been hearing more and more about you and what you stand for. Any predictions on the election."

MARTIN: "Absolutely. I predict there will be an election this year."

AMBER: [Laughing hard, obviously taken by his sense of humor.] "There you have it. You heard it yourself. [Ha ha] Right from the mouth of Martin Truth, very possibly our next congressman. [Ha ha] Thanks so much, Mr. Truth. It's been a real pleasure!"

MARTIN: "The pleasure's been all mine. Are you married?" [Big Martin Truth grin.]

AMBER: [Now so giddy, she's unable to sign off the interview. She just nods and winks at the camera. They cut to a commercial. It was the Matt Gardner pledge ad.]

Jamila couldn't let it go by.

"Loved the toilet paper comment. Real class, Martin."

"You told me I needed to rough up my image."

"And I really dug your hitting on her."

"It was a real human touch, eh?"

The truth was, Jamila was beside herself with the excitement. Between the press release, portions of which was even showing up in the national media in one context or another, and coverage his comments were getting via more than a dozen back-to-back regional interviews, the campaign had a whole new set of legs. People were starting to take notice.

The toilet paper comment itself really caught fire. A 5-second video snippet just of Martin's little snipe — 'Most of what professional politicians promise during election season is best written on toilet paper' — went viral. It appeared on thousands of YouTube channels. When it was featured in the tabloid media, it usually was headlined with a comment to the effect of: *Candidate says campaign promises great for wiping your butt.*

Soon candidates around the country at all different levels were quoted as saying that their opponents were running toilet paper campaigns. One Democrat running for Congress in Texas changed his campaign motto to: *There's no TP in USA*.

As more of this nonsense kept coming up, Martin just shook his head and laughed.

"The country has truly gone insane."

Jamila had her own take on its success.

"Hey, Martin. Like they always say. Imitation is the highest form of flattery."

"I guess."

"Another thought. If you don't get elected, you might be able to get a product endorsement gig with Charmin. Or Scott Tissue."

"We're not going to lose."

"Is that a campaign promise? You know what they say …"

"Put 100 monkeys in a room with …? I forget the rest."

"That did it! I'm convinced. You *are* going to win!"

"You're just prejudiced."

"Some of my best white people are friends."

"Wow! You're crazier than I am."

Chapter Nine

Two weeks before the election the attack dogs were out in full force.

Martin and his staffers naturally expected it. But one aspect did take them by surprise.

Conservative action groups like the Heartland Institute, Karl Rove's American Crossroads, the Koch brothers' Americans For Prosperity, Veterans For A Strong America, all following in the reptilian footsteps of the noxious Swift Boat Veterans and the Club For Growth, often swept into districts just like Martin's and targeted candidates they wanted to defeat using huge amounts of cash and a deceptive advertising blitzkrieg designed to destroy voter support. Usually, however, these assaults on the public consciousness were directed at Democrats. Or in some instances at Republicans who in the view of the rabid right were too 'moderate', maybe too willing to work with the Democrats. The fact that this time they directed their venomous political assassination at a third-party candidate — Green Party, no less — was unprecedented.

The ads were sad affairs, obviously slapped together at the last minute. They looked somewhat amateurish, but were still powerful. They left little to the imagination.

Martin was portrayed as a traitorous socialist pinko, a loser, an advocate of free love orgies, a druggie, a 60s hippie wannabe, and an immature spoiled brat.

As a swipe at his youthfulness, in one television ad he was rendered as a badly drawn cartoon baby, in diapers no less, throwing a crying tantrum because he couldn't get his way. They alleged that he wanted to put a statue of Marx and Lenin on the front lawns of all of the area public schools.

In another, someone had taken video footage of him driving the Future Perfect delivery truck, then hurrying into a building to deliver a package. It was captioned, *"Your future congressman? Don't you deserve better?"*

There was an extremely sleazy ad produced by a PAC called Family Counts, an organization which was probably cobbled together purely to attack Martin. They had no website or contact information. It attempted to contrast the family life of the Republican incumbent and the wild orgiastic single life of his Green Party opponent. It was a hodgepodge of incriminating video clips juxtaposed against shots of Gardner at home with his family, in the yard playing with his kids, at a picnic in the neighborhood, coaching a little league team. The incriminating clips directed at Martin included pole dancers in a strip club, tattooed motorcyclists, wild youths passing a joint and partying at a rock concert, and even hookers strutting around in front of an adult book store. Apparently the Family Counts folks counted on no one noticing that Martin wasn't *in* any of these displays of drug abuse and wanton hedonism.

One particularly onerous smear, paid for by a mysterious organization which called itself Americans For Drug Free Politics, took the viewer on a tour through an opium den, using stock black-and-white film footage from a half century ago. In the paternalistic patter of a concerned patriot, the mellow voice of the narrator let the questions pose as the answers the district voters allegedly were looking for:

"When Martin Truth says he loves America, is he
seeing the same America as you and I? When Martin
Truth talks about the American Dream, is this the same
American Dream you and I have? Or does his dream begin
and end here? Is Martin Truth telling you the whole truth?
When Martin Truth and his buddies on the lunatic fringe
talk about smoke and mirrors, you might want to
to ask what they've been smoking?"

This last nasty gem was clearly a riposte to a campaign poster Bill and Jamila had recently put together, which was a laundry list of Gardner's betrayals:

When you blow away the smoke and put away
the mirrors, this is what you see:

Congressman Gardner says he supports Medicare.
But his voting record says otherwise.

Congressman Gardner says he believes the rich
should pay their fair share in taxes.
But he votes against it.

Congressman Gardner says he wants to protect
retirees from cuts in Social Security.
Yet he votes against it.

Citizens gave him a chance to give us his solemn
commitment in the form of pledges.
He wouldn't sign them.

Martin Truth signed them.
Martin Truth lays it on the line.
Martin Truth will represent <u>you</u> and
do the job you elect him to do.
No smoke and mirrors.

Martin Truth for U.S. Congress.
3rd District Ohio.

Apparently the poster had raised some hackles.
Sometimes the truth really hurts.

• • •

Martin's core advisory committee had been getting together every night for over a month.

They trooped through the front office area, now filled with volunteers of all ages, manning a bank of twelve lines Phyllis had installed for their final push up through election day. It was very crowded and quite a din resulted from the many conversations going on simultaneously. Most of the calls were made to thank people for their donations, confirm that they were registered to vote, determine if they needed a ride to the polls on voting day, and to suggest that if they hadn't already, they tell their neighbors and friends about Martin Truth. Sometimes they were confronted with questions raised by the smear ads Gardner and the PACs were running. The volunteers were counseled on how to calmly and politely allay any concerns. Phyllis and Lincoln had prepared incisive replies to the most common questions, scripts that didn't sound scripted but which fully rebutted the nonsensical, unfounded personal attacks on Martin. Every call was concluded with a critical reminder:

> *"By the way, to prove his commitment to serving you and the needs of this district, Mr. Truth has signed four pledges which legally bind him to do everything he can to protect Social Security and Medicare, increase taxes on the rich before the country goes bankrupt, raise the federal minimum wage, and bring our soldiers back home safe and sound from Afghanistan. He has made legally binding contracts with you as a voter, personally guaranteeing that you will get the representation you want and deserve in Congress."*

The volunteers were reporting that most people were already familiar with the pledges, and if they brought up Gardner, it was usually to ask if anyone had heard whether he had signed them or not. A sizable majority thought it was the right thing to do. Word was definitely getting out, not in small part due to Gardner himself drawing attention to the issue by putting out his own phony pledges. The obviously staged hoopla of him signing them had backfired big time.

This particular evening, Lincoln and Bill were the last to arrive. With all of the noise in the front area, Helen closed the door to the conference room so they could hear themselves think.

Imogene opened tonight's meeting with a dramatic, wholly unexpected announcement.

"Looks like you've got Bob and I full-time. We've been relieved of our duties over at Job and Family Services."

Everyone started talking at once.

"What happened?"

"But you guys have been there forever. What, twenty some years?"

"No way! They fired you? Is that possible?"

"That is truly *fucked up!*"

Bob didn't look all that shook up about it. He was actually smiling.

"We're on mandatory administrative leave. We're appealing it."

Imogene was equally stoic.

"They're probably going to try to fire us. But they're taking their time. I should say, they're being real careful. They know the have no cause. We're suspended pending a final evaluation and ruling which is due within 15 days. We'll be formally apprised of the official reasons and decision at that time."

Martin looked chagrined.

"So what was it? Did working on my campaign have anything to do with it?"

Bob just chuckled.

"Indirectly. Though we didn't actually break any rules. It probably came down to the petitions. Somebody is punishing us."

Phyllis showed the early symptoms of her recurrent cold sweat.

"Maybe they put two and two together? Do they suspect you're working on this campaign? Did someone turn you in?"

Imogene seemed very sure of the situation.

"There's nothing barring us from having party affiliations, Phyllis. We just can't advertise them while we're at work. Working on someone's campaign is not prohibited. But they'll try to twist things around and suggest that the petitions were somehow showing political favoritism. It's a joke. They don't have a leg to stand on."

Bob shook his head dismissively.

"They're just slapping us around."

"Exactly. Our management, God help them, are rabidly right wing, Republican to the core. Sure, they knew about the petitions all along but never said a word. They couldn't. There was nothing political about them. All the caseworkers were circulating them, collecting signatures. But I think when the pledges became a liability for their good buddy Gardner, they started to view our good citizen efforts in a different light. It pissed them off."

Phyllis looked mortified.

"I knew this would happen. So what are you saying? They tracked them to the two of you?"

Imogene laughed.

"You could say that. We kept a low profile. But there are no secrets anymore ..."

The all-too-familiar look of *total dread* now permeated Phyllis's entire face. Imogene tried to backtrack and give her some reassurance.

"... except some things, of course. Like ... like the connection between the pledges and this campaign."

Trying to be helpful, Bill made things even worse.

"People understandably are going to be a little suspicious. At least curious. Everyone who comes into my shop knows I'm campaigning for Martin here, so I've had a couple people ask me if the petitions had anything to do with us. I just point to the logo and tell them. 'See here? It's a citizens group. Something called Committee on Public Policy Preferences.' I've had no one question it any further. They take it at face value."

Now Phyllis was bent over with her hands stretched out in front of her. She looked like she was going to start banging her head on the table. Martin came to the rescue.

"Look. We've got two weeks. Nothing's going to happen. The pledges have done their job. No one can challenge their validity. Certainly no one can make the 90,000 signatures on the petitions go away. Our biggest fear was that people would see the petitions and pledges as a political trick. Dismiss them as a personal smear or a campaign stunt. Well, Gardner took care of that with his own stunt. He sealed the credibility of our pledges by trying to replace them with those fraudulent ones of his. At this point, he's the one with the credibility problem. And like I said, we've only got two weeks left. We got the ball rolling. Nothing's going to stop it now, not at this late stage, even if they accuse us of orchestrating the whole thing."

Lincoln hoped to put the matter to rest.

"Which they won't … because they can't."

Martin looked over at Imogene and Bob. His expression betrayed both his enormous respect for them and his immediate concern for their well-being.

"Are you going to be alright? I assume you won't get paid during this administrative leave."

Bob shrugged.

"I bought Apple stock when it was $36 a share."

Imogene smiled.

"I love Top Ramen."

• • •

Maybe the press smelled blood, maybe voter awareness had pushed it to the forefront.

Gardner was now being regularly dogged about the pledge issue. Without fail, it came up in every interview. With only twelve days left before people would be going to the polls, one particularly insistent reporter pushed the wrong button too many times and the congressman lost it.

> *"What's with you guys? Are you all nuts? This whole pledge thing is being blown out of proportion by bozos just like you. I've been representing this district for nearly ten years. I've done great things here. Now I'm just trying to run a good, civil, above-the-board campaign and jokers like you want to turn it into mud wrestling. Well, Mr. Smart Ass Reporter, whoever the hell you are, let me tell you something. I know where this is coming from.*

And I've known all along who's behind this smear campaign. It's that Martin Truth Green Party bunch of creeps, who don't stand for anything and can't make a respectable run for office. So they've resorted to this cheap stunt to distract everyone, to get guys like you all hot and bothered about a piece of paper. If you were a real reporter and didn't have your head up your ass, you'd be covering the real story. You'd ask some tough questions. You'd find out what I already know. These pledges are just a rotten trick to fool the good voters of this district, to seed suspicion and doubt, to slander me and my long service to this community and our great nation. This interview is over. Get a life!"

Even with the expletives bleeped out, it made for great TV.

Gardner had really blown it. If the footage of him beating up the protester hadn't totally ruined his good-guy, distinguished-public-servant image, this outburst certainly did.

At the same time, Phyllis was beside herself.

"How did he find out? How does he know?"

Lincoln and Martin were with her in her office, doing all they could to calm her down.

"He didn't and he doesn't."

"Gardner was just blowing smoke."

"But you heard what he said."

"It doesn't mean anything. The guy was pissed. It was obviously a bunch of idiotic ranting. He was just shooting in the dark. Grasping at straws. If he really thought we were behind it, he would have come out with it a long time ago. He would have used it in his campaign ads, at least done a press conference and made some serious political hay with it."

"Should we come out with a refutation? Of course we'll be lying. Then if we get caught, we're in really big trouble. Oh god! This is so … phew!"

"If we jump right on it, it'll make us look guilty as charged. People will assume there's something behind what Gardner said."

"Let's wait. Let them come to us."

They didn't have to wait long.

Next morning the phone starting ringing. It was the usual suspects, local newspaper and television reporters, asking Martin to comment on what Gardner said.

It was in situations like these that Martin really showed his prowess. For better or worse, he definitely had the makings of a politician. Before talking to the media, he sat down, collected his thoughts, and came up with a statement which he repeated almost word for word in each of several brief interviews.

"I fully support the work of the Committee on Public Policy Preferences, the citizens group that did the petitions and found out where the voters of this district stand on certain key issues. This is democracy in action, in its purest form. The pledges are a natural

extension of the polling process. People have a right to demand of their elected representatives firm commitments. Frankly, I was more than happy to sign the pledges. At least for Social Security, Medicare, fair tax policy, the minimum wage, and ending the war in Afghanistan, it took all the guesswork out. If I'm elected, I know exactly what I'm expected to do and intend to do it. As for Mr. Gardner's frantic pointing of fingers, I can honestly say that the petitions and pledges were not my idea. Frankly, I wish I had thought of it. It's a fantastic concept and the perfect way to keep us politicians honest. I applaud the CPPP and all of the hard work that they've put into this."

Jamila sat and listened as Martin gave his spiel on the phone to a reporter from the Dayton Daily News. When he hung up, she just shook her head and smiled.

"Martin Truth. You are too smooth for words. You're better than Bill Clinton!"

"Uh, thanks … I guess that's a compliment."

"It is. But don't let it go to your head."

"Of course not. I can't touch the guy on saxophone."

• • •

There was so much to do. Everyone spent as much time as they could at campaign headquarters. Jamila, Phyllis, Helen, Martin, Bob and Imogene were there morning to night. Bill and Lincoln were in and out throughout the day. Volunteers came in sporadically morning and afternoons, making calls, picking up campaign literature to distribute as they spread out like a citizen army wherever they were sent in the city. Evenings were a packed house, the front area full of eager faces, young and old, gabbing away on the phones. To add to the cacophony, they had pooled their resources and come up with three TV sets which were tuned to the local network stations to monitor any relevant stories.

Suddenly, Jamila yelled out from the front.

"Hey, everybody. You might want to watch this. My my, Martin Truth. I didn't know you were a special ambassador to the Far East."

They knew it had to be something interesting. Everyone flocked to the front.

A very petite, very attractive, very pregnant Asian-American girl was being interviewed on WKEF-TV Fox 45 by Chelby Kosto, one of their star reporters.

"He took me for a weekend at a beautiful luxury hotel in Chicago. He was quite the charmer, a real playboy type. He kept telling me how he had been waiting his whole life for a girl like me. We made love like it was our honeymoon. After we got back here, I never heard from him again."

"So you're saying that this baby is Martin Truth's child? And he's not taking responsibility for it?"

"It's his kid alright. Not taking responsibility? He's blown me off completely. I've seen this type of man before. He's probably out chasing other women and figured I would just go away. It's very painful to be treated like this. But even worse for his baby. What kind of man acts like this? That's what I want to know. A sex-addicted womanizer, that's who!"

Jamila sported a big taunting grin.

"Martin, you devil you! I had no idea you were such a ladies' man. Are we in store for any more surprises?"

"She told me she was Yoko Ono's niece. I just wanted to send Yoko some of my haiku."

Next evening, they got probably a bigger surprise.

On the same station, being interviewed by the same reporter, was the last person Martin thought would come to his defense. Chelby Kosto kicked it off.

"Last night in an exclusive interview, we reported some serious allegations against local candidate for U.S. Congress, Martin Truth. We have here with us someone who would like to speak in his defense, Alison Baker. What can you tell us, Alison?"

"I was Martin's fiancé back then, at the time of the alleged impregnation. I can assure you that Martin did nothing of the kind. He is the most loyal, dependable, trustworthy person I have ever met. We had been together nearly eight years and the guy never looked at another woman. He sure wasn't gone for a whole weekend. We were living together at the time. I think I would have noticed."

"So you're saying Mr. Truth is not the father."

"I'm saying that this is just a cheap political stunt to discredit a good person. If every politician were as moral as Martin Truth, this country wouldn't be in the mess it's in."

Alison then turned and looked directly into the camera.

"I decided to end my relationship with Martin for personal reasons and haven't spoken to him since. But I can say this. It's truly disgusting to see this kind of malicious attack. There is no better person, no more honest, no more dedicated, no more selfless and giving individual than he is. He would be a great congressman. The voters of this district should know that, and see this kind of

sick stunt for precisely what it is: An attempt to slander the only person who is qualified and worthy of the job."

Martin, master and maestro of the English language, blessed with the gift of great orational powers, expressed the enormity of his feelings with characteristic conciseness and precision.

"Wow!"

Jamila, of course, had her own spin.

"This is great!"

"Great?"

"Listen. Any publicity, good or bad, is good. At least there's some chance people will actually know who Martin Truth is. Somewhere in the midst of this bloodletting, they might have even gotten the message that he's running for Congress."

"And?"

"And? I'll give you an 'and'. *And* no more Martin Mannikin. You've got two hot babes on TV in a cat fight over you. Maybe this won't exactly dazzle the Christian Right. But trust me, this does wonders for your image. Do you know how many women voters watch soap operas?"

Jamila let out a laugh that nearly shattered the front window.

Martin just paced, somewhat relieved but still incredulous as to the emotional roller coaster he'd been riding for the last 24 hours. Even more incredulous that right there on television only moments ago was his ex, actually standing up for him, telling the public to vote for him.

He stopped pacing and looked over at Jamila. She was as beautiful as ever.

Crazy beautiful. Crazy intelligent. Crazy mad sexy beautiful.

"Jamila Parks, you are so twisted."

"I am! I am!"

• • •

Eight days before the election, they buried themselves in their computers and phones. The petitions had included requests for contact information. Surprisingly, most people had written in a phone number or an email address. Sometimes both.

A typical conversation …

"Mrs. Davison, hope you're well. The election is coming up in next week. You're planning to vote?"

"Haven't missed in forty years."

"Back in July you signed a petition about Social Security. You said that you would only support a candidate who promised to leave Social Security alone."

"I'm on Social Security. What there is of it. Do these politicians have any idea what it's like to try to survive on what I get? Yes, it's very important to me."

"You know that the local citizens group which circulated the petitions, the CPPP, asked the incumbent from this district, Congressman Gardner, to sign a pledge which required him to do everything he could in Congress to protect Social Security, to make sure that recipients like yourself aren't hurt by changes in the law. But he refused to sign."

"Gosh. He's been around for a while, hasn't he? I voted for him every time. It's hard to believe that he's being stubborn about this."

"He has I believe promised in every campaign to do the right thing by retirees like yourself. But the fact is, in Congress he's been on the wrong side of the issue. He's been voting for bills that cut benefits."

"Are you sure about this? I hate to kick a good man out of his job."

"Well, he looks good on television, doesn't he? He's got a nice smile. A beautiful family. But I wouldn't worry about kicking him out of a job. He has a law degree, you know, and has made a very good living in the past with his law practice in Dayton. I don't think someone who on his last tax return said he made over a million and a half dollars in one year is someone you need to worry about."

"A million and a half dollars? Good grief!"

"Just to remind you. There is another very good man running for office. His name is Martin Truth and he did sign the pledge. He signed the Social Security pledge. That same pledge also protects Medicare since the—"

"Good for him. Medicare. That's another thing I really depend on. I have diabetes, you know."

"Martin Truth also signed a pledge to have the wealthy in this country pay their fair share in taxes, so that we don't have to cut Social Security, Medicare, education and all of the other things that have made America great."

"Martin Truth, eh. I'll bet he's always on the side of truth." She giggled like a little kid.

"He's on your side, Mrs. Evans. That's what counts. Listen. I've taken up a lot of your time. I really appreciate this. Thanks for listening. It's been great talking with you. Do you need a ride on election day? That's this coming Tuesday."

"That's so kind, sweetheart. But I'll get a lift with my neighbor. Thanks for asking, though."

"My pleasure. We're here to help. Don't forget now. That's Martin Truth. I know him personally and I can honestly say, Mr. Truth really appreciates your support."

After a few days of this, they ran into a slight snag.

Phyllis got the call at 7:00 o'clock in the morning. It was from Company 32 of the City of Kettering Fire Department.

"I've got some bad news for you, ma'am."

The Martin Truth For Congress office had burned to the ground.

Fortunately, no one was hurt. It happened in the middle of the night.

Close to tears, Phyllis threw on some clothes and immediately drove to the smoldering shell of her former office.

She was in shock. The shock quickly gave way to horror. The horror centered around practical issues.

How were they going to mount their final blitz on the voting public over these last few crucial days before the election? How were they going to send the emails, make the calls?

By noon she got the answers she was looking for.

Over the course of the last six months, Martin had accumulated a very sizable, enthusiastic following among students at University of Dayton. His youthfulness, progressive ideas, perceived accessibility, outsider status, hip casual persona, and the strong stand he had taken in advocating free college education, and if that was not achievable, then at bare minimum interest-free student loans, had made him enormously popular.

As soon as word of the fire got out, they were overwhelmed with volunteers. Hundreds of students with iPhones, Galaxies, Motorolas, and every other cell phone on the market, showed up in front of the charred remains of Martin Truth for Congress world headquarters. Phyllis suddenly had at her disposal a small army of eager young people outraged by what was viewed as a blatant act of political sabotage. They didn't need to wait for the official results of the fire department's investigators to know arson when they saw it.

Thus the diabolical attempt to shut them down backfired. Martin Truth For Congress now had more than ten times the number of volunteers they had previously had. Phyllis — God bless the iron lady of organization — had duplicate lists with all of the contact information from the petitions tucked away for safekeeping at her home. Bill immediately suggested they set up new headquarters at his coffee shop, Solid Grounds. From 2 pm to 12 midnight every day, the campaign took over tables and every other available flat surface, to set up laptops, organize literature, distribute the petition call lists, compare notes, and put the fine points on anything that needed to get done in these last few critical days. The student volunteers typically came by and picked up call sheets, then went back to campus or their favorite haunts to make the calls using their own cell phones. Phyllis had put together very effective scripts for them to work off of, scripts which kept the calls on target but allowed a lot of flexibility and creativity on the part of each volunteer.

Three weeks ago, Martin's staff had been resigned to the fact that there was no way they could possibly call everyone who had signed a petition. Now it was likely that not only everyone would get such a courtesy call, but it should be possible to contact most of them more than once.

The student callers — and they didn't just call but emailed, tweeted, posted online, and used every available means to connect and interact with the local voters — were reporting a lot of very sympathetic ears. Some individuals literally thanked them for making contact. News of the fire, and a generally unfavorable reaction to the incivility of the smear campaign and crude personal attacks on Martin in the television ads, had resulted in an underdog backlash. Ironically, people who had barely noticed his candidacy were now paying attention. Not only did they sympathize with him as a victim of foul play, they started to look more closely at what he stood for as a congressional candidate. People started identifying him as the guy who *did* sign a number of firm pledges to properly represent them in Congress, the guy who would vote the way the majority of voters wanted on the five key issues, or resign from office. Here was someone who would put his job on the line for the good voters of Ohio 3rd U.S. Congressional District — no nonsense, no excuses.

Politics seemed with each election cycle to descend to new depths of depravity and deceit.

But in a world polluted with the stench of evil ways and seedy players, if you stand on your tiptoes, hold your head high, and look straight up to the sky, sometimes you can still find some clean air up there to breathe.

• • •

Monday evening. Late. Very late.

Solid Grounds, ad hoc headquarters of Martin Truth For Congress.

Actually it was Tuesday morning. The sun would be up in a few hours.

There was nothing more they could do. It was election day.

Two long years. They had pushed themselves as hard as they could right up to the very end.

Jamila was sipping on an herbal tea. Martin was leaning back with his eyes closed, a still life portrait of exhaustion, as limp as the bean bag chair he was draped over.

Everyone else had gone home. Bill left Martin the key to his café in order to lock up when they got around to leaving. Sitting there in the empty café, it all seemed so anticlimactic.

Even Jamila, who always seemed to be a limitless fount of energy, looked very very tired.

Martin kept shifting, trying to get comfortable. He put his hands behind his head and gazed at some invisible point on the wood beam ceiling above.

"Well, Jamila. We did it."

"We did something."

"Why do I feel so empty?"

"Fatigue? Lack of closure? Makes sense. The cards aren't all on the table yet."

"No, it's beyond that. It's … I mean, even if I win it'll be a Pyrrhic victory."

"You wild-eyed optimist."

"Look around you. Look at the world. Look at this country."

"Things have always been messy. You think World War II was a movie with a John Williams soundtrack and a Hollywood ending? America has always been a comedy of errors."

"It's never been this messy, so strewn with corruption."

"Well, Martin, I don't want to even get started on that argument. Your problem is just seeing things in black-and-white. Good versus evil. Like there are clear lines of victory. It's all just a myth. Especially now, the American Way is just another show on the Disney channel."

"What? You can't be serious. There are no good guys, no bad guys?"

"There are no fairy tales. Not ones that end well. I'll tell you what's different now. It used to be that adults told fairy tales to kids, to entertain them, to give them hope for the future. Now they tell them to one another. The narratives that are being pushed by the major parties, the complete dumbing down of anything newsworthy by the media, reducing every dialogue, every legitimate issue to a sports contest, it's all cartoon stuff. Comic strips for us adults. It's like professional wrestling. We all know it's a joke. It's fixed. But we still want to see it played out. It lets us have the reality we want. The good guy kicks the bad guy's ass. The prince slays the dragon."

"So what are we doing, Jamila? Why try? What have we accomplished with this campaign? All of this work trying to get rid of Gardner. The speeches. The pledges. Is it all just make believe?"

"Not unless we let it be.

"You haven't answered my question."

"What have we been doing? Here's my take. The folks in the Death Star point the beam and we build a mirror. We do what we can do. That's all we can do."

"And that's not a fairy tale?"

"It's whatever you make it."

They sat again in silence for several minutes.

"Oh my god! I just thought of something. I know exactly what this campaign feels like."

"Ladies and gentlemen! Martin Truth has an epiphany! An epic breakthrough!"

"This is so weird. Actually it's embarrassing. I haven't thought about this … I mean, this goes back maybe twenty years."

"This should be good. Is this before or after you were potty trained?"

"It had to be like the fourth or fifth grade. Hmm … yep. Fifth grade … fifth grade …"

"Fifth grade. Got it."

"Naw! I can't tell you this. Way too humiliating. One of my worst childhood memories."

"Hold on, buddy! Not fair at all! You started this. Now you *have* to tell me."

"Alright. But try not to laugh. I mean, it's kind of funny, so you can laugh. But don't laugh *at* me. Okay… so this kid comes up to me in the fifth grade. Can't remember his name. He was the class bully and a totally obnoxious little fucker. Except he wasn't so little. He was twice my size. Anyway, he says to me, 'You want to have a contest?' I say, what kind of a contest? He says, 'It's just a contest to see who can punch the softest. Like who can hit the other guy the lightest.' Now considering this guy was always showing everyone how strong he was and even at his age had muscles popping out all over him, it didn't make much sense. But I said, 'Sure. I'm game.' So he says, 'Remember, it's who can hit the softest. You go first.' So I made a fist. He turned sideways and rolled up his sleeve. And I laid the ever-so-gentlest little nudge against his arm. My punch was probably lighter than if a butterfly had landed on him. He said, 'Wow! That was really soft. Okay, now it's my turn.' Suddenly he threw a roundhouse right hook that felt like he had crushed the whole side of my ribcage. He hit me so hard, I flew halfway across the room and had a big bruise for two weeks. Then he looked down at me and said, 'You win.' He and his buddies just walked away laughing their asses off. That was it. That's my story."

Martin naturally expected some kind of reaction. But Jamila was just staring at him with a totally impenetrable look on her face. He had no idea what she was thinking. Finally she spoke.

"Yes. I can picture that."

"Don't you think it's funny?"

"I'm tempted to laugh. But it's so … it's just so …"

"Pathetic?"

They sat in silence for a few moments. Martin wasn't sure if he was sorry he had told her the story or not. But he was definitely leaning that way. Jamila continued her enigmatic stare.

"Martin. I do have something to say. But I don't know how to put it … uh … tactfully."

"Jamila. I can honestly say that 'tactful' is *never* a word that pops up when I think of you."

"Score one for the burly candidate. His intern is reeling in pain. She staggers and falls back on the ropes, waiting for more blows to rain on her frail body."

"I was just joking!"

"I know."

Again they sat in silence for a while.

"Okay, Martin. I've got it. I know what I want to say about your story."

"And that is?"

There was a slight twinkling in her eyes and the tiniest hint of amusement lurking about her lovely lips. But she spoke in a deadpan, almost reverent tone.

"There's actually something quite noble about being *that* stupid."

After maybe ten seconds which rivaled the silent void of deep space, they both suddenly broke into convulsive, outrageous, bombs-bursting-in-mid-air peals of uncontrollable laughter. It went on and on. They'd almost stop, then would look at one another and start laughing again.

It took several minutes before they settled back into the quiet meditation that had preceded their outburst. They each again became lost in their own private thoughts.

Then in the same exact moment, as if they were both obeying the same silent command, they stood up to leave, to go home and get a few hours of sleep.

Jamila stood outside in the chilly November air and watched as Martin locked up the café.

Before they parted to go to their respective automobiles, Martin turned and faced her.

"Yes, Martin Truth?"

"Thanks, Jamila Parks."

Chapter Ten

There was no way to predict how this would turn out.

Martin and his dedicated staff had done all they could. A lot had gone his way by both luck and design.

But the simple truth remained: People were creatures of habit. They were always going to try to quit smoking but bought that last pack of cigarettes again and again. Tomorrow they were going to go on a diet and start eating right, but there was that one last cheeseburger and fries. Tomorrow never came.

Maybe they were truly impressed by Martin. Maybe this time they wouldn't just pull that lever for a Democrat or a Republican like they had been doing for the past twenty years. Maybe they were convinced that this time when they went to the polls, they'd try something new. They'd take the chance and see if America could get on a better track by giving their vote to a third-party candidate.

But when they stepped in that voting booth …

Well, who could say?

Old habits die hard.

• • •

Martin was a strange fellow in some ways.

Not in ways that made him unpleasant or less endearing.

He just sometimes did things differently.

As for example on election day.

He voted quite early. He was the third or fourth in his precinct to show up.

He spent the rest of the morning and afternoon at the library, then the Dayton Art Institute.

He reread almost half of Howard Zinn's *A People's History of the United States*.

Then he made a decision.

Tonight he wanted to be alone.

Of course, everyone else would be at Bill's café, Solid Grounds. He loved and respected each and every one of them. He just couldn't handle sitting there, squirming in his seat, biting his nails, watching the play-by-play news updates as the election returns started trickling in.

In fact, he decided he wouldn't watch TV at all. Not until late in the evening. Not until a sure winner had been declared.

• • •

At 11:47 pm, an announcement by Jerry Revish of WBNS-TV10 in Columbus, one of the anchors reporting the election results, said it all.

"Well, here's a shocker. We've got a final on that very contentious, topsy-turvy, nearly impossible to predict race for U.S. Congress, 3rd Congressional District. With 97% of the precincts reporting, there is a winner. Are you ready for this? Martin Truth has been declared victorious in a political race that will go down in the history books. In a contest that has resulted in record voter turnout, Mr. Truth has pulled 92,897 votes, Matt Gardner, the Republican incumbent who was favored to win this one, received 85,113 votes, and running close behind him, the Democratic contender Chris Castiglia with 83,887 votes. You will recall that Martin Truth is running on the Green Party ticket. We're looking for an acceptance speech by Mr. Truth, live from his campaign headquarters, if our roving reporter can find it. And if his opponents are available, we will broadcast their concession speeches as well. How about that, Therese?"

"And I believe, Mr. Truth is the first Green Party candidate to ever be elected to national office."

"This is a truth we hold to be self-evident."

"My my, Jerry. You have such a way with words. By the way, isn't that the guy that got shot at?"

"It is indeed. Maybe that's what you need to get elected these days, eh?"

"Maybe that's what I need to do to get a raise around here."

"Whatever spins your chamber. You wanna borrow my gun?"

"Thanks. I have my own right here in my purse."

• • •

It took Martin eight minutes to get there. When he pulled up to Solid Grounds, his official campaign headquarters for at least a few more hours, someone had taken a felt-tip pen and changed the wording on the poster in the window. It now read ...

Congressman

Martin Truth

For ~~Congress~~ *a*

better America!

After the victory celebration, Martin got a surprise that came close to rivaling his unlikely win in the election.

After giving an acceptance speech standing on a chair on the sidewalk in front of Solid Grounds, thanking everyone involved in his victory, shaking so many hands he thought his arm was going to fall off, he headed home. It was close to 3 am. He was exhausted but he seriously doubted he could sleep.

As he got out of his car, Jamila pulled up.

The conversation took an unexpected turn.

"So Mr. Congressman, do you have any beer in your refrigerator?"

"Are you inviting yourself in?"

"You could say that."

As soon as they got in the door, she gave a sharp tug at his arm. When he turned, she planted a huge wet kiss on his shocked face, her tongue leaving little doubt about what she was up to. She probed his mouth, pressing her body tightly against his, her hands sliding down his back, across his butt and to the front of his jeans.

"I thought you were a lesbian."

"You converted me. You're such a hunk, I don't like women any more."

"Alright. What's the game?"

"Do you want to talk or get on with this? I've been watching you stare at my body now for seven months. I don't think you were guessing my height and weight."

And they did. Get on with it, that is.

Jamila turned out to be everything Martin had imagined and more. His fantasies of the shape of her body, the texture of her skin, her *smell*, the delectability of her nipples and the delights of her vagina, didn't even come close. For once, imagination took a sorry back seat to reality. Lucky him.

After four hours, the longings, the deprivation, the sheer horniness built up over almost a year without sex, and the considerable lustful fantasies about Jamila, had been exhausted by more intense lovemaking than he thought he was capable of.

"Martin! You have such a great smile! You keep it too locked up most of the time."

"Beer. You wanted a beer."

"It was only a pretext. But sure, I'd love a beer."

He returned from the kitchen with two bottles of Dos Equis and two mugs.

My god! She was so beautiful! And thoughtful enough to not get dressed.

He sat on the edge of the bed.

"Okay. The lesbian bit. Come on, tell me what's going on."

"We had a professional relationship, Martin. I don't believe in mixing business and pleasure. But the work is done."

"You aren't … you never were—"

"Martin, you might just be the sweetest guy in the whole world."

"Why?"

"Because you're so gullible! And honestly, I knew what was going on in your head. Because it was going on in my head too. From the first time I met you, I felt it. I thought I was being silly. School girl crush and all that. But as I got to know you …"

"Is this a joke? Are you putting me on again?"

"What do you think? All I'm saying, Martin, is I could tell you were really attracted to me. Not like most guys either. I never saw you checking out every babe that came your way. So it wasn't the slicky meat kind of attraction."

"Slicky meat? Jamila, you are one-of-a-kind."

"Anyway, with you, dear boy, I was surprised, amazed, intrigued. You're not like anyone I've ever met before. You have integrity. I like that. I really like that."

They just stared at each other for the longest time.

Then Martin got a rascally look on his otherwise handsome face and started laughing.

"You're something else! 'Jamila' means 'lover of labia'. Isn't that what you said?"

"Swahili is difficult. That's a very loose translation. I took some liberties."

"Do you know what 'Martin' means? Roughly speaking?"

She glanced down between his legs.

"If I'm not mistaken, it means 'seize the moment'. I think the beers will have to wait."

He placed them on the floor and crawled back in bed.

"Hear ye! Hear ye!"

"Congress is in session!"

Epilogue

John Irving says in his extraordinary novel *The World According To Garp*, that an epilogue which fulfills its essential function is not about the past. It is a warning about the future.

It would be heartening but Pollyannaish to claim the Martin made some huge difference during his first term as a congressman.

A sickly economy and pervasive ignorance as to what caused it, vast sums of money from multinational corporations and Wall Street pouring into the political campaigns of conservative play-for-pay lap dogs, the thousands of deceptive and grotesque television ads by PACs and SuperPACs misinforming the public concerning just about everything, and the patently partisan editorializing by the talking heads on the most watched TV station in America, Fox News, all combined to sweep into office even more extreme, fanatic, and unseemly right wing ideologues. The few sane and constructive contributors to the national and congressional dialogue like Martin, were often drowned out in a cacophony of irrational, vituperative, flag-waving, patronizing speeches by toadies of the corporate oligarchy.

Thus, there remained over the course of his first term a huge disconnect between what the clear will of the American people was — prodded, tested and polled with compulsive fervor by the media — and what came out of both legislative houses.

Predictably, Martin was painted by the attack dogs — snarling thugs who now openly and arrogantly prowled the revered halls of Congress — as a whiny, irrelevant, anti-American socialist, much as Bernie Sanders (Ind-VT) had been maligned in the Senate over the course of his remarkable career. The ruthless and rabid right wing went out of their way to make Martin's life miserable. Martin's addresses on the floor were cut short by a highly partial and overtly dismissive Speaker of the House. He was given subcommittee assignments which were uninteresting and frivolous. He was frequently subjected publicly to verbal abuse, snide comments, and ridicule. At times as he wandered from his tiny office to and from the floor of Congress, it felt to him like the locker room for a high school gym class. Not a few times did he hear someone mumble in passing, 'traitor', 'tree hugger', even 'commie fag!'

On the other hand, his campaign and victory did set a new standard and model for the future. Over the next several congressional electoral cycles, candidate pledges were increasingly deployed with some success. Some of the worst conservative mouthpieces for the corporate elite were one-by-one painstakingly replaced with elected officials who had the greater interest of the country and the majority of its citizens at heart.

The incumbents targeted by the candidate pledges, of course, screamed bloody murder and even attempted to pass legislation outlawing the strategy. They tried to claim that unlike their own bullying tactics, the pledges were blackmail. In perhaps a vestigial allusion which honored Martin's initial groundbreaking use of them, the rallying cry defending their use became, "*Demanding truth is never blackmail.*"

Over the next decade, pressure continued to mount from liberals of a reinvigorated left. While there was never a dramatic landslide reversal of the balance of power, district-by-district progress could be seen. Corporations using front organizations to smear and marginalize progressive candidates, badgering and browbeating by unscrupulous and mercenary lobbyists, bribes in the guise of campaign donations, all still persisted in their assault on democracy. But gradually these onerous forces became less a match for the line-in-the-sand legal demand by voters that their elected officials guarantee in writing the representation they voted for and deserved. The candidate pledges gave the voice of the people a loud megaphone and that voice was finally being heard above the roar of money.

It was too soon to say if the plodding revival of a liberal center and the mounting pressure from a progressive left would be enough to save the republic. A lot of damage had been done. The wounds were deep and slow to heal. The scars were tender ugly swaths, which could easily rupture and reinfect. Perhaps the battle ground would for a time become calmer. But in effect, the respite was more of a cease fire than a peace treaty. The dogged opponents still glared at one another with frustration and bitterness over a narrow and tense demilitarized zone, which marked ideological lines too antithetical to permit compromise or even civil discussion.

The passage of time might or might not bridge the differences.

Either way history would record the results.

More Books by John Rachel

If you liked this book, you might want to check out these other novels by this author and political blogger.

"Blinders Keepers"

In this dark comedy, a young man who escapes his hopelessly hayseed home town in Missouri is mistakenly labeled a terrorist and must survive a manhunt by government security agencies, while the President of an America in chaos and collapse perpetrates an end-of-the-world hoax, attempting to reclaim control and get himself re-elected.

"From Thailand With Love"

In this street-tough thriller, a low-crime slacker is set up as the fall guy for an international trafficking operation bringing adolescent Asian girls into the U.S. for prostitution, and goes head-to-head with his brutal crime syndicate bosses in a life-or-death struggle for supremacy.

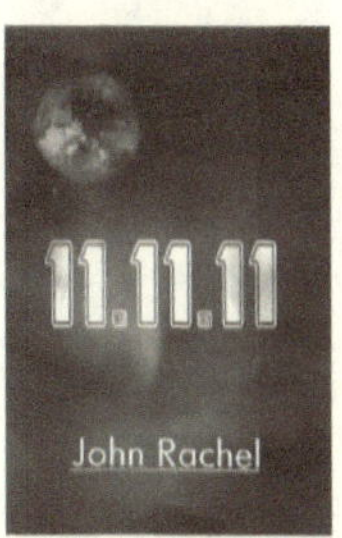

"11 - 11 - 11"

Noah was turning 23 and desperate to get out of town. Pulnick, Missouri had always been bland and soporific, but now it was now being invaded by white supremacist meth heads, plagued by an unprecedented crime wave, exploited by spiritualists and local politicos, and driven to hysteria by paranoid rumors that the world would end on November 11th.

"12 - 12 - 12"

Welcome to the parallel universe of "12-12-12". This not what actually happens during 2012. But what unfolds is not more implausible. Nor is it less implausible. It is dark satire, a portrayal of reality with healthy doses of surreality and comedy, spawned by the tragic absurdity of our times. One reviewer calls it "laugh-out-loud brain food for hungry minds."

Coming Soon

"The Man Who Loved Too Much" Trilogy!!

Billy Green is bright, enigmatic, and lost. He has spent his first 28 years trying to figure out who he is and where he fits in. His life has been a wild, unpredictable quest to attach himself to some reality he can grasp and live with. He grew up in an abysmal suburb of Detroit, escaped to university life at Cornell, got married and divorced before being thrown headlong and entirely unprepared into the crazy social chaos of New York City. Billy's adventure is proof that not every member of Generation Y is doomed to live surrogate lives within the electronic confines of smart phones, TVs, computers, or the chemical prison of drugs and alcohol.

. . . and in 2015 - 2016 . . .

"The Naked American"

"Love Connection"

"The Last Giraffe"

"Happy Happy Dreaming Girl"

"St. Jerome's Home For The Sexually Insane"

About The Author

John Rachel has a B. A. in Philosophy, has traveled extensively, is a songwriter and music producer, a left-of-left liberal, and has spent his life trying to resolve the intrinsic clash between the metaphysical purity of Buddhism and the overwhelming appeal of narcissism. Prompted by the trauma of graduating high school and having to leave his beloved city of Detroit to attend college, the development his social skills and world view was arrested at age 18. This affliction figures prominently in all of his creative work.

In October of 2008, while living in Japan, he completed his first novel, *From Thailand With Love*. It is a thriller about the trafficking of adolescent Asian girls for prostitution in America. It is set in Brooklyn but ranges over a number of locations, including Chicago, Duluth, Seattle, St. Louis and San Francisco, and overseas in Thailand, Myanmar, Laos, Vietnam, Malaysia and Singapore.

In November of 2009, he completed his second novel, *The Man Who Loved Too Much*, written over ten months, as he lived in and traveled through Japan, China, Nepal, and India. It follows the convoluted life of a young man from age 4 to 28, as he tries to find his place in the world. The story is set in Detroit, upstate New York, and New York City. At 800+ pages, it is an epic. Perhaps it should have been titled *The Man Who Wrote Too Much*.

While writing his third and fourth novels in 2010 and 2011 — *11-11-11* and *12-12-12* — which track two years in the life of a young man who was the hapless victim of being born in a hopelessly hayseed town in Bible-belt Missouri, the author hopped around between Japan, Taiwan, Indonesia, South Korea and the Philippines.

He is now somewhat rooted in a small traditional farming village in Japan near Osaka. It was there, immediately after poking himself in the forehead with chopsticks, that he was inspired to plant soybeans and sweet potatoes in his small but promising vegetable garden, and to write *An Unlikely Truth*.

After the publication of his *The Man Who Loved Too Much* trilogy, he has two more novels in the pipeline: *Love Connection*, a thriller set in Japan, and *The Last Giraffe*, an anthropological drama which takes place in sub-Saharan Africa.

His next project, as he slumps in a hammock he purchased in Vietnam and waits for harvest time, is a creative non-fiction work, *The Naked American*. It is allegedly an account of his travels since leaving America August 2006, but more likely the product of the voices in his head which have plagued him since puberty.

The author's last permanent residence in America was Portland, Oregon where he had a state-of-the-art ProTools recording studio, music production house, and a radio promotion and music publishing company. He recorded and produced several artists in the Pacific Northwest, releasing and promoting their music on radio across the U.S.

• • •

You can follow John Rachel's adventures and developing world view at:

http://jdrachel.com

Since the open mind recognizes no borders, you are also invited to join us in the ongoing dialogue about the writing arts here:

http://literaryvagabond.com

Legal Notifications and Disclaimers

An Unlikely Truth is entirely a work of fiction. Names, characters, places, brands, media, and incidents are either the product of the author's imagination or are used fictitiously. Any references to celebrities and nationally-known figures and their roles in the story are likewise fictional. No participation in the writing of this novel or their endorsement of its point of view and message is claimed or implied. For example, several real individuals who are known media figures in Ohio are cited. Among these are Jana Collier editor-in-chief of the Dayton Daily News, Jerry Revish of WBNS-TV10 in Columbus, Amber Watson of Dayton's WRGT-TV, and Chelby Kosto of Dayton's WKEF-TV Fox 45. They are used to add an element of authenticity to the story. All of the dialogue attributed to them, opinions expressed or implied, interactions cited, or characterizations offered, are merely the creation for effect by the author, thus are purely fictional representations made in the context of a work of fiction. They should be judged accordingly.

The author acknowledges the trademarked status and trademark owners of various products referenced in this work of fiction, which have been used without permission. The publication/use of these trademarks is not authorized, associated with, or sponsored by the trademark owners, but appear as common features in the story as they are common features in modern everyday life. No product endorsements are meant or implied by their use.

The Man Who Loved Too Much
Book 1: Archipelago (Excerpt)

Chapter 1: THE EARLY YEARS

Balloons — 1986

It was an especially cold Thanksgiving on Woodward Avenue in Detroit. Today was the annual Thanksgiving Day Parade and the crowd alternated between shivering and cheering. People shuffled and stomped, attempting to keep their feet from freezing. Gusts of steamy cold blew from their dripping noses and through clenched teeth.

Suddenly Billy started screaming. "My balloon!! My Balloon!!"

"Harold, do something. His balloon!"

"Goddamit, Irene. Do I look like I have wings? It's too late."

Up up it went. The string had slipped from Billy's grasp and the balloon was off to wherever balloons go. The stratosphere? Balloon heaven?

"You stupid little fuck. I told you to let me tie it to your wrist. But you're so goddam smart. See what happens when you don't listen."

Billy's face instantly melted into a chastened mask of humiliation and defeat, as he started to cry like his puppy had been crushed under a bus.

"Nice work, Harold. Give the kid a complex. Let's find a vendor and get him another one."

"Over my dead body! He'll learn something from this. Next time something is so goddam important to him as that there balloon ..." Harold jerked his thumb skyward at the latex dot which was all but invisible by now. "... maybe he'll take better care of it."

"Jesus Christ, he's only three. How could I have married such a heartless man? Come here, sweetheart." She reached down and picked up the heartbroken and tremulously sobbing young boy, face streaked and blotchy, mittens wet with the fresh tears of tragedy.

Another parade float approached and would soon be right in front of them.

She pointed. "Look, Billy. Look at the dinosaur."

Sure enough, big as a moving van, bloated with helium, tethered to the 8-wheel steel flatbed of a float frame covered with artificial turf, and looking about as realistic as cardboard and crayons, was a Tyrannosaurus Rex. Its mouth was agape in what was supposed to be a scary, imminent man-devouring chomp. Several repairs were visible on the rubber underside, patches which were poorly matched in color to the skin of the faux beast. To underscore the implausibility of the threat, eight baton twirlers circled around the float, dancing, kicking their bare legs high, tossing and twirling gleaming chrome batons in the clear November air.

"Grrr!! Grrr!! Careful he doesn't eat you up." She tickled his cheek with her wool-gloved finger and tried to elicit a smile.

Billy had already stopped crying and just looked confused. He seemed more interested in the baton twirlers than the gas bag monster.

Next came a landlocked riverboat float, bearing the Flint Banjo Club players. This was their historic parade debut and they enthusiastically picked and twanged their way through various Dixieland and bluegrass favorites to a crowd which almost seemed to notice. Two mounted policemen followed, their horses snorting and blowing foggy jets from their wet nostrils.

"Harold, I need to powder my nose. Can you take him?" Giving her husband no real choice in the matter, she abruptly reached over and placed the boy up against his father's chest.

"Mommy, I have to—"

"Just sit tight, Billy. Mommy will be right back."

"But, Mom ... "

His father took Billy, obviously under protest, and slung him up on his shoulders. The boy completely caught off guard by the sudden and heavy-handed move, grabbed on desperately to keep from falling, wrapping his arms tightly around his father's neck.

"Easy! Easy! You don't have to choke me to death."

Billy knew better than to try to talk to him and just settled in an uncomfortable slump against his father's head. Before she had left, he was trying to tell his mom that he had to pee. But she was off to find a ladies room and it would have to wait until she got back. He had to go. Really bad.

To make matters worse, his father was bouncing him. Whether this was to entertain Billy or just to try to stay warm was a moot point. The pressure of the full kidneys built quickly and all Billy could do was concentrate on holding it in. He couldn't even look at the parade floats. He closed his eyes and bit on his lower lip. All he could think of was the critical pressure building in his groin. He clamped his legs together as hard as he could against the urgent and painful need for release.

"What the fuck are you doing up there? This ain't no wrestling match. Back off with the leg lock."

His dad reached up under Billy's arms and shook him to drive home his point. That was all it took for the dam to burst. Billy let out a tiny whimpering cry. Then silence. He tried to stop it but his urethral valve was open and it wasn't about to be turned off until the job was done.

At first Billy's father only noticed a slight increase in the temperature around and below the collar of his coat. Then he felt the wetness and sensed the faint odor of the boy's young pee.

"Is that what I think it is? You little shit!"

Billy was swallowed whole by shame and fear. He fought desperately to keep from crying and covered his face with both hands as his father roughly lifted him off and held him out in front of him to confirm his worst suspicions. Billy was still going. Pee dripped from the bottom of his wet trousers, past his shoes, onto the pavement.

Billy's father was fast to act. Still holding Billy at arms length, he turned around and headed away from the street, towards the public restrooms, just as Billy's mom was making her way back to join them.

"I asked for a son and you gave me this piece of trash."

She tried to grab for Billy, both to rescue him from his father's rage and offer him whatever comfort might be needed. But Harold was too quick. He muscled past her and walked over to a large wire trashbasket, already nearly full of newspapers, crumpled lunch bags and food wrappings.

He dropped Billy in head first and stormed away.

www.ingramcontent.com/pod-product-compliance
Lightning Source LLC
LaVergne TN
LVHW090941080826
845145LV00003B/840

* 9 7 8 0 6 1 5 9 7 4 1 0 1 *